SAVING
Aiden

KRISTIN MONDA

SAVING AIDEN

Author's photo by Photos With Flair • Jennifer LeBaron

Cover design and page layout by Ace Book Covers

Acknowledgements

First and foremost, I want to thank my best friend, my partner in everything, Buddy Rivera. You inspire me daily. You've been my constant source of encouragement and support. Thank you for believing in me. Without you this story would still be just a bunch of words on a zip drive. Now its a legacy, my fathers name, in print for eternity. I can't begin to express my gratitude. Thank you for reassuring me it was safe to take a leap of faith. For taking us "off the grid for a little while," and for teaching me more than I thought I could learn. For pushing me to reach higher, for showing me its possible to achieve more, no matter how many times I've failed. "Fall down seven times, stand up eight."

For my father, Danial Leroy Monda; 1939-1983. Thank you for my beautiful life. The memory of you drives me to think bigger, love better, run harder and to never ever quit.

Thank you to my Mother, for always being my biggest fan. And to my sisters, and to my enormous family, thank you for your unwavering support. For my friends, my incredible friends, my fellow goal getters and dream chasers... two words, thank you. Two more, never stop.

And a special thank you to my amazing kids, Stacy, Katie, Jake, Jesse and Chris. Thank you for listening for hours and hours about these characters. Thank you for all of your perfect suggestions, for the ability to give unbiased opinions when needed, but mostly for your patients while I checked out from time-to-time over the past six years to write this story and bring it to life. I love you guys.

... "*I stand in the cold. In the shadow between life and death.*

In a place where warmth doesn't exist."

For my Father, Danial

I

Close Enough

A dim ray of light broke through the glass window. Raindrops streamed over the weathered pane as I leaned my head against the cool surface. For days I sat still in my chair staring out the terrace window. I gazed through the tiny breaks in the streaming water to the well-manicured garden in the courtyard outside. I released the brake from my wheelchair, thrusting myself through the open doors out into the rain. Heavy drops streamed down my thin, pale face as I gazed up at the sculpture in the center of the garden. A cold, gray statue of stone towered over the courtyard. The statue of an angel that watched over those left here for one reason or another. We were lost souls, lost to the world. To outsiders we were the challenged, the weak. Those who couldn't hack it after some sort of traumatic event took place in our lives leaving us in this pathetic state, institutionalized.

We were sent here to rehabilitate. To rot was more like it. If I had to be here, it was definitely better to be out here with her. She was my saving grace. This place was a hell hole. Drugs, needles, poking and prodding us like a lab rats trying to give our disorders a description. I knew all too well what my problem was and there was no cure. Out here there was far better company, and I preferred watching over her as she watched over me.

Not long ago I fell in love. She meant everything to me. But she's gone now and I spend every minute of my pitiful existence dwelling on the smallest detail of our last moments together. She made me a promise the night she left. She promised she would come back to me. I couldn't let her go. No matter how much time passed, I couldn't let her go.

I was in the rehabilitation unit at Wescott Memorial Hospital. As least I assumed I was. It didn't really matter to me. Nothing did. I didn't care enough to ask. I needed rehabilitation. That's what they kept telling me. To rehabilitate only meant one thing... to get back to the way I was before. I needed to let go of the past to face the future. I had no future. Not without Tess. It was like they were forcing me to let her go, let go of her memory. Letting go of everything we had together would take much more than what they offered here. I glanced down at my legs. They're so frail and weak. Once, thick with muscle now just a fraction of what they were. I was wasting away. I knew if I got up out of this chair I could go and look for her, but it was going to take more than I had inside to do it. I didn't trust anyone here. No one was real. Just a bunch of white coats with badges using medical terms and pretending to actually care. Their job was to pushing meds left and right, shuffling each of us one by one through the so called "rehabilitation process." It was all part of the system they said. A process they call "restoring." To restore to the physical and/or psychological state prior to trauma. Restore. A word that meant nothing before Tess.

I wiped the rain from my face as I gazed up at the statue. I stared into her eyes, desperately searching for a sign. The darkening clouds rumbled above us. The rain fell even harder as if the heavens were attempting to wash me away. No one would miss me if it succeeded. Well, maybe one. This angel looking down at me. Her somber face completely covered in beaded raindrops. I don't know what I was expecting from a statue made of stone. Maybe I was waiting for her to send me a subliminal message, instructions on how to move on. Maybe something in the form of a whisper. A soft, delicate voice telling me what to do, how to feel, how to move on.

I closed my eyes and squeezed the arm rest trying to pull myself forward. I slid my feet off the steel plates and planted them onto the wet pavement. Slowly, I pulled myself toward the edge of the padded leather seat. My arms began to shake. I was just too weak. The cold rain pelted against my skin as I looked up at her. There was just nothing left inside to give.

All I thought about was Tess. There was nothing I wanted more than to find her again, to hear her voice. I struggled to remember the sound of it, the softness of her whisper. I put my hands over my face, desperate to find her in the darkness... to feel her somehow. I felt a warm tear stream down my cool, wet skin. There was no way to get my life back. Not without her.

"Good morning, Aiden," a loud, feminine voice announced from inside the terrace. "You're getting wet." I glanced over my shoulder to the doorway where there stood yet another doctor. So many have tried to help, but none of them have come up with any specific diagnosis. I knew the drill. After a series of tests, a scan or two, I'm shuffled along and forwarded to yet another group of doctors. They all come to the same conclusion. I wasn't sick. I was broken.

"Do you know where you are?"

I clenched my fists and muttered, "Yes." I sat there just outside the terrace in the pouring rain. "How about if I bring you back inside and we talk. Would that be okay with you Aiden?" I didn't respond. I looked back at the statue.

"It's time to return to the living." she announced in a low voice.

I yanked my chair around and glared at her. I thought about her statement. I furrowed my brow as I pondered on just one word.

"Living?" I shouted. "Is that what you call this?" I asked wiping the rain from my face.

"It doesn't have to be this hard, Aiden," she said softly. I could see she was reaching for just the right words, trying to avoid upsetting me any more than she already had. She folded her hands in front of her leaning on the large door holding it open.

"It doesn't?" I shouted. My voice cracked.

"No. I can help you. I know I can. You just have to trust me." There was something different about her. I watched her as she slowly stepped out into the rain. She just stood there waiting for my response. She gave me a gentle smile as the rain quickly saturated every inch of her. In that moment, I thought maybe I could trust her. Besides, I had nothing else to lose.

"Okay," I whispered. Before I could say another word, she darted toward me grabbing the handles of my wheelchair and pulled me inside.

"Do you know who I am?" she asked, as she picked through the soaked pieces of her hair, pulling them away from her face. She snatched two towels from inside the small restroom near the hallway. She tossed one to me and used the other to dab over her face.

"Yes. I know who you are. Another doctor," I groaned. I could hear the water drops hitting the floor under me.

"I'm Dr. Gloria Bennett."

"That's good. You know who you are," I whispered sarcastically, sitting lifelessly in my chair.

Dr. Bennett wasn't just another doctor. She was the Chief of Psychiatry at the hospital. She had been following my case since I arrived. She stopped by to see me after her morning rounds to check my progress.

I turned toward her. I wanted to avoid eye contact at all costs. She just stood there with a ridiculous smirk on her face. She was a little too confident in herself if you asked me. She wore a gold suit that matched the highlights in her dampened hair. I could see her suit collar from under her white coat.

"Are you going to use that?" she asked, pointing at the towel in my lap. I just sat there, unresponsive.

I had no intention of using it. I thought she was going about this trust building idea of hers all wrong. I wondered what happened to the warm smile, the soft voice. I liked that approach much better. She pulled out a pen from inside her pocket.

"Do you mind if I sit?" She reached for one of the two chairs near the doorway sliding it across the uneven stone floor. I didn't answer. It wasn't like she was actually asking for my permission.

"Can I ask you something?" She took a seat in the chair and moved toward me. Suddenly, I felt every ounce of blood in my body rushing through my veins. She was now officially irritating the hell out of me. My facial expression must have given her a hint that things were going from bad to worse rather quickly.

"For some reason I believe a 'no' wouldn't settle with you." I whispered, as I sat up.

Shifting around in her chair, she caught the edge of her skirt. She began to tug on it as she turned her eyes back toward me. There it was. The same warm smile I had already become fond of. It was much more appealing, much less like a doctor. Her smile grew wider. I could feel the corners of my mouth draw up as I snatched the towel and ran it through my hair.

"You're right. It wouldn't."

I wasn't quite sure what it was but there was definitely something about her. Something different and I liked it. "Then, I guess, the answer is yes," I muttered.

"If I told you that you could trust me, would you believe me?"

"What do you mean?"

"I want you to know that I'm going to help you. But you have to trust me." She looked so serious, almost believable. "I want you to tell me about Tess," she said, softening her voice to a gentle whisper. I could feel my bloodshot eyes widen. I glared at Dr. Bennett. She calmly pulled a small note pad from her pocket and began to write.

"How-how do you know her name?" I made sure to never say her name to anyone here.

"It's okay. I told you, you can trust me," Dr. Bennett assured me. "I want you to tell me everything." She whispered.

I was unsure whether to respond or not. I glared at her desperately searching for the slightest sign of sincerity.

"You can't go on like this forever, Aiden. You know that."

She was right. I could feel my muscles in my hands releasing the fists that I had clenched. Maybe it was time to talk about her. I felt a knot tighten in my stomach. I didn't know where to start.

"How about if we start from the beginning. Would that be alright?" she asked.

I turned back toward the garden to see the angel. I watched as rain streamed steadily down her tarnished face. A darkness had fallen here, over this place, over me. A lump swelled in my throat as I swallowed. I could feel the emotion welling up inside me. Emotion that I had buried deep inside for so long.

"The beginning?" I whispered, as I ran my hands over my cold colorless face. I was a wreck. I felt the prickly stubble of my beard scratch my fingers. I took in a heavy breath of air and held it. I closed my eyes and was surrounded once again by the blackness that consumed me for so long. The beginning felt like a lifetime ago.

"Do you remember the first time you saw her?"

I closed my eyes tightly and let out the deep breath. I began thinking back. Back to a time away from this place. Before all of this.

"Yes," I replied. "On the mountain. That was the beginning." I whispered. My voice was a bit shaky, but I think Dr. Bennett was expecting it to be. I had completely detached from everything. I hadn't really spoken to anyone for a very long time. I guess I just didn't have anything to say.

"That's when you first saw her?" Dr. Bennett asked, eagerly.

"Yeah, on that mountain. I was desperate when I first saw her."

"What do you mean, Aiden? Why were you desperate?" She moved to the edge of her seat inching her way closer to me.

"My equipment was failing" I whispered. I dropped my chin to my chest and closed my eyes. "I bargained with some invisible force making all kinds of promises," I confessed.

"Invisible force?"

"You know. Whatever it is that watches over us."

"I see." She said, scribbling on the notepad.

"I was going to die. So, I begged for my life."

"When was this?"

"I don't know. September, two, maybe three years ago." I had no idea how long I had been in the hospital. The concept of time was another one of those meaningless subjects I no longer had any interest in.

My mind wandered back to that day on the mountain. I remembered the view near the top. "The sunsets at twelve hundred feet were something to see, especially that time of year." I muttered. I could almost feel the cool mountain breeze, the warmth of the sun on my face.

"I loved the climb." I blurted as I shifted in my chair.

"I see. So, you're a rock climber?"

"Yeah. But this climb was a little out of the ordinary. I was in a pretty bad situation." I whispered. It wasn't easy to recall the events that day on the mountain. It was the closest I ever came to dying. "It's kind of hard to forget. Even if I wanted to and believe me, I've tried." I closed my eyes and searched in the never ending darkness for her. "I remember when I first saw her."

"Can you tell me what happened?" Dr. Bennett asked.

"I was having trouble with my equipment. My line had snapped after three anchor pins pulled from the rock. I had my safety line and one pin left holding me up."

"Sounds like you were in a pretty bad predicament."

"You could say that. I remember looking down at the rock below." My voice dropped to a shallow whisper. I could feel the anxiety begin to build as I spoke. It was difficult to bring it all back…the thought of dying. I remembered it so vividly. Beads of sweat began to form mixing with the water still covering my face. I quickly became filled with emotion. I felt the tears as they began to well in my eyes.

"Maybe you're not ready to talk about it, Aiden. I don't want to push you," she whispered.

I glanced at Dr. Bennett. There was something genuine about her. She made me feel comfortable. Finally, I thought. I didn't need to hold it all in.

"I'm okay." I could feel the adrenaline begin to flow. My heart began to pump a little faster. I gave her a tiny smile. "This is good." I said, as I perked up in my chair. I took a deep breath and let it out. "I'm good," I assured her. "It's been a long time. I haven't felt anything." I glanced out the window at the statue and then back at Dr. Bennett. "I need to feel this," I whispered.

"I thought I was going to die. I knew I couldn't survive a fall like that." She scribbled in her notepad and turned her attention back to me.

"Were you prepared to die?" She took her glasses from her pocket, unfolded them, and put them on.

"No." I ran my hands through my hair and looked at her. "I had things to do, you know? Lots of things! I had my whole life ahead of me! No way was I ready to die... not like that!" I shouted, as I sat there gripping my forehead.

"I'm sorry," I mumbled, shaking my head.

"Please don't apologize. It's ok. It's all part of getting you through this," she whispered. "Aiden, can I ask you a question?"

I hesitated but eventually nodded.

"I don't want to upset you any more than I already have bringing up these buried emotions, but don't you think when it's time it's just your time?" she asked in a soft tone. Her eyes quickly dropped to her notepad. It was obvious she knew she was gambling with this line of questioning.

"No, I don't," I mumbled, while attempting to keep my emotions in check. "I needed a miracle," I confessed.

"Do you believe in miracles?" She removed her glasses and carefully placed them in her lap.

"I do. I got my miracle that day. I'm here talking to you, aren't I?" I replied without hesitation. I ran my fingers through my damp hair and looked up at the stark white ceiling.

"I remember looking up at the pin. It was separating from the rock." I let out a deep breath. "I thought I had only seconds left." It was difficult to talk about. More difficult that I had anticipated.

"What was going through your mind?"

"I thought of my mother. She believed in..." I caught myself and stopped mid-sentence. I glanced at Doctor Bennett. I wanted

9

to tell her everything but I was afraid. I didn't want another doctor diagnosing me as delusional or a schizophrenic, strapping me to a bed forcing mind-numbing meds into my veins.

"In what, Aiden? Miracles?"

I sat there, silent. I wasn't sure how to proceed. I felt a sudden trembling in my left hand. I clenched a fist and released it over and over trying to get the shaking to stop. Dr. Bennett looked at me.

"Aiden?"

I couldn't answer. I gazed back toward the statue in the garden. I wanted to make sure she was still there.

"It's alright. You can tell me. What did she believe in?" she asked.

I moved my chair forward, closer to her.

"In guardians," I whispered.

"I see." Dr. Bennett smiled and sat up in her chair. She crossed her legs away from me. Just the kind of body language I didn't want to see.

"Crazy. I know," I said under my breath, followed with a heavy sigh.

"No, not crazy. Not at all," she announced, leaning in toward me. She glanced at her posture and quickly uncrossed her legs. She tugged at her chair and moved it closer to mine.

"Tell me about your mother, Aiden," she whispered. She was definitely different. She didn't pass judgment; she didn't change her demeanor. She was still gazing at me with genuine interest, eagerly awaiting more from me which I couldn't understand. I was left here to wither away for so long. As if a label was printed on my chart, one hopeless case. All of the sudden, I felt not so hopeless.

"I remember the last thing she said to me." I wiped the wetness from my eyes as I spoke. "What was it, what did she say?"

"She told me they were out there," I said quietly. I knew what Dr. Bennett was thinking. I couldn't bring myself to look at her. This was the exact point in time where doctors in the past came to the conclusion there was absolutely nothing wrong with me physically. Eager to free up a bed, they transferred me here to this God forsaken place they call the mental ward.

The knot in my stomach tightened. I slowly lifted my head to look at her. Dr. Bennett didn't budge. She was still with me awaiting more.

"Guardians?" She asked, dropping her elbows to her lap. It was funny how into it she was.

"Yes," I replied, "she told me they were out there... watching us." I exhaled. One I felt I had held for far too long. "She said she knew because she spoke to one of them once."

"That's very interesting. And I'm sure you believed her," she replied, as she added to her notes.

"Of course I believed her. She was my mother."

"Can I ask what happened to her?"

"She and her team were killed when a mine collapsed." I could feel a lump forming in my throat as I looked back toward the courtyard.

"I'm sorry, Aiden." I felt her sincerity. It was way she looked at me. She wasn't here to add to the list of prescriptions or therapy sessions. She wasn't here to interrogate me or remind me of the risks I take not eating or taking my meds. Not to warn me of the threat I become during my random, somewhat violent outbursts. How I'm a danger to myself with the potential to harm other patients and staff. I glanced back at her and she smiled. I knew she was here to help.

"She died two weeks after my ninth birthday," I mumbled. It was hard to think about and even harder to talk about.

Dr. Bennett sat up in her chair and dabbed her nose with a wadded tissue she took from her pocket. She gazed at me as she folded her arms.

"Do you believe in fate?" she asked.

"I don't know, maybe." I couldn't help but wonder what she meant. Maybe it was a trick question.

"I think we have some control over our future, but what happens before we get there may be out of our control," she explained.

"I guess," I reluctantly agreed. Dr. Bennett pulled out a fresh tissue from a plastic package and offered it to me.

"If your mother were here she would want you to get better," Dr. Bennett whispered.

"Yeah, she would," I mumbled in a low voice. She was right. I knew it would hurt my mother to see me like this. Dr. Bennett reached for the folder from the counter. I could see my name written in heavy black ink on the tab. She flipped it open and rummaged through my chart.

"I see you majored in art as well, just like your mother?" "Yes."

"You had a very busy schedule, I see." She ruffled through a few more pages before tucking them neatly inside and closing it. She sat her notepad on top flipping to a new page.

"So, it's kind of a way for you to escape, climbing the mountain?" Removing the cap to her pen, she scribbled tiny circles trying to get the ink to flow. She looked up at me to find a tiny grin.

"I suppose it was my way of getting lost for a while. Ever since I heard about the castle tucked inside the mountain I wanted to climb it. I wanted to see it. And it wasn't easy. I probably wouldn't have climbed it as often if it were easy," I snickered. "The rush of adrenaline I felt after making it to the top… all I wanted to do was to feel that rush. But, this time it was different. It was the first time I almost didn't make it. I was just waiting there."

"Waiting for what, Aiden?"

"Waiting to fall," I whispered, taking a deep breath. "Waiting to die. And that's when I saw her."

Just then, I felt it. Sitting in that wheelchair, talking to Dr. Bennett something happened. Something came over me. A rush of emotion, a sensation unlike any I had ever felt. I looked down at my pale hands. I held them out turning them over and back. The grayish color of my skin flickered with warmth. "She was there with me on that mountain. She was all around me and the imminent danger I was in just faded away. Either I was hallucinating or I was dead. It didn't matter. All I saw, all I felt was her."

"She was so perfect, so beautiful." I could feel my heart beating heavily in my chest as I spoke. I kept glancing at my hands. For a brief moment the color of my skin went from a cold gray to a warm bronze. I knew what it would take to get out of the chair that I confined myself to for so long. The mere thought of her brought back a flicker of life inside me.

"Who was she? Did you recognize her?"

"No. Not then I didn't."

"You feel better when you think of her, don't you?"

"What do you mean?"

"I can see it in your eyes. They've been so dark and lifeless. When you talk about her, something happens. It's like the light returns."

"That's good right?"

"Yes, Aiden. That's very good," she said, smiling. "What else do you remember about her?"

"She had a warmth that consumed me. I felt it. At the time, I thought that it must be one of those out of body experiences that happen to people in extreme duress. Like an adrenaline induced hallucination." I went on and on. She seemed content with my babbling. She even let a tiny giggle slip out as she wrote. "It was either an out of body or quite possibly out of mind experience. Whichever it was, it didn't matter to me." I let out a sarcastic grunt followed by a short lived laugh. I shook my head as I peered through the window. Just like that, the rain stopped. The sun began to force its way through the clouds and into the garden. "Nothing mattered." I mumbled. "I wasn't in any pain from falling. I wasn't in danger at all when she showed up. She appeared out of nowhere. It was like she took it all away, the fear of falling... the fear of death... it was gone."

"But you didn't know who she was?"

"It didn't matter. My line shifted jolting me back to reality. And in the same second, just like that she was gone. I braced myself for impact. I closed my eyes and waited."

"But you didn't fall. What happened?"

"When I opened my eyes there was a pin right where I needed it to be. I clipped to it just as the one above broke free. So, there it was. I had my miracle."

"A very close call," she blurted, as she sunk back into her chair. "So, Aiden, do you think she was your guardian?"

"I know it sounds impossible, right?" I asked, with a laugh. I must have sounded like a complete lunatic.

"You think I'm crazy don't you?" I asked with a little more depth to my voice. "I know what comes next. You proceed to tell me that it was a hallucination. None of it ever really happened, right?" I could feel tension beginning to build in my arms and hands as they began to shake. I was definitely afraid of what she was going to say.

"You're not crazy," she whispered. I exhaled in relief dropping my hands into my lap. "I think we can get you better, Aiden. I really do. And this is a great start." She inched her chair closer to me. I could feel the tightness in my stomach begin to loosen making it little easier to breathe. I gave her a smile. My pale, unshaven face began to break from the gravitational pull that had consumed me. The morning sun came through the window, filling the cold, damp room with radiant warmth. I closed my eyes as it moved over me, consuming me.

"She was the light that brought me back to life," I whispered.

"Tell me about her, Aiden. What happened after you came down from that mountain?"

2

Reflections

As I made my way down, I couldn't help but think about her. She saved me from falling. I had no idea who she was, what she was. But she saved me.

It was late. I packed the last of my gear and tossed it into my Jeep and got in. I flicked on the dome light, tugged on the rear-view mirror, and gazed at my reflection. Not a scratch. I wiped the dirt from my face and brushed the dust from my hair. I sat there for a moment, thinking about how close I was to falling. I was lucky. It could have been much worse. I didn't tell anyone I was going. Not even my roommate, Ben. I usually told him when I headed up to climb. Occasionally I would mention my weekend plans when I talked to my Dad, but not this time. I told no one that I was climbing that day. No one would have known to send help if I didn't return. It could have been much worse.

I took a deep breath and let it out as I started the engine. The spinning tires formed a cloud of dust as they left the shoulder and gripped the road. It was worth the danger to me. To get to the top, that's what I lived for. I headed down the black road that hugged the edge of the mountain. There was no one out there, no one for miles. I loved the quiet serenity of the mountain. I considered inviting Ben along but changed my mind at the last minute. Ben's a chronic complainer. He's definitely good for making petty conversation, but always one sided. He rambled on and on about his relationship with his latest girlfriend, Maggie. I heard enough of the drama at home. I wanted to keep this place free from the insignificant conversation of everyday life. This is what I do. What I need for me. Just get off the grid for a little while.

Darkness came quickly over the mountain. No glorious sunset as ordered earlier that evening on the drive up. Next time, I thought. I made it through a pretty bad situation. That was the important thing. Tall trees and mountain ledges blocked the dim moonlight from the road ahead. Good thing it wasn't raining like the forecasters were predicting. Wet, dark mountain passes are no easy task, especially after dark. The wind thrashed against the side of my Jeep as I took each curve. I could feel the strength of each gust pushing me off to the shoulder as I made my way down the mountain. I took my foot off the gas and coasted through the dense patches of fog that had just settled in. Ahead in the distance, I noticed two people walking on the side of the road. I slowed as I approached them. They struggled with the wind as they fought their way up the steep mountain road. For a second I thought to stop and see if they needed help but something told me to stay away. I wondered where they were headed. There was nothing around for miles, nothing but the old castle at the top of the mountain. As I made my way past them, I noticed one of them was a young woman. Her eyes peered at me from above her scarf. Deep blue eyes. In this darkest of nights, in a blustering wind storm, with her face close to completely covered, I saw the color of her eyes. The most piercing blue eyes I had ever seen. Soon the two strangers faded into the darkness. I couldn't help but wonder where they were headed that late on such a blustery night. There was nothing up there. Nothing but the castle owned by Father Andrews. I worked for him part-time for the past couple of years. The ancient castle had been in his family for centuries. Father Andrews had been known to take in young drifters and runaways who were in need of a place to stay. Maybe that's where the two were headed.

Father Andrews kept it somewhat a secret. The castle and those that stayed there. The town of Princeton had been gossiping about Father Andrews and his family for years. Some thought that Father used the castle as a halfway house. He adopted his daughter, Sarah a few years ago. But others just came and went. Some thought his behavior was odd the way he kept them, secretly. Each of them had a story, a past. The stories of the guests of the castle go back hundreds of years. In a book written by Father Andrews' Great Grandfather, he told about the ancient carvings on the walls in the cellar of the castle. He kept records of each visitor that came over the centuries. Some of the guests stayed for a short time while others stayed and joined the community. They attended church, they were musicians and artists, teachers and students attending the University. Not your typical drifters. But Father Andrews was definitely a positive role model. Many could attest to that. Myself included.

I made it back to town just as it started to rain. The street lights were flashing, sending a faint red glow through my window. Lighted signs from the quaint little shops of downtown Princeton reflected off the dampened pavement. Ben and I rented an old two story just off campus a few blocks from town. Perfect spot for two broke college students. Close enough to walk to class if we made a couple bad decisions with what to do with gas money.

As I pulled into the driveway, I noticed that Ben was still up. The light was on in the kitchen. I stepped over the bicycle that had tipped over in the walkway and quietly opened the screen door. He was in the kitchen with Maggie. They were sitting at the table sharing a bottle of beer. There was a tiny pile of paper bits from the label next to the bottle. Ben enjoyed making a mess.

"It was part of his boyish charm." Maggie admitted at a party we all went to not too long ago.

"Hey you!" Maggie shouted, as I walked in. She quickly glanced to the unopened bottle on the table. She gave Ben a scowl nudging him to offer it to me.

"Hey, Bro. Want one?" Ben asked, as he slid the bottle across the table.

"No thanks, I'm good. It's been a long day," I muttered, snatching a water bottle from inside the refrigerator door. "I think I'll just hit the shower and turn in," I answered. "Thanks, though."

"Hey, Aiden, do you want to come to our sorority block party next Friday?" Maggie asked. "It's going to be a lot of fun. You can keep Ben under control," she said as she laughed at Ben.

She gave him a soft punch on the shoulder remembering the last party they had thrown. "Sounds fun. I wouldn't miss it," I snickered.

"What do you mean you wouldn't miss it? You told me you couldn't make it two days ago. Now you wouldn't miss it? Where's your loyalty man?" Ben whined.

"Oh Ben, face it. He likes me better than he likes you," Maggie said, giggling. "Night, Aiden." Maggie said sweetly as she backed out of her chair. "Night, Ben," she replied in an overly sweet tone. She leaned over to kiss Ben on the cheek as she darted toward the door.

"Hey, wait!" Ben shouted, as he chased her outside.

I picked up the unopened bottle of beer off the table, placed it into the cardboard slot next to the others on the shelf in the refrigerator, and headed for the shower. I noticed the laundry basket filled with neatly folded towels near the stairs. "Good for Ben," I thought. It was his turn to do towels and he did towels. I'm sure Maggie had a hand in it. Nothing Ben does is that neat. I snatched one tossing it over my shoulder as I tromped up the stairs. I carefully pulled my shirt off making sure not to catch the heavy medallion that I wore around my neck. I untied it and carefully placed in inside a small wooden box on my dresser. I always wore it, but tonight it meant more to me. I brushed my fingers over the shiny metal face as my mind raced back to those desperate moments on the mountain.

My mother found it. She discovered lots of ancient artifacts. Some she donated to museums and institutes but most she kept. So many in fact, we had to open a Gallery back in Boston to display them. Incredible pieces of time so well preserved, saved by my mother and her team. Tales of their discovery introduced a new and exciting world to the locals. But to me, the necklace she found was the greatest of them all.

"It's good to have keepsakes," Dr. Bennett whispered. "You're not wearing it, Aiden. Did you lose it?"

"I guess you could say that," I answered, "but I'm hoping it'll turn up."

"You were so young. It's good that you remember her," she said smiling.

I remember her stories. She would tell me all about her exciting adventures how she got paid to find hidden treasures. Sometimes she would take me along. I wanted to be just like her. I remember the last trip she took. I begged her to take me with her.

"I'll be back before you know it. Besides, I need you to stay here and take care of your father," she whispered as she held me close in her arms.

I remember the night she was expected to return home. I remember listening to the rain pounding against my bedroom window. Any minute she would come through the front door, dripping wet, carrying her tattered suitcases into the foyer. She would drop them with a thud pretending to be upset no one was waiting at the door. We were always hiding close by. An enormous smile would cover her face as soon as she saw me.

I remember her soaked navy overcoat she wore over her faded beige suit. Her jacket buttoned up to her chin with big heavy buttons. She wore horribly unattractive, yet completely practical, brown shoes that were covered in mud. And her dampened, unmanageable curly hair drooped from under her hat. She would hold her arms out to me as I flew down the stairs. But that night she wouldn't be there. No thud of her bags, no mud on her shoes. No open arms to fly into. Instead, I remember my father knocking on my bedroom door. He walked toward the window and slowly closed it as the evening rain had soaked the pane. I remember the expression on his face as he turned toward me.

"There's been an accident, Aiden," he whispered, as he sat next to me. "Tears welled in his eyes. He took me in his arms and held me. He stayed with me in my room that night."

"He told me about how she and her team were searching for an angelic sculpture when the cave collapsed. He never really got over the loss of my mother. My mother died trying to find an angel. That's why I love the statues, the sculptures. I need to believe there was an angel with her when that cave collapsed," I whispered.

Doctor Bennett scribbled the last of her notes onto the pad and looked back at me. I had focused my attention on the broken cobblestone near the wheel of my chair. She pulled her chair up next to me.

"I'm sorry about your mother. We can stop here if you want."

"I'm alright. I like talking to you, Dr. Bennett."

"I'm glad, Aiden," she said, smiling as she nodded. "I like listening."

3

Inspiring

I got to the park earlier than usual that next afternoon. I took my sander and moved it over the stone, gently smoothing the angles of her face polishing away years of wear. It was my job to restore the angelic sculptures in the park. The one I had been working on was unique. I took more time on her than the others. She inspired me. Even more so that day than the day before. Some days I hated my job. The dull monotony, the long, tiresome hours. But I was glad to be there with her that day. I took my block and brushed it over her shoulder, smoothing away the dust and pebble to expose the perfect stone underneath. I studied the sculptures, the history of angelic carvings, and why they were created. I read about these beautiful shadows of stone to better understand the true purpose of each piece.

I was fortunate enough to get the job with the Restoration Foundation through the community outreach program. It didn't hurt that I came highly recommended by Father Andrews, who happened to be the chairman of the board. It was a dream job. My first project was to restore this particular angelic sculpture that had been carved in the early Fifteenth Century. This one was my favorite. She was the oldest of all the pieces in Albany Wescott Park. And after the near death experience last night, I had a new mission and that was to work as much as I could to finish her. I moved my kneeling board across the grass in front of her. I needed to get closer to carefully sand her delicate features of her face. I pulled my pads up over my knees and dusted off my tattered jeans. I drew myself closer to her as I continued to work. It was getting late, daylight began to fade and there was a chill in the air. There weren't many people left in the park. It would be closing soon. The lamps were lit to light the path around the park connecting the sculptures like a maze. There were a few students across the lawn sprawled on a blanket under the oak tree. There were a small group of grounds men gathering their tools onto their truck near the back gate. I stood in front of her as evening came. "I'll be back tomorrow," I whispered softly, as I gazed at her freshly polished face. I packed up the last of my tools and placed them inside my bag. As I headed for the gate, I noticed a young woman sitting on the bench nestled deeply in a book. Her dark jacket covered most of her face yet a slight profile peered from her heavy hood. A few strands of her dark hair, the delicate tips of her lips. The subtle hints of her silhouette were beautiful. She dropped the book suddenly to turn the page. I was staring. I couldn't help it, there was just something about her. She didn't notice as I began to walk toward her. I watched as she gently played with the tips of the pages with her fingers as she read. As I approached the bench, I made a bit more noise shifting my heavy bag. I threw it recklessly from one shoulder to the other in an attempt to get her attention. The tools inside made a loud clanging as they slammed against my back. It worked. She glanced up at me. The corners of her mouth drew back forming subtle smile as her eyes met mine. I smiled back as I shuffled slowly past. She quickly returned her attention back to her book. I needed to stay focused on anything but her. I just needed to go about my business and not appear too desperate or too confident until I was out of the park. I couldn't have her thinking I was an obsessive stalker type who couldn't stop staring, fumbling around like an idiot. Once again, she glanced up at me. My intentions must have been so obvious.

Clearly she was uninterested, focusing right back to her book. But this time she repositioned herself on the bench, shifting away from me. Maybe Ben was right. On more than one occasion he's mentioned that I had a negative aura. I think I'm a pretty nice guy and I'm definitely approachable. Why do these things have to be so difficult? I thought to myself as I walked toward the gate. Whatever. I won't be too hard on myself. Ben doesn't know what he's talking about half the time anyway. Whoever she is... she'll be back. She was in the park tonight. She'll be here again.

The next morning I rushed through the pouring rain to the lecture hall. Surprisingly, I was on time. The large double doors were locked and a sign was posted. Class was cancelled. Of course it was. Of all days to be cancelled, it had to be a day I was on time.

My mind quickly shifted gears. I decided to head over to the library to read through a couple of chapters before my next class. I attempted to do that last night but I found it difficult to concentrate on anything but the girl in the park.

I stumbled into the library, pulled a dirty sweatshirt from my backpack, and ran it quickly through my wet hair. After a second or two, I noticed it had an odor. It was overwhelmingly horrid. It was a little late to be worried about the smell. I yanked it over my head shoving each arm through the appropriate sleeve and settled into a desk. It really couldn't get much worse, I thought as I leaned beside the desk gasping for air. No shower, no time to shave, and now a nearly unbearable smelly sweatshirt. I sunk into my seat and opened my book, peering around to see if anyone had caught wind of my existence.

The stillness of the library quickly turned into chaos as a small mass of drenched, out of control students raced inside to escape the rain. And wouldn't you know the loudest of them all was Ben herding several female students to one table. Within seconds he had spotted me and waved me over. The one single wave turned into several frantic waves in a desperate attempt to get me to join him at his table. I tried to ignore him and his theatrical display but it was no use. He wasn't going to give up. He would continue flapping his arms like a lunatic, disrupting the entire library, until I acknowledged him. I held up my hand and smiled briefly and jumped right back into my textbook. I heard him exhale. Everyone did. Clearly he wasn't satisfied. There was no question about it, Ben had issues. He could very well be the most dramatic male ever. He blamed his anxiety on his on again, off again relationship with Maggie. But even with all his pathetic faults, he was a lot of fun. He was the guy that everyone picked on for a guaranteed laugh.

Ben was from Chicago and to attend Princeton was always his plan. He's a big city boy with big expectations of himself, sometimes too big. He's a hyper sensitive, overly dramatic, exaggerator who has been known to fly off the handle every now and then for absolutely no reason. But I wouldn't change a thing about him. I never had too much going on so Ben and all the drama that came along with him, was exactly what I needed. He definitely kept life interesting.

"Hey, Bro! What's your problem?" Ben screeched. "Didn't you see me waving you over?" I looked at him with a scowl. "Whoa, dude. What's that horrible smell?" Ben pressed his nose against my shoulder. "Wow. Man, that's pretty bad. You can just stand far enough away. They may not smell you. Come on, come meet these girls. They really want to meet you and you're making me look bad," he whined.

"Can't you see that I'm trying to get through this chapter?" I snarled. Sometimes I needed to be firm with him. Otherwise he would never stop hounding.

"Yea, but this will only take a minute. Come on," he insisted. I put my sleeve up to my nose taking a big whiff of the biting odor.

"Maybe now isn't the best time, Ben. I've had the worst morning," I whined.

"Whatever dude. Just come on," he snapped.

We shuffled across the library to the table where Ben and his friends had set up for their morning study group. Ben shoved me toward the table.

"Ladies... this, this is my roommate, Aiden."

The girls each said hello. I stood back a safe distance from the table. The girls all seemed content with the gap between us. None of them seemed to be offended by my presence. They smiled at me. I must have looked alright. My wet stringy dark hair and slightly grungy look must have been more powerful than the nasty smell of my sweatshirt. Just as I began to make idle conversation for the sake of my roommate's reputation, I saw her. Or at least I thought it was her. Over in the corner of the library. She was sitting in a chair by the window reading. I instantly disconnected from Ben and the girls. I completely blocked them out. No one else existed in that moment. In the crowded library, with several quiet conversations consuming the atmosphere, nothing else existed. Just her sitting there. Her hair swept back around her ear. Her delicate profile. It was her. My heart began to race, my eyes glassed over as I glared toward her chair. I could feel a slight smile creeping over my lips. A nervous smile just at the thought of her. The girls let out a quiet giggle.

"Wow," Ben mumbled in embarrassment, "Aiden, hello?" Their quiet giggling turned into full blown laughter when I failed to respond. At that point, I realized I had completely removed myself from the conversation. I felt a slight reddish tint warm my pale, dampened face. The girls noticed my pitiful display of admiration for a certain young woman sitting at the other end of the library. I peered at Ben with a dumbfounded look on my face.

"Sorry, Ben. What did you say?" I desperately searched for a reasonable excuse to walk away. Nothing came to mind.

"Man. You really need to get a clue," Ben sneered.

"Excuse me ladies. Ben, I'll talk to you later. I have to go," I blurted, while giving him a pat on the shoulder to lighten his mood. Clearly he was perturbed by his negative facial expression.

"Aiden!" Ben shouted.

"Hey, it was nice meeting all of you," I whispered, as I darted away. I focused my sights to the newly emptied chair over by the window. I rushed over to where she was sitting just seconds before but there was no sign of her. I quickly scanned the entire west wing of the library looking for her. Unfortunately, it skipped my mind to pay any attention to what was in front of me. Obstacles like desks, books, chairs, all of the typical solid objects found in a library were left in utter ruin. The quiet hum of the library quickly began to buzz with gossip and sneering at my obvious desperation. She was gone. I just stood there for a moment in the open doorway. I glanced back to see the path of mild destruction brought on by my impulsive yet chivalrous attempt to talk to her. A path that led to back to Ben and his friends who, at that point, were mortified that I had been associated with them in the first place. I gave them an apologetic wave confirming what everyone at his table didn't want me to confirm. That yes, he is with us. I must have appeared completely frazzled. Everyone in the room was consumed with curiosity, their eyes fixated on my every move. I looked at Ben stuffing his hands deeply into his pockets as if to tell everyone that the show was most definitely over. They all needed to get back to whatever it was they were doing before I made a complete jackass of myself. I was pretty disappointed.

Once again I missed an opportunity to talk to her. Sooner or later I'll see her again. I pulled my damp stringy hair away from my forehead looking around in embarrassment. Ben and the girls stuffed their faces into their books as if to disown me. It was time for damage control. I was pretty good at charming the ladies. I quickly made eye contact with one of the girls at Ben's table. She turned and patted the arm of her friend as they both gazed my way. The poor, helpless romantic. That's what I was to them. I gave a wave and a sappy smile that instantly melted them into submission. They each returned a sympathetic wave. Ben sat groveling in his chair. I'd make it up to him later. A large pizza, a six pack, and a good game playing. And conveniently, his Sox were playing my Reds that weekend. Hanging out together for a big rival game like that would definitely render him "over it."

"I like Ben," Dr. Bennett said, chuckling.

"He's a good guy." I replied.

"I read in your chart he came to visit you."

"I don't remember. I'm sure it was hard for him to see me like this. For anyone to see me wasting away like this. I'm not a quitter. Anyone who knows me knows that." I whispered. "But it must look like I've given up."

"Have you?" she whispered. I know these questions were not easy for her to ask. I could sense it in the tone of her voice. She was trying to be careful and not ask the wrong questions.

"I guess, maybe."

"We'll get you back. Get some sleep. We need you to be well rested to continue. That is if you're comfortable continuing..."

"This is good. Right?" I asked, as I looked over at her. She smiled and nodded. I felt tears welling up in my eyes. I hated feeling so weak but I knew I had no one to blame but myself. I had to take responsibility for allowing this darkness to take over me. I felt a glimmer of hope talking about her. She was like a candle in a hurricane.

4

Walk With Me

The next morning I was up earlier than usual. I knew Dr. Bennett was standing in the doorway behind me. I could hear her sipping her coffee. In the first quiet moments I knew she was attempting to assess my mood.

"Good morning. How are you feeling?" she asked.

"Better. I suppose," I replied.

"Did you sleep well?"

I was reluctant to respond. I hadn't been sleeping much. I definitely didn't need more medication to help me sleep. Tremors, cold sweats, feeling like I fell deeper into a blackness? No thanks. Dredging up the past was harder than I thought. I needed to get clean. I had to get rid of the mind numbing effects brought on by the meds they pushed. I suppose I would find out soon enough if I had the strength to relive it without them.

"Do you want to continue Aiden?" Dr. Bennett flipped through her tattered leather notepad.

"Yeah. I'm good," I replied turning my chair toward her.

"Where did we leave off? Ah yes, the library," she said, as she sipped her coffee. She was definitely a morning person. I, on the other hand, wasn't. She stood there patiently waiting for me to respond. She drove her hand into the large front pocket of her coat searching for her pen. Out popped several slips of paper, wads of yellow sticky notes, gum wrappers, breath mints, tissues… you name it, she had it. Maybe she had a little too much coffee this morning. I couldn't help but smile at her as she struggled to get organized. It felt good having someone so eager to listen.

"Good. Okay, we're good," she exclaimed, as she proudly held up her pen. "That's where we left off… the disruption in the library." She gazed at me smiling, eager for me to continue.

Yeah. Well, that next morning I woke up late. Nothing was going right. I overslept. I didn't set the alarm. Who knows. It didn't go off. It didn't matter. What did matter is that it was obvious I was going to be late for class. Professor Williams didn't like his class rudely interrupted by late students.

Professor Williams was one my father's oldest and dearest friends. They went to high school together back in Boston. My father and the professor even attended Harvard together. Best men in each other's weddings, Godfathers to their children. They were close. But after Professor Williams' divorce he took the job teaching at Princeton. According to my father, he referred to the opportunity as being his "dream job." Guess he wanted to lessen the guilt he felt for leaving his two young daughters back in Boston. I raced down the stairs still wearing the old t-shirt that I had slept in. No time to change. No time for a desperately needed shower to help wake me up. I thrust open the screen door slamming it against the house and launched off the porch, skidded across the wet pavement both hands buried in my pockets searching for my keys. I hated being late. The look on Professor Williams' face popped into my mind as I jumped in the driver's seat. He wasn't going to give me special treatment. Even if I thought I deserved it as his Godson. The muffler made a raucous rumble as I pumped the gas pedal. It sounded a little louder than usual, like it was in need of repair. Everything was working against me. I spun the volume button to ditch the annoying morning talk show as I raced thru town. I looked at my watch. It was now 8:06. I was unquestionably late, I thought as I pulled into the last open spot in the student lot. I remained hopeful that Professor Williams wouldn't make a mockery of me to get a laugh out of the class to get even for my tardiness. Maybe I could just sneak in undetected. The large double doors rattled as I entered the hall. All eyes headed to my direction. Unfortunately, that wasn't going to be the case. I was definitely a distraction. Professor glared at me for a moment and, thankfully, jumped right back to his book. I settled deep into my chair in an attempt to discourage the ongoing stares from my classmates. I took a deep breath relieved that I had arrived, unscathed and without a second look from the professor.

Professor Williams had been teaching Art History and Greek Mythology at the University for eighteen years. He believed that his understanding of the subject matter reached far beyond the intellectual capacity of any author of any book in his lecture hall. He began to read a section from a novel about Angelic spirits. Everyone in the class was eagerly anticipating his interpretation of this chapter.

"Which of you has read this book and are familiar with this author and his conclusions?"

He had a subtle way of luring gullible students into what would seem to be an innocent discussion. But with just the right spark, would turn it into a grand debate. I glanced around the room. I knew a little bit about the book. I read several books by the author and was quite familiar with his theories. But I wouldn't be raising my hand. Not this particular morning. That would more than likely start a slew of questions regarding my whereabouts prior to 8:08 am. I sunk deeper into my chair. Professor knew I had plenty to say on this topic but the way I was avoiding eye contact. He snapped the novel shut as he approached my desk.

"Let's see, who has something to share?" He scrolled the room pointing the book in a circular motion. He stopped and pointed the book at a student directly behind me. "Mr. Rice. Do you have an opinion on the author?"

"Not really, I guess." He quickly slouched pretending to take notes. Professor probed the room while standing next to my desk.

"Miss Hamilton. How about you?" He asked politely. I was off the hook. For now. I turned in my chair to catch a glimpse of the poor girl who Professor Williams had sunk his claws into. It was her. I didn't notice her before. She was sitting a few rows over toward the back. She didn't seem to notice me. Her long brown hair was pulled back away from her face.

Only a few spiraling strands cascade down her cheek. She was obviously prepared to respond as she smiled at the Professor with confidence.

"Actually, Professor, I do. The author gives his description of the guardian angels." She spoke so eloquently. "He discusses in several chapters the different roles of the guardians. Some are assigned to mortals. Some are to appoint other angelic spirits. Some are protectors. He also discusses theories of how each level of these groups governs themselves," she explained to the class.

"Very good, Miss Hamilton. Thank you. For tomorrow, you will all read the last four chapters. Be prepared for discussion. That's means everyone. Mr. Rice, Mr. McCarthy."

I glanced over to her as Professor Williams strutted back to his desk. She was beautiful. The most beautiful girl I'd ever seen.

"Also, go over the notes taken from Wednesday's discussion. Make sure you have a clear understanding of the material. There may be a pop quiz later in the week," Professor Williams announced, turning back to the class now moaning in response.

32

He noticed my lack of interest in the topic and more interest in Miss Hamilton. He knocked on my desk as he spoke to grab my attention. It worked. For a few moments anyway. I was completely enthralled. And not with Professor Williams. Once again I found myself leaning around to look at her. She pushed the curl draped in front of her eyes away from her face tucking it back into her pony tail. Her lips delicately pink with a slight shimmer of gloss. I wanted to get her attention. But I had no idea how. I deliberately dropped my pen to the floor. I reached over to pick it up. She noticed my pathetic gesture to get her attention. It worked. She smiled at me, a sweet smile. She was incredibly captivating. She turned her attention back to the Professor who was obviously getting impatient with me.

"Do you mind if we continue, Mr. McCarthy?"

"Not at all." I whispered turning back toward him. "...sorry." I added slowly sinking in my chair.

"So, in this writer's view, various studies of saints and of guardians have uncovered interesting findings. The author believes that certain protectors are capable of seeing into the depths of mortal souls. To go a step further, he goes on to say that the souls of mortals are seen in shades of colors. For instance, those mortals who are envious are a shade of green. Those who are filled with hatred are shaded red. Those who are shaded yellow are afraid to do what is right, and are classified as cowardly. That would be you, Mr. Stiles. Am I right?" Professor Williams looked up above the rims of his glasses to find the desk of one particular student. With his menacing stare he directed the classrooms attention to Howard Styles. The room quickly filled with low pitched snickering. Mostly by the students who were involved with latest hazing prank. Everyone involved was either caught or confessed. Everyone but Howard, giving him the new nickname "Howard the coward".

"Funny." Howard whispered to the offensive cackling. His face scrunched up with anger. After the short lived fun, the Professor's eyes returned to his book. He cleared his throat as he shuffled back to his podium.

"The contents of this chapter will be included in your midterm," he shouted over the low grumbling as we dispersed.

She was packing up her bag as I glanced over to her. She latched her buckle, threw her bag over her shoulder, and headed down the aisle toward my desk. I wanted to talk to her. I needed to get her attention and keep it so I could introduce myself. I slid my book off my desk and it hit the floor with a loud thud. She looked down at it. She then raised her eyes to mine. She shook her head, smiled, and turned to walk away. I rushed around to greet her.

"Hello. I'm Aiden." I blurted.

"I'm Tess. It's nice to meet you," she replied, as she held out her hand. I touched her gently. I didn't want to let her go. I didn't say a word.. I could barely move. I held onto her hand as if my life depended on the connection. She couldn't move either. I was standing in her way. She smiled at me. She realized that I wasn't going to walk away with just a simple handshake. She pulled her hand away to once again tuck the stubborn lock of hair behind her ear.

"So, you're into Art History, too, I take it?" I asked.

"Hmm, you think?" She chuckled as she tipped her books toward me. Each of her books included the words "Ancient and Art" in their titles. I smiled and blurted out a laugh.

"Where are you headed?" I asked, nervously.

"I'm going to walk to the coffee shop on eleventh and grab a cappuccino. I had a rough morning. Maybe you did, too..." She chuckled again. She was breathtaking. I couldn't take my eyes off of her. "... and that would explain you coming in late?" she added, twirling the tips of her hair that had fallen from her ponytail.

"You noticed, huh?" I replied.

"I did. It was kind of hard not to. At least Professor Williams didn't embarrass you like he usually does to everyone else who comes in late." She said as she giggled. I darted in front of her to open the door. The sun was shining. A definite improvement from the rough battle I had with the elements earlier that morning.

"Thank you." She whispered as we made our way through the doors. She seemed comfortable with me. A gentle smile lit up her face as we walked together through the courtyard.

It was a perfect day. There was a gentle breeze that encircled us. A perfect few first moments to be with her. I didn't want to make her feel uncomfortable by asking too many questions even though I had plenty. For instance, where had she been all my life.

I hadn't actually been invited to join her for coffee. But at the same time I wasn't going to let her get away so easily.

"Do you mind if I walk with you?" I asked. I was mesmerized by her beauty. Her skin glistened in the sunlight, strands of her dark hair draped over her shoulder like the finest silk. And her eyes... her eyes were endless blue. They pierced through me.

"Not at all," she replied. "Would you like to join me?" she asked, tugging on the straps of her backpack.

"Sure." I quickly responded. I took her bag from her shoulder and threw it around mine in a chivalrous act of kindness. I walked closer to her as made our way toward the corner cafe.

"So, Aiden, are you a sculptor as well as a restorer?" she asked. I looked at her completely puzzled. "I saw you sanding the sculpture... the angel in the park."

"Did you?" I pretended to be surprised. I wasn't surprised. I shouldn't have second guessed myself that night thinking I didn't leave an impression. I must have. I smiled at her. I wanted her think I didn't see her just for a moment or two before confessing that I more than noticed her, too.

"You were so gentle with her. You must be very talented to be working with the sculptures in the park. Father Andrews is pretty selective. He doesn't give that job to just anyone."

"That's for sure. So, I take it you know Father Andrews?"

"You could say that." She giggled.

"He's my father." She smiled as she spoke. "He adopted me just before I turned eighteen. I needed a place to stay after my foster Mom split. I was with her for a long time. She wasn't around much so I basically raised myself. I don't remember my parents. They died in when I was little."

"I'm sorry," I said softly. I knew that sadness all too well.

"Thanks. But that was a long time ago. There are a lot of us that stay with Father Andrews. He's pretty great for taking us all in." She smiled and nudged my arm. I drifted from the conversation. It must have been her walking in the storm that night. Those piercing blue eyes... impossible to forget. They were definitely hers peering at me from her scarf as I drove past.

"It was me," she whispered.

"What do you mean, it was you?" I asked. I was definitely a little puzzled.

"You're putting two and two together, aren't you? I can tell," she said with a smile. "Father Andrews, the castle, that the night on the mountain road?"

"I was just sort of figuring it all out," I stuttered.

"Well, it was me. And Thomas. He lives with Father too. That wind storm kind of came out of nowhere." She picked up the pace like she was in more of a hurry to get to the coffee shop.

"It sure did," I replied.

"Well, the sculptures are very precious to Father Andrews," she quickly added. "You're very good with her. I'm not sure why but she does something for me. I guess maybe she just calms me," she said in a soft tone. She caught me in an intense stare as I waited for her to finish.

"I know what you mean. I feel the same way," I whispered. She gave a gentle smile and quickly looked down at the rustling leaves at her feet.

"I saw you, too," I confessed. "... in the park last night. You were sitting on the bench."

"That was somewhat embarrassing. You caught me staring. Didn't you?" she asked while blushing.

"You were staring?" I nudged her, pretending not to have noticed.

"We have a lot in common, Tess. My mother died when I was young. It's a pain that runs deeper than anything," I whispered, leaning into her. There was something there, something between us. I felt it. I think she did too.

As we approached the coffee shop, I rushed ahead to open the door for her. She brushed by me as she entered. I caught the delicate aroma of her perfume. Her innocence was invigorating. Her honesty, stimulating. As we walked through the café, Tess pulled the end of her dark ribbon untying it from her hair. She pulled a book from her bag and gently placed the ribbon inside the pages and returned it to her bag. She was so beautiful. Everything about her. I noticed some students watching her as she made her way through the shop. There was no denying that she was extraordinary. I felt a deep desire to be near her. As close as I could, as close as she would allow. She reached the end of the line and turned to ask me what I wanted to order. The cafe was extremely busy that morning. When she turned to me she was slightly embarrassed as we were sharing one spot in line. She tried to back up but there was no room.

Students were all bunched up together eagerly awaiting their beverages. She gazed up at me, searching for a sign that her closeness was acceptable.

"Busy this morning, isn't it?" I asked with a smile.

"Yes, it is," she replied, as she leaned to the counter.

After we both had our cups, we took a corner booth where it was a little quieter. There we sat. Face to face. She took a sip of her coffee leaving a bit of froth on her cheek. I reached toward her with my hand and pressed it gently against her skin removing the foam. Her hand cupped mine. For a moment we had connected.

"So, Aiden. How do you like Princeton?" she asked.

"The Art program here is amazing. I guess I'm following in my mother's footsteps. She majored in Art History as well. She went on to become an archaeologist. I think I'll stay more with the restoration process," I said, chuckling, as I sipped my coffee. I was rambling. No question about it but she didn't seem to mind.

"Where are you from?" she asked.

"Boston. And you? Where are you from?"

"Here, all my life. In Princeton. I love it here. I have zero desire to be anywhere else. It's peaceful here... you know? Even with all the students, the hustle, the mass chaos at times." She giggled as she spoke.

She continuously played with the tiny floating heart carefully designed in cream. "I'm sure you know what I mean... the grind of college life. It can be overwhelming, but there's just something tranquil about it here," she said, as she flicked the froth from the rim of her cup.

I nodded. "I know what you mean."

"Well, I should head back. I picked up a job working part time at the library." She grabbed her phone from the front pouch of her bag quickly checking it for the time. "I have to be there in exactly eleven minutes," she whined, as she tucked it back inside her backpack.

I pulled her chair from behind her and picked up her bag draping it over my shoulder. I took her scarf from the back of her chair and carefully wrapped it around her neck. Whatever I could do to leave an impression on her... that's what I needed to do. I had to see her again.

"Thank you, Aiden. You're too sweet," she whispered with a warm smile.

"You're more than welcome," I said in a soft, low voice. "That's a good thing I'm hoping," I whispered, leaning closer to her ear. I stuck close to her as we head toward the door.

"That's definitely a good thing." She answered. Her lips pursed together forming a flirtatious smile. The way she looked back at me I knew something was brewing between us. Something incredible.

As we made our way through the crowded café, Tess saw a familiar face through the window. She hesitated to move any further. I looked to see who she was staring at. He was blonde, a white blonde and well built. Nothing I couldn't handle. He definitely appeared to be angry. He was looking for her and she knew it. He was dressed completely in black, arms covered in scrolling tattoos, hair cut very short except for a few random tough guy spikes. Definitely an identity crisis going on there. A big time Billy Idol wannabe. Someone needed to tell him that look was long gone. And for good reason. Clearly no one wanted to mess with him and his obvious badass attitude, so I suppose it ultimately worked for him.

The path was cleared as he stormed toward the coffee shop. No one wanted to get in his way as he pushed through the busy line of students. He headed directly toward us, toward Tess.

In route, he bumped a waitress carrying a tray of coffee tipping it spilling several cups. Customers quickly scattered to avoid being burned. Everyone was able to escape the scorching liquid but Tess. It completely saturated her sleeve. Quickly she began brushing the hot coffee from her shirt while everyone rushed around trying to help her. Vincent realized the damage he caused and the scene he had created. Tess glared at him. It didn't take him long to turn around and head back the way he came. And just as rudely. I could feel my heart pounding, rushing blood through my veins. I couldn't believe the nerve of this guy. What a coward, he just walked away. He didn't apologize, or try and help. He didn't say a word.

Another time, another place, he would get his. I thought. And I'd be the one to give it to him.

"That guy was the worst! I'm so sorry!" the waitress shouted, as she leaned over toward Tess dabbing up the coffee.

"Are you okay?" I asked Tess, helping to clean her sleeve. "It's fine, really. It was an accident. I'm fine," she insisted.

"You must be burned," the waitress demanded, as she yanked on Tess' sleeve. Tess pulled away in an attempt to stop the waitress from examining her.

"I'm fine," she insisted. I knew she couldn't have been fine. But I understood her desire to stop the whispers from the other students gawking at her. "I'll be fine," she said, as she attempted to roll her sleeve back down over her arm. "Aiden, please. Let's just go," she begged. I took her hand and we headed for the door.

The crowd began to settle back into their spots in line and the chaotic buzz faded just as quickly. With Vincent gone, Tess insisting she was ok, no one gave it a second thought.

I noticed her arm during the struggle. There was no burn. No redness, no mark at all. I was relieved that she wasn't hurt, but wondered how it was possible.

"You're not burned. Not even a little," I whispered. "That's strange. That coffee was scalding hot, but you're not at all burned,"

I murmured to her, as I escorted her out of the shop.

"I was lucky then I guess," she said, smiling.

Once we made our way outside it didn't take long before we ran into Vincent. "Tess, you need to come with me," he said in an angry tone, as he rushed toward us.

"Vincent, go home. I will meet you later, after work. Just go!" she shouted. I was ready. No one would hurt her. Not while I was breathing.

Vincent stormed away after looking directly at me with obvious disdain. Oh yeah, pal. We got a problem, I thought, as I clenched my fist.

"Who was that?"

"Vincent. He lives with Father Andrews, too. He has issues. Mostly with me. I'm sorry for all that, Aiden. He sometimes goes into these rages when he realizes that he doesn't have complete control over me."

"It's not your fault, Tess. There's no reason to apologize. Just tell me you're not with that guy."

"No! He's like my brother! I thought you would assume that when I said he lives with us," she shouted.

"I'm sorry. All I wanted to do was set him straight for treating you like that," I said, firmly. "I wish you didn't have to deal with a guy like that." I took her by the hand as we headed back toward the library.

"I'm a little surprised Father Andrews would let a guy stay there with an attitude like that."

"He helps Vincent with his issues. He better with him than any of us." She confessed. "I need to hurry back. I'm late which isn't a big deal if it's just a few minutes." She said flashing a somewhat frantic smile. Maybe she was a little uncomfortable talking about her family. I didn't want to push, and yes, we were out of time which explained why she wanted to change the subject. There was a desperation in her eyes, in the way she looked at me. I can't quite explain it. But from that moment on, I knew I would do anything for her. Including extinguishing the overwhelming desire to go after Vincent. Brother or not, he could use a good lesson in manners.

"So, what is it that keeps you busy other than working on the sculptures?"

"Well, I keep myself pretty busy. I'm on the row team, which is quite demanding. And I like rock climbing. I try to head up to Seraph every Sunday. It helps to clear my head. That's why I was up there the other night. I was driving back from my climb," I replied. She leaned into me wrapping her hands tightly around my arm as if helping to hold her up. Having her close to me felt natural. Like we've always been together.

"Oh, I see. That's very interesting. And adventurous." She giggled as she spoke.

"So, how about you? What do you like to do besides reading in your spare time?" I asked.

"I dance... with the Princeton Dance Company."

"Really? I would love to come see you sometime."

"Well, ok! There just so happens to be a performance Friday night, if you're not busy." She squeezed as she held onto me grinning. "I could leave a ticket for you at the theater door. If you'd like. It starts at seven."

"I'll definitely be there," I said, as we reached the steps of the library.

"Good," she replied. "And do me a favor..."

"Anything," I said, handing her bag to her.

"Find me after."

"I'll find you," I assured her.

She skipped up the cement steps. "I'll see you tomorrow, then. In class?"

"Yes, tomorrow. See you then," I answered. She gave me a quick wave as she opened the door and went inside.

Dr. Bennett put the cap on her silver pen and set it on the table. She appeared to be confused. She let out a heavy breath as if she had been holding it the entire time. She moved closer to me with a funny look on her face. A look of disbelief which wasn't one I was used to seeing from her.

"Interesting," she muttered, crossing her legs. "I'll bet you were relieved she wasn't burned by the coffee."

"Very," I answered, calmly. I needed to keep my emotions in check. No jumping to conclusions with where she was headed with these questions.

"And this Vincent fellow, he seems to have anger issues."

"Yes. And he didn't seem to like me much," I whispered.

"And Professor Williams, being a close friend of your fathers, it must be nice having him so close. Have you ever shared any of this with him?"

"Some things."

"What does he think?"

"I don't know. I think he only listens as a favor to my Father."

She took in each of my responses, displaying no emotion. I didn't quite know how to read her. She kept her opinions to herself and chose to stay focused. She played the role of the doctor to a "T", jotting down bits and pieces of our conversation. I knew this could go one of two ways. If I continued to be completely honest, I risk losing her believing me. Believing she could actually help me. Or I could stop here. I could shut down and go back to the dark, cold nothing where I'd been for months.

"Aiden?" She put her pen down and folded her hands. She gazed at me with no expression. I hesitated to answer, afraid what she was going to say.

"Did I lose you Dr. Bennett?" I asked. My voice cracked a little from the lump forming in my throat.

"No. I'm with you. I'm just trying to figure out why no one's come to see you. Your father for instance, or Professor Williams. There's nothing in your file that says you've refused visitors," she mumbled sympathetically.

Maybe that was the reason for the change in her demeanor. She was simply confused as to why no one cared. They cared. I cleared my throat and looked at her.

"I know why they don't come. I made it clear to everyone that unless they brought her to me I wanted nothing... no one. No visits, no cards, no calls. Nothing. I don't want pity. I only asked for one thing. If they couldn't bring Tess, I didn't want them to come. I can't have them here hovering over me, feeling sorry for me."

"I see. Alrighty then, let's keep going shall we?"

5

Intrigued

The next morning, I arrived to class on time. Professor Williams gave me a sluggish smile as I entered the lecture hall. I cased the auditorium to see if she had arrived. She wasn't there. Not yet anyway. I opened my bag, took out my book and tossed my backpack under my seat. I proceeded to open to the chapter for the days discussion with enthusiasm. And there she was strolling through the doors with a couple other students. She was wearing a dress, a short, light pink dress. Her hair was tied loosely away from her face. She glanced up and noticed me watching her. She gave me a quick smile and took her seat.

After class, I waited by the door for her. "Hey there!"

"Hey yourself," she replied, shoving her books in her bag. "I wanted to ask you... if you're not too busy..."

"Spit it out." She giggled and nudged me.

"Well, I have a row competition Saturday. I was thinking maybe you would like to come?"

"I'd love to."

"Cool."

"See you later... gotta run," she shouted, darting down the hall to catch up with awaiting friends.

"Who was that you were you talking to?" Ben asked, charging toward me. He had a class at the same time across the hall.

"Tess, the girl from the library. We're in Williams' class together," I replied. "I don't know, Ben. There's something about her. Something amazing."

"Man, you say that about them all. Oh, this girl is so special, she's the one... Whatever. You fall in love too often my friend. Too easily." Ben reached down and snatched up the ribbon that had fallen from Tess' book. He draped it over my shoulder in a girly gesture to tease me. I grabbed it and tucked it inside my pocket.

"You're a hopeless romantic," Ben teased, pointing to his pocket.

"Coming from you... the serial monogamist." I said sarcastically shaking my head. "You're nuts,"

"Come on, we got practice. Coach called. He's moved it up an hour. We got to get going. You drive," Ben yelled, as he ran ahead.

"What do you mean, I drive? You don't even have a car," I shouted as I caught up to him giving him a shove.

"I could drive your Jeep, but I'm too emotional. Maggie didn't call me back last night. So, you should drive," Ben whimpered. I couldn't imagine him experiencing an actual crisis. He wouldn't be able to handle it. It's my belief, he lived a very sheltered life. He must have. Theres no other explanation for his stupidity.

After practice I rushed home to get ready to go watch Tess. I couldn't wait to see her. I adjusted my collar in the bathroom mirror, tucking my necklace inside my shirt. through the opened buttons. The theater was just down the block from the flower shop where I picked up a dozen white roses.

"Lucky lady," the shop owner said, as she handed me my change.

I'm the lucky one, I thought, thanking her and returning the smile. I took Tess' ribbon from my pocket and tied it around the stems.

The Theater in downtown Princeton was spectacular. The lights of the marquis sign lit up the entire street. Couples dressed in their very best ushered in from every corner. I couldn't wait to see her. I was dressed in a dark fitted suit, my hair slicked back with a waxy shine. Sophisticated, dashing, and extremely uncomfortable. What if she had forgotten to leave a ticket? I felt a slight panic warm my insides. Maybe she wasn't that into me to remember. That would be devastating. I stuffed my hand into my pocket feeling around for my wallet as I approached the ticket counter. If she forgot to leave a ticket, I would purchase one. There was no way I was going to miss this.

"My name is Aiden McCarthy. I believe there is a ticket here for me?"

"Yes, there is," the attendant said. He fumbled through a small box of tickets covered with yellow sticky notes. Finally, he came across one with my name boldly printed on the yellow tab.

"Here you go, Mr. McCarthy." He handed me the ticket. "Enjoy the performance."

"Thank you."

Father Andrews spotted me right away. "Aiden, I'm glad you could make it." His arm stretched around my shoulders as he gave me a gentle shake.

"It's nice to see you."

"You too, son. So, I hear that you've met my Tess." He raised an eyebrow at the roses.

"Yes. I have. She's incredible."

"That she is. Well, good. Very good. Enjoy the show, Aiden. Oh, and find me after. I've been given specific instructions to escort you to the meet and greet after the performance."

"I will. Thank you."

An usher directed me to a balcony seat with clear view of the stage. The theater was incredible. Enormous gold and crystal chandeliers hung from the colorfully painted ceiling and red tapestry draped from every balcony. It was perfect. From the tuning of instruments in the orchestra pit to the humming of the audience. Tonight's performance was about to begin.

As the lights dimmed, the violinist stood and began to play. A soft, enchanting sound that echoed throughout the theater. I scanned over each of the dancers as they entered the stage looking for her. And there she was, second from the end.

They were dressed in white with their hair pulled tightly back. Each wore feathery wings that raised high above their shoulders, floating delicately as they moved. The performance was breathtaking. Several of the dancers were lifted into the air, high above the stage as if to fly like the angels they were made up to be. Tess floated out into the crowd right in front of me. A spectacular final scene that left everyone in the audience cheering with excitement. All eyes were on Tess. The applause grew as she soared above them. But she kept her eyes focused on mine as if I were the only one watching and in that moment I knew I would love her forever.

"Well, by the look on your face I take it you approve of the performance?" Father Andrews was beaming with pride as he should.

"Incredible," I whimpered, nearly speechless as I came down the staircase toward him.

"I thought you'd enjoy it. Now let's get you backstage."

We entered a big room filled with dancers and several guests. I felt my hands tremble as I held the roses tightly. There she was. Resting on a long bench removing the ribbons of her shoes wrapped high around her ankles.

There was a younger, somewhat good looking guy sitting next to her. Very close to her. Too close in my opinion. Tess stood holding out her hands helping him to his feet. He was pale. Maybe he was sick. He had heavy dark circles around his eyes and seemed to have trouble standing. Tess immediately looked up as we came through the open doors. Her eyes grew with excitement which I had to admit was a slight relief. I didn't want her with anyone else. I was now emotionally invested and wanted to let her know how I felt before we went any further.

"Aiden!"

"These are for you, Tess." I handed her the roses.

"They're beautiful... and you found my ribbon! Thank you. It means so much to me, even more now." She kissed my cheek tenderly, which completely melted me.

"You're welcome. You're amazing, you know."

"Thank you. I'm so glad that you could come," she whispered, pulling my arm escorting me toward the bench.

"Aiden, this is Dominic. He's a friend of our family. He just arrived in town and will be staying with us."

"Dominic, it's nice to meet you," I said, reaching out my hand.

"And you as well, Aiden. Nice to meet you," He replied as he shook my hand.

"You were brilliant tonight my dear, Sophia and Daniela too. You were all simply magnificent," Father Andrews whispered as he hugged her. "Dominic, you can ride with me. You will need to get some rest. I'm afraid you will have plenty of excitement once we get you home. But rest is what you need. See you at home, Tess."

"It was nice to meet you, Aiden," Dominic said, struggling to maintain his balance. "I'm sure we will be seeing each other again." Father Andrews was right. He was in need of rest at the very least.

"You, too. Yes, we will. Very soon."

"Thank you Tess," Dominic whispered.

"You're very welcome."

"Aiden, my boy... you're doing a good job and staying on schedule. We'll catch up Monday."

"Thanks. Monday it is."

"I'm so glad you're here," Tess whispered, gripping my arm tightly. Here it was. The moment I needed. I wrapped my arms around her pulling her closer to me.

"There's nowhere I'd rather be in the world, than here with you."

She leaned toward me looking at me, deep into my eyes. She didn't say a word. She didn't have to. I cupped her face with my hands and gazed at her. We shared a moment together, away from the chatter happening around us in the room, away from everything. So much was said with not a single word spoken. The color of her eyes, the intensity of my stare, her face, her lips. She was flawless. And there was something building between us. We both felt it now. Her eyes dropped for a moment as she broke from my embrace. She backed up while looking around to see if anyone was watching our romantic display. She looked back at me smiling.

"You look very handsome."

"Thank you."

"Where did you get this?" She asked as she pulled my necklace from behind my shirt. She gently ran fingers over the medallion.

"... the sign of the angel," she whispered.

"What did you say?"

"It's the sign of Saint Thomas, the angel," she replied. She gently stroked the carved symbol.

"How did you know that?"

"I know a lot." She giggled. "I think I've read just about every book ever printed about guardian angels."

"Me, too," I replied.

"Where did you get this?"

"My mother gave it to me."

"... your mother? Your mother is Betsy McCarthy."

"Yes."

"Incredible. I'm familiar with her work," she said, smiling.

"You are?"

"Yes. She was an amazing archeologist. I remember her," she added, "..I mean, I remember reading about her passing."

She looked at me to see if I noticed her fumble of words. She would have been just six or seven years old when my mother died. Too young to possibly know her.

"I was going to say something before you corrected yourself. Either you were a child prodigy, which I wouldn't doubt, or you are much older than you look," I said, sarcastically.

"You're funny." She giggled. "Seriously though. I feel special hanging out with you. Your mother is famous. In our world, any-way. Our amazing world of historical artifacts."

"You are special," I said, nudging her.

"She would be very proud of you, Aiden."

"I'd like to think so."

"Well I know so. And I also know it's getting late and I need to get home."

"Can I drive you?"

"My sisters are here. Sofia, she dances, too. And Daniela. She was the violinist tonight. We came together."

"You have a big family. You're very lucky."

"I don't know about being lucky. It definitely has its perks. But as you saw with Vincent, it also comes with drama."

"How many live there?"

"Thirteen all together now with Dominic joining our family. Sofia, Daniela, and three more sisters at home — Rachel, Sarah and Elaina. And my brothers, Thomas, Nathaniel, Frederic, Angelo and Avery. Oh, and Vincent. We were all adopted by Father over the years. We just refuse to leave."

"It's nice to have so many people to love and care for. And love you back."

"Yeah, it is. It can get hectic but most of the time it's great. I really should go. Here's my number." She snatched a pen from the bench and wrote her number on the palm of my hand. "No paper. This works. Call me later?" The smile she gave me was enough to weaken my knees. It took every ounce of energy to stand there next to her and not pull her to me and kiss her.

"I will definitely call you, Tess." I watched her run out the doors.

Dr. Bennett shifted in her chair. She struggled with her skirt as she yanked it down over her knees. The distraction brought me back. Back to the hospital terrace where I sat in a wheelchair. But something was happening the more I talked. I was beginning to feel better somehow. Better than I had in months.

Remembering the conversations with Tess, the moments we spent together, the intensity of the feelings I felt for her all came rushing back.

"She's talented."

"Incredibly," I answered.

"And this young man you met that night, Dominic? What do you think of him?"

"He seemed alright. He was definitely not well. Father Andrews took care of them. Or they took care of him, I don't know. It wasn't really my place to ask too many questions."

"You're probably right. Intrusive questions this early in the game probably wouldn't have been good."

"That's what I was worried about. I always wanted to know about that place. Every climb I would try to imagine who he kept there, what they were like. And now that I knew, it didn't matter. I only cared about Tess."

"It's all somewhat ironic if you think about it, Aiden. Wouldn't you agree?"

"Yeah. Pretty ironic when you think about it."

"Let's stop here for today. Your lunch will be ready soon. One of the nurses will be here soon to take you," she said. She lifted herself from her chair. Still fighting with her skirt, she yanked it back into position covering her knees. "I'll see you tomorrow."

"Sounds good."

As she walked away she turned back toward me stuffing her hands into her pockets. She pondered on her thoughts for a moment before she said anything.

"You're making great progress Aiden. I'd say at the rate we're going you'll be able to get out of here before you know it... and back to your life where you belong," she said, smiling at me.

I didn't respond with words. I really didn't see a need to. Besides the fact that I was left speechless, the enormous smile covering my face more than spoke for me.

6

The Others

After the ballet, Father Andrews returned to the castle with Dominic who, at that point, was very frail. He needed help and he needed it quickly. Tess and her sisters came in shortly after and helped to get him safely inside.

"We're home," he announced. "Come quickly please, all of you."

They took him into the living room and sat him in the chair next to the fire. He was going from bad to worse very quickly.

"Thank you for bringing me here," he whispered in a weak voice.

"You're home, Dominic. There's no need to thank us," Tess whispered as she knelt down beside him. "You belong here, with us."

"How many are here?" he asked. His voice grew more faint with every breath. "There are thirteen of us now including you." She replied.

"So many."

Father Andrews handed Dominic a glass of water.

"Yes. And each of you are welcome to stay as long as you wish," he said patting Dominic on the shoulder. One by one they came running into the living room. Little Sarah came hopping down the staircase happy to see everyone including the newest addition to the family.

"Sarah is the youngest but has been here the longest. She's five."

"Say hello, Sarah."

"Hello," she whispered as she leaned into him. She took her tiny hand and pushed his hair away from his eyes.

"Hi, Sarah. It's a pleasure meeting you."

"As you can see she's very affectionate. Helping newcomers to feel welcome is her specialty. She's been five years old for over four hundred years."

"I've heard stories of you, Sarah," Dominic whispered, as he stroked her rosy cheek. He gazed at each of them and his beautiful surroundings. "This place is incredible. I'm so glad I found you all."

Father smiled. He was very proud of his family and more than happy to welcome another.

"Thomas, Tess, and Vincent came together. The three of them came to the castle over sixty years ago when I was just a child. But I remember when they came." Father put his arm around Thomas. "We grew up together. Thomas is like a brother to me. But after I kept aging and he didn't, I naturally became more like a father," He explained.

"He may appear older but I am still the big brother," Thomas interjected, teasing Father Andrews.

"Tess and Vincent were very close when they first came. They were always together. They stayed with my mother most of the time. Tess was especially close to her. Father Andrews reached out for Tess' hand as he spoke. She took his hand giving him a warm smile. "It was very hard on her when she passed."

"She was an amazing teacher, mother... sister. I miss her," Tess confessed.

"Me, too, Tess," Father whispered, as he kissed her forehead. "Nathaniel came seven years after Thomas, Tess and Vincent. And... Frederic, Angelo, Daniela, and Alaina came twelve years after. Sofia and Rachel came four years later and Sarah found Avery one year later."

Dominic smiled at Father Andrews. He knew that he was finally safe with them. "That was what… thirty years ago?"

"Thirty-two," Tess whispered.

"And no one has come since." Father added.

"We try to blend in. As much as humanly possible," Thomas said. "We're no different than anyone else. As long as we stay focused on our tasks, we can coexist. We're able to live among them. It can get tricky attempting to blend in to a society when you've been around for centuries. We've traveled the world. We've visited many places.

"Many times over, in fact. We've experienced wars, famine, plagues, disasters, all of it. Many mortal experiences in which, unfortunately, we cannot interfere. And we must heal ourselves or we can't be what we are. We go to a place where we restore. Otherwise we simply can't stay." Thomas explained. He glanced at Tess. She knew what he was getting at. She scowled at him trying to keep him focused on more urgent matters.

"How far back do you remember, Dominic?" Tess asked.

"Not long. I remember meeting Isabella. I don't know how long it's been since I've seen her. Or when I left them. They were weak. I couldn't watch them wither away. There was nothing I could do for them. None of us knew what to do.

"Isabella warned me that I would soon be just like them and we needed to stay together. I didn't believe I would get sick. I was stronger than they were. I didn't understand and I just left them. I've been wandering on my own for a while now… growing weaker by the day. My very first memory was the desire to just soar. To be as free as the wind. I wanted to see as much as I could. But something was happening to me and the more I tried to ignore it the worst it got. I remember her telling me to find her, or to find this place before it was too late. I didn't know what she meant, but now I understand."

"We've never met Isabella," Tess whispered. "But it's possible they found the falls on their own. There are signs showing us the way. I've known others like Isabella, and from what you've said about her I can tell she's smart and strong. I'm sure she's ok." Tess assured him.

"I'm guessing he must be young," Tess whispered to Thomas.

"I'd say so, yes. And probably hasn't been assigned."

"Assigned? What do you mean?" Dominic asked.

This was all so new to him. Nothing he'd ever heard before.

"Well, some of us have mortals to protect. That's what we do," Thomas explained.

"I see. That's why you're with them like this, living among them."

"Yes. The only mortal we're close to or let get close to us is Father Andrews. But, we don't believe that he's mortal. He's more of a protector to us than we could ever be to the mortals."

"You need to take him now Thomas," Father whispered. "We can talk more later."

"See what I mean? Always looking out for us," Thomas replied.

They all gathered around Dominic. He needed to restore and soon.

"You know where to go?" Dominic asked.

"Yes." Thomas whispered putting his arm around him helping him to stand. "We all go together. And often. Whenever sadness, hurt or any human emotion begins to wear us down or effects our judgement we go to restore. If we don't, we age. Rapidly."

"That's why we don't interfere," Vincent interjected from the dark corner of the room. "We can't. We're only here to guide them. Not get involved," he grumbled. "We're very discrete." He glared at Tess. "We have to be." He was clearly upset with her by tone of his voice and the angry look on his face.

"We have to convince mortals that we are just like them. Yet we never age, never hurt, never hunger. It never comes into question with mortals. It's all just a part of our power over them. Part of our existence," Tess explained, as she held Dominic's hand.

"Isabella." Dominic's voice grew more faint. "We need to find her first, before we go." His head fell to his chest.

"He can't wait. He must go now," Father Andrews insisted.

"Angelo and I will take him, Father," Thomas insisted. "Vincent you should come, too."

"When Tess goes, I'll go," he snapped.

"Vincent… please…" Tess pleaded.

"We'll go together Tess."

"Off you go then. Quickly," Father said, ushering them toward the door. "Hello there, friend. I'm Angelo. It's good to meet you."

"Same to you, Angelo."

"You're going to be as good as new in no time," Thomas assured him as they made their way through the opened doors whisking him out into the night sky.

Sharing all this with Dr. Bennett was a relief. She believed every word. At least she appeared to. Her notebook began to look more like a mini novel. One she wasn't only proud of but one she was on a mission to finish.

"Hello, Aiden," Doctor Bennett whispered, as she tapped her knuckles softly against the door. She usually came to see me in the morning, but not today. I had just finished dinner. Surprisingly the meals were pretty decent for hospital food. I started to put on some of the weight I had lost when I first arrived. Back then, nutrition came in liquid form. Intravenously or through straws. Regaining an appetite was a definite sign things were improving.

"I wondered where you were when I didn't see you this morning."

"I'm sorry, Aiden. It seems I've fallen a little behind, so I had to play catch up with some unfinished paperwork. I can't seem to concentrate lately. I'm having difficulty working on any other case but yours. So that makes you a special case."

"I'm not sure if I like the sound of that," I said, chuckling.

"It's just a term, Aiden. Nothing to worry about. Let's just say I've made you a priority."

"I'm good with that."

"Good." She nodded. "You're making great progress. And did I just hear one of your nurses say you were ready to lose the chair?"

"It was a thought," I replied. "I know I need to."

"It's a good thought. Would you like to continue tonight or should we wait and get a fresh start in the morning?"

"You must have absolutely no life," I joked. I still possessed a sense of humor. That was a good thing. And, thankfully, so did Dr. Bennett. "Don't you have a family waiting for you?" I asked.

"Unfortunately, I don't," She replied, smiling. "My career took most of my time. I was too busy to think about anything else especially a relationship. Don't get me wrong, I've done my share of dating. But it never amounted to anything. No one special. Let's just say your life is much more interesting than mine." She smiled and flipped her notepad open to a new sheet.

"It was more interesting. So, what exactly do you write in that notepad?"

"I just take notes, Aiden. To help figure this all out."

She was becoming less and less like a doctor and more like a friend.

"I think you left off saying your goodbyes at the theater," she said, still smiling from the comment I made about her lack of having a life outside the hospital.

I returned home that night to find Ben snoring on the couch. I quietly closed the door behind me trying not to disturb him. He was definitely out. Various body parts dangling off the sofa, his glasses pushed up against his forehead. I carefully removed them and placed them on the table. I snatched a blanket from the chair and tossed it over him. He shifted a little and mumbled, "Thanks, Ma."

I laughed at him as I went up the stairs. All I wanted to do was call Tess. I grabbed my phone from my bag and dug for the small piece of paper that Tess gave me at the theater. I got her voicemail. It was pretty late. She may have been tired after the ballet and fallen asleep. I left her a voicemail so she knew I remembered.

"Hey Tess, it's Aiden. Just thought I'd give you a call. I'll try you later."

Dr. Bennett noticed as I reached for the cup of water near my bed. She stood and handed it to me. "Thanks."

"Of course."

"I had a pretty crazy dream that night. The first of many."

"I saw that in your file. Bad dreams?" She asked.

"You could call them bad. More stressful than anything."

She sat up in her chair crossing her legs to get comfortable. "I thought maybe these dreams had something to do with how you ended up here."

"Maybe."

"Describe the first one you had. As much as you can remember."

7

Bitter First

I was on an old school bus. I couldn't tell where I was. There were two students sitting in the seat in front of me and another across from me. I couldn't see much through the mud covered windows. The only thing I could see were branches hitting the bus as we whipped past. I gripped tightly to the seat in front of me trying to hang on. The muddy road was filled with potholes and tight curves. Up ahead I could see parts of it had washed away from the storm.

The students around me were silent, seemingly unaffected by our situation. Their eyes kept straight ahead. I looked up at the driver. He struggled to keep us on the road clenching the wheel tightly maneuvering through the rough terrain. We were going too fast. Way too fast.

A muddy drizzle covered the windshield making it difficult for him to see the road ahead. Large branches slapped against the glass after being torn from the trees by the wind. The wipers were unable to keep up with the rain pellets and debris. I braced myself thinking any minute something bad was going to happen. The driver jerked on the wheel as the back of the bus slid off of the road. We began to roll backwards down a deep embankment headed straight for a ravine. There was nothing he could do. Nothing but to save himself. He gripped the lever to the double doors thrusting them open and in an instant he was gone.

Windows began to shatter sending a shower of glass, mud, and rain into the bus. We hit large rocks and trees making it nearly impossible to hang on. The three students were tossed to the back against the emergency doors as we sunk further down the embankment. I clung to the seats around me but the wet leather made it hard to grip and I, too, was thrown to the back.

The bus slowly tipped to its side as we slid down the muddy embankment. Two of the students disappeared through a large hole at the top of the bus ripped open by a large branch. I needed to do something to help them. If they were clinging to the bus outside I needed to act quickly. I slowly moved toward the opening but I heard faint whimpering from behind me. A frightened young girl, the third student was left clinging to the handle of the emergency door. She was terrified. Her face was pale white and covered in mud. A cut over her right eye sent a stream of blood down her face. I extended my hand to her as the bus skidded farther down embankment.

"Take my hand, I'll pull you up!" I shouted. She was frozen. She didn't move.

"Don't be afraid. I'm not going to leave you. I'll get you out. I promise," I shouted. "As soon as you can, just reach up and take my hand."

Slowly she began to pull herself up toward me. I took her by the hands anchoring my body to the metal frame of the seat in front of me. Her wet hands slipped from mine and she fell back into the corner of the seat.

That's when I saw him. That's when I saw Vincent. He was there. At the front of the bus next to the driver's seat completely unscathed. Not a scratch, completely dry. No mud, no rain. He stood upright which in that moment was physically impossible. Basic gravity wouldn't allow it. It was like he orchestrated some form of freakish optical illusion and by the look on his face it was for his own entertainment.

"Are you here to help?" I yelled to him. He just stood there watching me struggle. A sadistic smile covered his face.

"Vincent?" I shouted. Still he didn't answer. He had no intention of helping me or this poor girl.

The bus had slowed in the heavy mud and it began to spin and shift. If we were going to escape, now was our chance. I looked back at her. She hovered on the floor between the two seats.

"Come on, get up!" I shouted, as I clutched onto her hand. She began to step over seats moving back toward me.

"Hang on!" I shouted. I reached up towards the hole above me. I took of my jacket and threw it over the opening to protect us from the jagged metal. I jumped for the opening and pulled myself out.

There was no sign of the two students. There was nothing I could do for them. I needed to stay focused. We only had seconds before the bus reached the river at the bottom of the ravine. A violent river. I needed to get her out. I reached in for her and glanced toward the front of the bus. No Vincent. No surprise.

I took her by both hands pulling her up just as the bus slammed into the river. Raging water poured over seats filling the bus within minutes. I held her tightly as the bus traveled with the turbulent current. I spotted a shallow bed of sand and together we jumped. The bus bobbed in and out of the river as it traveled until it was completely submerged.

I sat there with her tightly in my arms on the side of the river. I remember trying to catch my breath thinking I should have reacted quicker. I should have helped the other two. But I did save one. And that was it. That's when I woke up.

"Well, Aiden. It sounds like you were a hero," Dr. Bennett declared. She finished scribbling in her pad and flipped the cover closed.

"I suppose you could say that if you can take credit for heroic acts while you're sleeping," I snickered. "But, that's just it. It wasn't like a typical dream. I'm sure you know how you feel after you wake up. It's difficult trying to recollect most of the details. It's not like our dreams are crystal clear. But I'm telling you... mine was. I remember every second so vividly... like it actually happened. I was even exhausted when I woke up."

"Dreams can be exhausting. How many of these dreams did you say you had?"

"I lost count."

"And they were all this type with you playing the role of a hero?"

"Yes."

"Very good progress tonight. Let's stop here and let you some rest. Bringing up your past dreams may trigger them to start up again. If you have trouble, ring your nurse. She can give you something to help you sleep." She gently tapped her pen on the rail of my bed. "I'll see you in the morning."

"Alright," I whispered.

8

Conquering Rivals

I didn't sleep much that night. I didn't call for the nurse like Dr. Bennett instructed if I had trouble sleeping simply because my sleeplessness wasn't brought on by dreams, not by anxiety, none of the usual issues. It was more of a restless feeling. Eager to talk to Dr. Bennett. Eager to get out of this place. I noticed a small white paper cup on my nightstand. I knew what was inside. There were two tiny red sleeping pills. Looks like Dr. Bennett took the precautionary approach. I can't blame her, but the pills never really helped anyway. They made me feel groggy and lose track of time. Days went by, weeks, months. No more losing track of time. Dr. Bennett asked me to trust her. And I did. Sleep or no sleep I felt stronger. I finally had the motivation to get my life back.

"Hello, Mr. McCarthy." A nurse from the physical therapy department stood patiently at my door. "Are you ready?

"I am."

"Do you need help?" she asked.

"No thanks, I got it." My arms shook as I lifted myself from the bed to the chair. This was the first time I refused help but I had to start doing more on my own.

After therapy, I wandered to the abandoned parts of the hospital. I liked the privacy of the east wing. It was rarely used. There were no patient rooms, no elevators, and no distractions. Only a single hallway paved with cobblestone leading to the former lobby of the two-hundred-year old hospital. And the stillness of the terrace brought me back to a familiar sense of tranquility.

"Good morning," Dr. Bennett announced, as she approached from behind me. "Are you ready to continue?" she asked gripping the handles of my chair. "Would you like to have our session here this morning?"

"Yes, I would."

"Tell me what happened when you woke up. How did you feel?"

"Exhausted, disoriented. I sat up in bed looking around to see where I was. I realized that it was just a dream. The girl, the bus, all of it. Just a dream. But it seemed so real. My sheets were thrown in every direction as if I had struggled with them for hours. I stretched out my arms attempting to pull myself out of bed. It was no use. I decided on hitting the snooze button and rolling over instead. The second and third snooze had run its course. I had plenty of things to do that day and my plan was to get an early start.

First things first and that was my morning coffee. I shuffled down the stairs and staggered through the living room. I noticed Ben thrashing around the couch as I reached to turn on the television. He made some groaning noises in an attempt to get a few more minutes of sleep and was quickly angered by the chatter of the morning news.

"What's going on? What time is it?" He bellowed.

"It's almost seven."

"a.m?"

"Yes a.m, get up." I snapped tossing a pillow at his head.

"Yeah, yeah. I'm up."

A live broadcast caught my eye. A reporter was at the scene of an accident in Pennsylvania. A small aircraft, carrying medical students from John's Hopkins, had crashed. The scene was chaotic. The mangled plane was being pulled from a steep embankment, out of a river. There were three fatalities. Two students and the pilot. Only one student survived. A young girl. Emergency personnel were everywhere. They were treating her for what looked to be minor cuts and scrapes. She was sitting on the back of the ambulance behind the reporter. The scene was just like in my dream. And the girl, she looked exactly like the girl on the bus. I rubbed my hands across my unshaven face. How could it be her? But I remember every detail. Her blue coat, her tan leather backpack, her tangled brown hair, the tiny cut above her right eye that was now covered by a white bandage. How strange was this? I thought to myself. I was stunned. It made absolutely no sense so I dismissed the possibility. There was no way... just a crazy coincidence.

Dr. Bennett had a puzzled look on her face. She stood there gazing at me. It was pretty obvious that she was trying to make sense of it. Or finally tired of listening me go on and on about nonsense like this.

Nonsense that drove me to the verge of insanity. Maybe I crossed the line of what was actually believable and she was afraid to say anything. How difficult would it be for her to tell me that she was wrong and that I was, in fact, crazy. Her eyes squinted as she pondered. Any second she was going to announce that there was no need to continue.

"I'm baffled. I just can't get past the similarities. A single student, a young girl survived a plane crash with only a few scrapes. And you're telling me the scene was the same?"

"Exactly. Same girl. Same everything. Only it was a bus in my dream. But the plane was so mangled you couldn't tell what it was. It actually resembled the bus."

"That is such a strange coincidence. Well, some things I suppose are just impossible to explain," she admitted. She needed to come to some conclusion so she could let it go for now. I could see she wanted to move on. She rationalized it for herself too, not just for me. I like that about her. I like that Dr. Bennett and I were in this whole healing thing together.

"Impossible," I answered.

"Let's just keep going," Dr. Bennett whispered. "If you're able to, of course."

"I'm good." I was very eager to continue. I hadn't lost her interest or her faith in me. That was huge in my mind. It gave me the confidence to keep going no matter how far fetched or hard to believe it seemed.

From the kitchen I heard Ben mumbling on the couch. He announced that he had absolutely no reason to live. He was ridiculously dramatic. I snatched a second cup from the cupboard and poured two cups of coffee instead of just one. I needed to sacrifice a few extra minutes to listen to his woes. Unfortunately, this was my role on occasion, listening to his sob stories about his petty fights with Maggie. He would get upset when I refer to them as fights, which in fact they were but he seemed to prefer to call them disagreements.

"Why do I put up with her?" He moaned.

"What exactly did she do? I walked to the couch and handed him his cup. "Here, stop crying," I demanded.

"Thanks," he said, as he took a sip, "Nothing."

"She did nothing?"

"Yeah, well, you just don't get it."

"Get what?"

"She's making me crazy," he said, sniffling, "…why in the hell are you up so early?"

"It's too late Ben. You're already crazy."

Ben nodded, "True." His angry facial expression dissolved as he lifted his furrowed brow in agreement.

"So, I had a strange dream last night," I said.

"You're too stressed. That's what it is." Ben gulped his coffee.

"It can't be stress. I've been way more stressed out than I am now. I don't know what it is. But this morning, I turned on the television and the same girl from my dream, who I saved from a bus crash actually survived a plane crash. Now, that's impossible. Right?"

"Was she hot?"

"Ben, be serious."

"Of course that's not possible. I mean, come on. Are you listening to yourself?" He talked a bit louder as he wondered toward the kitchen.

"Let's go. Get dressed. We're going to be late," I scolded.

"Wait, do we have practice? What day is it?" he asked in a panic, slamming the last of his coffee. "What time is it?" He sprinted to the chair snatching his sweats and his wallet from the table.

"You already asked me that. You are unquestionably the most absent minded person I know. Seriously."

"It's women, Aiden. They'll be the death of me," Ben whined as he yanked on his sweat pants. He was the most unstable person I knew. I honestly don't know how Maggie put up with him.

Not living with him was a large part of it I'm sure. I felt more like a parent to him. He was the most needy person I'd ever met. Like toddler needy.

It was the morning of the row competition. Ben and I packed our gear into the back of my Jeep and headed out. I made a quick turn and pulled into the library parking lot.

"What are you doing?"

"Just a second. I'll be right back," I said, hopping out. I wanted to check and see if Tess was at the library. I wanted to make sure that she'd be there to watch today.

The row competitions were a big deal at Princeton. There was a pretty big crowd forming already with various lawn games happening all around the campus. The air was filled with the delicious smell of smoked ribs billowing from the food tents. And the band had just started playing, all in preparation for the day's festivities.

"Hey, Aiden!" Tess shouted, running out the door toward me.

"Hey there, Good morning! I tried to call you last night. I wanted to make sure that you were coming today."

"I know, I'm sorry. We stayed up pretty late talking with Dominic."

"Oh, that's right. I probably shouldn't have called."

"No, I'm glad you did. I like that you do as you're told," she whispered. "And how could you think I would forget? I wouldn't be anywhere else today."

Ben laid on the horn in the parking lot pointing to an oncoming truck loaded with their teammates yelling as they passed.

"Yo, Aiden! Come on, man! Let's go!" they shouted.

"Hey, I got to go. I'll see you later?" I asked as my hand brushed up her arm.

"See you later," she replied, "and good luck!"

"Thanks!"

The team gathered just across the lake. That's where the race began. The crowd roared as we cut across the water alongside of our competitors from Duke, which happened to be pretty big rivals. We took the lead just as we crossed the finish line. The crowd swelled around us as we exited the boat. I snatched a towel from my bag as I made my way through the crowd. I was completely covered in sweat but didn't care. All I wanted was to find Tess. I went a little harder to finish quicker. And a win was just icing on the cake. Knowing Tess was around somewhere watching made my heart pound even harder than the physical exertion of rowing.

I scanned the crowd searching for her. I really wanted to find her before Ben insisted that we head back to shower. That was the usual routine after a competition. Shower as fast as we could, then head to Johnny's Pub on Third. Exhausted, famished, and ready for a few beers and the best burgers in town to celebrate our victory was all we wanted to do. But for me, everything changed. Now all those petty desires such as hunger and thirst took a back seat to Tess.

There she was walking toward me with a few of her friends. At the same time, Ben came racing along side of me. Tess gave me a smile as our eyes met. I could feel my face light up returning a smile. I tossed my damp towel at Ben as I jogged toward her.

"Hang on Ben, I'll be right back."

"Come on! We gotta go man, I'm starving!" he shouted.

"Congratulations! That was so great!" she said taking my hand. She gently pulled me away from her friends who at that point began to whisper and giggle.

"Thanks, Tess," I said, while still trying to catch my breath. Sweat still beaded across my forehead. "I'm glad you're here."

I fumbled my fingers through my wet hair and pushed it away from my face.

"Aiden, come on!" Ben shouted from across the crowd.

"You guys were really great out there," Tess whispered.

"Let's go!" Ben screeched. A few of the others from the truck began to shout at me helping Ben in his rude crusade.

"Hang on!" I said angrily to end the shouting match. "I apologize for my ridiculous friends. They lack many things. Patients for one."

"Don't apologize. I know the feeling. You've met my family remember?" Tess smiled and took my hand. "There's a premier on Monday night at the Art Gallery. I was hoping you would come."

"I heard Professor Williams talking about it. A local artist, right?"

"Yes. Actually my sister, Elaina."

"Really? Wow. I had no idea."

"Yes. She's an amazing artist."

"Well then, I'll be there," I replied. I pulled her closer to me as we walked.

"I'm headed out with some friends tonight. Maybe we can meet up?" she asked. The look in her eyes pierced through me.

"Absolutely," I replied.

I didn't want to hang with the team. I didn't want to go to the pub. I wanted to be where she was. Hunger must have taken over the decision making part of Ben's brain. Nah, that wasn't it. He just had a lack of basic thoughts such as courtesy. Whichever it was it ended our shouting back and forth and brought him and the guys over in a hurry. They began stumbling all over each other the second they came into her presence.

I squeezed onto her hand tightly and pulled her even closer to me. She didn't seem to mind.

"Dude.. what's your deal?" Ben asked, rudely. He seemed to be unaffected by the extreme disapproving look on my face. The guy was oblivious.

"This is Tess." I proudly announced. All eyes were already fixated on her. Instantly I regretted making the introduction. These guys were the most immature, loudest, crudest males on campus… quite arguably ever known to mankind. And, now, I could easily add ill-mannered to their shameful resume.

Surprisingly, none of them said a word. They stood there staring at her like she was a zoo animal. Or they were the zoo animals and she was their next meal. It was embarrassing.

Ben broke from the trance and quickly began to fidget. Maggie was heading this way. He knew he needed to act fast.

"Hey sorry! I'm sorry we're so rude. Where are my manners? It's nice to meet you Tess!" he blurted.

"This is my roommate, Ben."

"Hey. It's nice to meet you. All of you," she said, with a smile which didn't help the situation. They were mesmerized. None of them responded. Breathing was difficult, let alone speaking. I think I even spotted a bit of drool. At this point, I decided it was necessary to re-evaluate my list of friends.

Maggie reached the group and quickly greeted Ben with a slap on the side of the head.

"Maggie… babe! So what did you think of my manly performance? I pushed myself harder today… just for you baby!" he gloated.

"Whatever," She scoffed.

"Aiden was just introducing us to Tess," Ben said, cautiously wrapping his arm around Maggie's shoulder.

"Hi, I'm Maggie. Ben's... well... you know...." She gave Ben an elbow to his rib. "It's very nice to meet you."

"You too, Maggie," Tess replied.

"What do you mean... you know? What is that? You know. You know what? Oh, now you're not my girlfriend?" he whimpered.

"Oh, Ben. Let it go," she mumbled.

"Let it go?" he snapped right back.

The two turned to disagree more privately. Maggie walked, Ben stomped. Maggie giggled. Ben shouted. He was completely frazzled by her decision to not add the crucial title to her introduction.

"If you do that to girls... do you do that to guys, too? Leave that part out?" he shouted.

The two continued their unpleasant discussion as they walked back toward the truck. The guys slowly followed behind still speechless.

"Beers and burgers or what?" Ben screamed back at the rest of us.

"Wings, let's do wings." One of the guys shouted. And another hollered voting for pizza. An argument was about to break out as they discussed the plan for the evening. I needed to break it up otherwise it could get very embarrassing. Even worse than the episode we just experienced.

"Sorry, Tess," I whispered, turning her away from the mounting madness. "So, I'll see you later?"

"For sure."

9

Narrow Pathways

We all made it back to our house. Hungry and tired but one thing was on our minds. It was definitely time for celebration. Devon, one of the guys on the team, rushed to the kitchen heading straight for the refrigerator. He propped open the door and began organizing the random items on the shelves making room for the several bottles of beer he pulled from inside a brown bag.

"Hey Ben, heads up!" Devon shouted, while peeking his head from inside the refrigerator door. He tossed Ben a bottle. "It's the last cold one."

"Atta boy," Ben replied. "Let's be quick. In and out. I need food ASAP."

I had no problem hustling. I couldn't wait to get in the shower, so I headed up the stairs.

"Where you going? We're playing cards, bro!" Ben announced, as he swung himself onto the broken recliner. Broken because it automatically threw you back into the fully reclined position due to repeated misuse.

"I was thinking a shower would be appropriate, don't you think?"

"Whatever, dude. It's just us guys anyway. Who cares if we're sweaty? We need to get a hand or two in and get to the pub for food."

"I do. And you definitely should. You smell bad. Really bad," I said laughing.

"I don't smell. Do I?"

"Trust me. You smell."

"Well, beer don't care. It doesn't judge, or hate either." Ben began to whisper to his beer as he gazed at the dark bottle. These were the moments I questioned his sanity. Cards were being shuffled behind him, chaotic clatter, mainly disagreements about who made the biggest impact on the day's victory yet Ben shut it off and went into his quiet little world. I stood there on the stairwell and listened to him whine quietly to himself, gently wiping the condensation from the bottle. I just shook my head and smiled before tromping up the stairs.

"TJ, you want one?" Devon shouted.

TJ was the tough one. A state champ wrestler in high school and pretty much good to go around with anyone at any time. He always had our backs. He constantly had Ben in a head lock. Ben was ridiculously hard headed and an ego that took hits nonstop. And the way Ben assessed his bouts with TJ made no sense. He'd say, "It's not about skill or strength. It's more about intelligence. Outsmarting your opponent... that's my approach." They weighed about the same. Ben was in pretty good shape and TJ was a beast. His approach never worked. He lost every time.

"What do you think?" he asked, as he caught the bottle Devon pitched. "Matt, Neil? How about you guys?"

They trickled from the living room to the kitchen to grab a bottle.

"Thanks, Dev," Neil replied, as he flipped the top into a small wicker basket on the table. Ben shot out of the man-eating chair to the table snatching it from the basket.

"Hey, that's Maggie's centerpiece. Show some respect, man."

"I'll take one, since you asked," Booner snapped. Travis Boon — aka "Booner" — was the comic of the group. He was a very likable guy. He could easily become a politician. He and his family had many friends in high places.

"So a few hands quick... who's in?" Chris sat at the table shuffling the deck. Chris was the boss. The one who took charge making all the decisions. So he thought anyway.

"I'm in. Hook me up, Chris," Matt ordered, as he knocked his knuckles on the table. Matt was the brains of the organization. He earned his law degree before he was twenty. He returned to Princeton just because thats what guys were doing at his age. He had plenty of time to make partner at a high pressure, high paying law firm.

"Aiden?

"You want in or what?" Chris shouted.

"Yeah. I'm in. I'll take Ben's spot." I elbowed Ben grabbing his beer from his hand. I took a swig shoving him from his chair. "Showers yours bro," I added, pulling cards from the center of the table. "Man, you're just mean." Ben sulked as he headed up the stairs.

The plan for the evening was to head to the Pub. Traditionally our crew victories were celebrated at Johnny's. It was a tiny little dive with hardwood floors covered in peanut shells, equipped with a dart board, a couple of ragged pool tables, and an old jukebox in the corner. The owner was a cool guy. He'd always brag about being an alum of the row team. He claimed his team set records but we can't seem to find his name anywhere on campus. We don't say much because he was a champ to us for occasionally losing count of the beers we added to our tabs or the few extra baskets of wings he'd throw in at the last minute. He was a "guy's guy." He honored the university and the row team by hanging flags and banners from one end of the pub to the other.

It was a comfortable spot. Perfect for us. And because it was so close, it became our second home.

On our way out the door, passing out a roady was the standard procedure. Number eight on the check list. Walking the quick five minutes to the pub wouldn't happen unless everyone had a beer in hand. Tradition isn't something we mess with. Every victory had its before and after "play by play" schedule of events that needed to occur. We even had the check list on a oversized white board behind the dining room table. If anything was missed it would most definitely throw off the winning vibe for the entire season. Calling us superstitious was an understatement. Ludicrous was a better word. But I'm a team player. I went along with it. Mainly because we won every single time these steps occurred before and after our competitions.

We all headed down the street toward the pub. All except Ben. He joined a few minutes later winded from the short sprint to catch up. It was obvious he was upset that we left without him.

"Wait up! What's your problem?"

"What's up with that shirt?" TJ asked pulling at it.

"What?" Ben yanked on it to see the entire front of what he thought was an extremely sweet shirt.

"It was a gift." He whimpered. "From an old girlfriend." Not one of us could hold back from laughing at him and his complete lack of manhood.

"What? It's cool. Don't you think it's cool?" Ben looked around the group of guys searching for just one of us to agree with him.

"Hey, I forgot my phone. I'll catch up or meet you guys at the pub." I shouted running back toward the house. The guys kept walking still teasing Ben.

"It's destroyed. Seriously, look at the holes, the stains. It's disgusting." Booner added putting his finger through one of one of the larger holes.

As I rushed back to the house the guys kept walking toward the Pub. None of them noticed, but there was a car headed their way speeding recklessly out of control. The back alley was narrow, barely enough room for a couple of bicycles let alone a truck with an intoxicated driver behind the wheel. He was heading right for them.

They had no idea what was about to happen. They continued to harass Ben about his shirt, laughing and goofing around as the reckless driver headed toward them.

"It has sentimental meaning," Ben explained in his own defense. "The girl was smokin' hot to say the least."

"Does Maggie know where you got your sentimental shirt?" TJ teased.

"You guys are always busting my balls."

"Were just giving you a hard time," Devon joked, darting over to Ben and squeezing his shoulders. Just then he heard the truck engine behind them. "Watch out!" Devon shouted, as he peered at the raging head lights heading right for them. They quickly scattered to get out of the way.

That's when I came running back toward them. I thought I was going to witness one or more of my friends get hit and I was too far away to do anything about it. That's when I witnessed something I couldn't explain. I saw someone I didn't recognize. It wasn't Chris, Ben, Matt or Booner. And definitely wasn't TJ or Devon. I didn't know who he was but he was there standing in front of Devon and TJ facing the oncoming truck. It was if this stranger somehow slowed time to a standstill. A point of impact, that's what was missing. I even braced for it. That's how fast it was all happening. I remember how I felt thinking there was no way they weren't crushed by the truck. But somehow it missed them. What I saw made no sense. And just as quickly as they came, both the truck and the strange guy who came out of nowhere disappeared into the night.

"What the hell?" Ben shouted. "Are you kidding me? He almost hit us! What an idiot!"

"Man, that was close!" Chris yelled, running back to Devon and TJ.

"Are you guys alright?" Matt shouted, as he checked each of them.

"Is everyone okay?"

"Fine. Man, TJ?

You okay?" Devon asked.

"Yea. That guy was crazy. He didn't even see us!"

"No, he didn't. I can't believe that just happened," Devon whimpered as he bent over putting his hands on his knees.

"Dude, that was crazy!" Chris screamed.

"Dev, man. Thanks. You just saved us. Seriously. You saw him coming before we did," Booner exclaimed, gasping for breath.

"You got all of us off the road. Man. Thanks," TJ muttered, patting Devon on the back. It didn't take long before he noticed his shirt was torn across the bottom.

"It looks like you and Ben belong to the same tattered t-shirt club, Teej," Booner snickered.

"Yea, thanks Dev. We all owe you one," Ben announced. "Let's buy his beers tonight, huh? It's the least we can do to repay this superhero."

"You guys okay?" I shouted. I couldn't explain what just happened. I wasn't sure what they saw. And at that point I was questioning my sanity. With the mirage on the mountain and the unexplainable, seemingly real life dream… I was hesitant to give my rendition of how it went down from where I was standing. I was just relieved they were all ok.

"Aiden!" Ben shouted. "You just missed it! A lunatic came barreling through here and almost hit us!"

"Yeah, I saw the whole thing fifty yards back. I couldn't get here fast enough. Everything moved in slow motion."

"No shit. That was out of control. Anyone get a good look at the truck?" TJ asked, stuffing his ripped shirt into the waist of his jeans. He went from scared to death to mad as hell.

"Nah. It happened so fast," Chris answered.

We finally got to the pub and headed for the pool tables. Ben and I went immediately to the bar. Ben spotted Maggie sitting with her friends. He waved at her. She waved back and blew him a kiss.

"You got this round or what? Grab 'em and meet me over by Mags!" Ben shouted, sprinting toward her table. I had no interest in following him. I grabbed the bottles from the bartender leaving one for Ben and headed back to the pool tables.

"You coming?" he shouted. "I left you one. Grab it. I'll bring these to the guys."

It was hard not to watch him as he approached Maggie's table. He threw his arms in air and began to flail them around wildly. His voice roared with excitement. It was obvious that he was telling Maggie and her friends about his near death experience. Chris and Booner walked over to join him after snatching a couple of bottles from me. I waved at Maggie and smiled. She was so normal. And pretty. I'd have to put her at the top of his list of girls he's dated. To put it nicely she was too good for him. He knew it too. I don't want to say he's the jealous insecure type but he was the jealous insecure type when it came to her.

She got a lot of attention. Wherever she went she was the center of it all. The "take charge" kind of girl. Organized, structured, punctual. Nothing at all like Ben who at this point was on the verge of tears describing every detail of what had happened.

She had the patients of a saint. She just sat there smiling giving him her undivided attention, every so often pulling her fingers through her long red hair to brush it away from her face. Half of our friends were just waiting for Ben to screw it up so they could ask her out. "Not in this lifetime," is what Ben would come back with when ever we brought up the topic.

I noticed TJ waving at me. He was pointing over toward a young woman sitting by the jukebox. It was Tess. She was sitting with a group of friends. Just as I started to walk over I noticed Vincent. Tess' constant and unwanted guardian. He was sitting back rocking on two of the four legs of the chair. And, of course, he was sitting at her table. A couple of the girls sitting with her got up and headed for the restroom. Vincent saw me looking over toward their table. I think he thought I was watching him. I wasn't interested in him. Not at all. He knew who I was interested in and he definitely noticed me looking at her. Maybe I needed to say something once and for all. Maybe tonight would be a good time. I had TJ who was now officially in a bad mood. After the brush with death, it would seem he would be thankful we were all still in one piece. He just wanted to get his hands on the driver of that truck. He couldn't let things go too easily. If he knew what kind of guy Vincent was... the lack of respect he showed Tess, and to me, he would be down for whatever I needed.

Vincent stood up and backed his chair with an abrupt shove. The other guy sitting at her table shot up and pushed him back into his chair. Tess noticed as I headed toward her table. She stood and rushed over trying to keeping me from getting any closer. There was obviously trouble brewing.

"I'm glad you're here," I whispered into her ear, wrapping my hands around her waist. I wanted this Vincent character to see her close to me. He needed to get use to it. "Aiden, maybe now's not the best time," she said. Her voice trembled.

"Don't worry," I assured her as I took her hand, keeping a steady pace toward the table. "Hello. I'm Aiden, a friend of Tess'." I held out my hand to the friendlier of the two.

"Hi, Aiden, I'm Thomas," he replied as he shook my hand. "And, this is Vincent." He added trying to help Tess out with the situation. I appreciated what Thomas was trying to do. He seemed like a good guy. Unlike Vincent who needed to check his attitude.

Vincent leaned in toward me as if to scare me away. It didn't work which obviously bothered him by the piercing glare he gave me. I wasn't in the least bit intimidated. Neither of us said a word. I was waiting for him to make the first move, knowing full well he had no intention of exchanging pleasantries. I was a threat to him. For whatever reason, I must have rubbed him the wrong way. I'd never met the guy before that day at the coffee shop. Which was a good thing. Guys like Vincent were toxic and I saw no need to associate myself with his type.

"Come on Aiden. I need some air." She pulled my arm turning me toward the door. His stare was hard to ignore but I needed to walk away. For now.

"Don't," Thomas whispered to Vincent.

"She needs the warning. Not me," Vincent barked. He stormed up to the bar and began watching a boxing match on the television.

"Hey, Johnny, a bottle of soda, if you please," Vincent demanded, slamming his money on the bar. "Sure thing, Vincent. No trouble tonight, right?" Johnny pleaded with a smile.

"Of course not, John! Just a soda." He noticed a couple of chain smoking regulars sitting at the bar joking with one another about his order.

"We got ourselves a hardcore boozer over here," one of them snickered.

"You got a problem with that?" Vincent snipped. His eyes flickered with red as he glared at them. They both felt an overwhelming fear that their lives were about to end right then and there.

"Not at all, pal. Sounds good. I think we'll have the same. Johnny, two cream sodas if you don't mind. And another for our friend here." The bigger of the two requested in the friendliest voice possible. "And put it on my tab," he added with an enormous smile.

"Sometimes I have to get away. I need to separate myself," Tess whispered. There was a chill in the air. I could see her breath as she spoke.

"Are you cold?"

"Not at all. I'm fine. More than fine when I'm with you."

I put my arms around her anyway. I was very warm, my body temperature had recently elevated by Vincent. The way he looked at me bothered me to no end. I felt the burning desire to protect her at all costs.

"This is nice." She whispered putting her arms around my waist.

"Don't let him bother you. I guarantee, I won't." I assured her holding her tighter.

"He's just a control freak. He doesn't bother me. He knows he has boundaries. He just pushes it, more and more lately. He's not very polite… I'm sorry."

"His actions have nothing to do with you. Don't apologize."

"Come on, let's go back inside." She darted in front of me gently pulling on my hands. "Thomas has a way of keeping him under control. If it turns into anything he can't handle, they just leave. We have an understanding." She moved in closer wrapping her arms around my waist.

There was something so intoxicating about her. Her long dark hair cascading softly over shoulders, her delicate lips, her soft skin and the way she looked at me, I knew something was happening. I pulled her back into me, embracing her once again. The way she felt in my arms was indescribable. She pressed herself against my chest.

"Thank you." She whispered.

"For what?"

"I don't know. Lots of things. But mostly for just being."

The way she gazed up at me, looking so deeply into my eyes as she spoke, she was falling for me. Nothing had ever made me feel so good. Nothing. And the way she thanked me for "being." I'm guessing she meant a lot of things. Being here tonight, being out here with her, being in this moment, being alive. I was ready to be anything she wanted, anything she needed. I realized holding her outside the pub that night that I would give anything to keep her close to me.

We went back inside and all we could hear was a bunch of shouting over by the pool tables. "Aiden! Come join us!"

"Come with me, Tess."

"Maybe this is a guy thing." She replied giggling, following close behind me.

"Nah, come on," I insisted, leading her across the bar.

"Gentleman, please. May I have your attention?" Neil announced. "Oh, and ladies..." he added with a wink directed toward Tess, "I'd like to make a toast."

The noise level in the pub was at an all-time high. It was pretty busy for how late it was. Maggie's table grew from just a couple girlfriends to more than half of her sorority. Ben was in his element. Giggling, joking, being the clown he loved to be.

Definitely in his element in full-on entertainment mode. That was until he saw Neil raise his bottle.

"Hey, hey, hey, fella's... come on, quiet down..." Ben screeched, as he darted across the floor from one end of the bar to the other. "Neil is attempting to propose a toast!" he announced, grabbing one of the two bottles in TJ's hand.

"Here's to Devon. For his quick thinking in a potentially bad situation. It could have been very tragic for many of our brothers tonight. To Devon, for being the hero." Everyone cheered as we raised our bottles.

"... and a toast to Aiden," Neil added, quickly shifting the groups attention to me and Tess. I have to admit I got a little nervous. For both of us. Who knows where this was going.

He placed his arm around my neck squeezing gently as he spoke.

"For his ability to acquire one of the rarest of beauties." He tipped his bottle toward Tess. Her cheeks slightly reddened. I gently squeezed her hand smiling. "To her sheer exquisiteness. With but a mere glance, blinding to helpless souls such as ours. May you never travel far from the eyes who seek your beauty."

As he finished, I raised my glass and toasted in complete agreement.

"Here, here!" They shouted swigging their bottles. At that point, she was more than embarrassed. She giggled as the cheering and toasting continued. I sat my bottle down on the table and took both of her hands pulling her back into a corner. I took my hand and brushed gently along her cheek. Her smile grew as I touched her. I put my lips to her ear as I spoke.

"May you never be out of my sight."

"I won't be." She said softly touching my hand.

"You belong with me." I whispered.

"I'm glad you kept your cool for her," Dr. Bennett whispered.

"It was hard to do. Believe me."

Our sessions became more frequent. Dr. Bennett stayed late into the night as often as she could. Talking about Tess, about all of it... it somehow brought me back to reality. And my story seemed to be more than just one of her patients talking about his life. The more I talked, the more interested Dr. Bennett became.

"So many things are working here. You're regaining strength. You're almost completely off your meds. The progress you're making is incredible. I'm so proud of you Aiden."

"Thank you, Dr. Bennett, for helping me. For listening."

"You're the best part of what I do," she whispered, smiling. "Recovery is the reward."

10

Conflict of Interest

Out of the corner of my eye I caught Vincent looking around the bar searching for Tess. He spotted us standing together in the corner and I'm guessing he was thinking we were too close by the look on his face. I watched as he finished his soda, slamming the bottle onto the bar. He then shouted at Johnny demanding a couple more.

"You got these, right?" Vincent snarled at the two guys who volunteered to pay for his last one. "I said no trouble tonight, Vince," Johnny said from the end of the bar.

"I know. We're good. Right guys? We good?"

"We're definitely good. It's alright, John. We got 'em."

Vincent gave Johnny a nod while snatching the bottles and headed our way.

"Tess, here!" Vincent shouted from across the bar as he held out the first opened bottle. Tess waved her hand mouthing the words "No, thanks."

"Don't worry about him," Tess whispered.

"Who's worried?" I replied, holding her tighter. She pulled me toward the dance floor. I could hear the music softly playing from the jukebox. "Shame on the Moon. Great song. One of my favorites," I whispered into her ear.

"Dance with me, Aiden." She asked as she spun around with

her arms raised. She was irresistible. The tiny white strap of her shirt fell off her shoulder as I moved with her. I held her so tightly, I didn't want to let her go. She felt it. My heart was racing. She opened the top of my shirt collar to rest her head on my skin. I could hardly breathe as she pressed her lips to my neck. The warmth of her breath made the urge to kiss her even stronger.

This was it. Being right here with her was absolutely the most perfect of all moments. I felt nothing but desire to be with her. I slipped my hands down and gripped her waist, touching her bare skin of her lower back. I felt her weaken in my arms. Her breaths drew deeper against my skin and it quickly became more than I could handle. She looked at me. She gazed into my eyes and just like that everyone, everything happening around us disappeared. It was just us. I couldn't take my eyes off of her. I felt the curves of her body pressed close to mine. I could take every part of her. She would let me. She wanted me to. I felt it in the way she held onto me. Clenching me. Tempting me. She licked the dryness from her tender lips. She trembled when I gripped her tighter pressing her against me.

"Do something, Thomas!" Vincent demanded.

"It's too late." Thomas warned.

Out of the corner of my eye I could see Vincent moving quickly toward us. He was pushing chairs, shoving tables, anything that was in his path. Johnny glanced over to Thomas signaling him that Vincent needed to calm down or go. Tess quickly broke from my embrace and moved herself into Vincent's path as he approached us.

"Thomas?" Tess shouted. Thomas jumped over his chair and spun around in front of Vincent. Angelo followed.

"What are you doing?" she snapped at Vincent.

"What do you mean what am I doing? What are you doing?" he scolded her. He was angry, too angry in my opinion.

"Don't talk to her like that!" I growled. I felt my fists as they clenched. He had gone too far.

"What are you gonna do about it?"

I let out a sigh. Followed by a heavy breath as I stepped in closer toward him. I could feel the adrenaline taking over. There was something wrong with him… besides the obvious, I mean. But something crazy with his eyes. They turned a fiery red. A horrible birth defect I assumed. He didn't scare me. He needed a lesson in manners. That's when the guys noticed what was up. TJ slammed his pool stick down on the table, rushed over and stood next to me. The rest of them followed.

"Please, don't," Tess begged as she pushed us away from each other.

"Hey, how about a game?" Angelo shouted from the open table. He was definitely good at steering Vincent away from trouble. A little friendly competition wouldn't hurt and Vincent was most definitely the type who couldn't resist. He would take on any challenge from anyone at any time and Angelo knew it.

Vincent scoped the room. I had a dozen or so ready to go if things escalated. And poor Johnny behind the bar waving at me, desperately signaling that this was a definite "no-go."

Vincent glared back at me. He knew he was about to make a very big mistake. His eyes dropped to Thomas' hand firmly gripping his arm, and then raised his attention to Thomas.

"Back down brother." Thomas whispered shaking his head.

"I'm game." Vincent shouted and peered around the bar for any quick takers. But quickly his attention directed back to me. "You're on!" TJ shouted as he raced back to the table. "Bro, you good?" he yelled back at me.

She stood there with a desperate look on her face. A pleading gaze. I had no choice but to back down. "I'm good." I replied. Tess needed me to stay calm. After all, he was her brother.

"Vincent? You got to step it up tonight, bro. Last time we played you got so mad you destroyed the stick. And then the table. You can handle this, right? A friendly game?" Angelo asked.

"What do you think?" Vincent answered, snatching the stick from behind me. Uncomfortably close, ridiculously disrespectful, desperately asking for me to make the first move. I felt his breath on my shoulder that's how close he came to me. There were plenty of sticks over by the table. I'm not much of a bar fighter. I'm not much of a fighter in general but after the scene at the coffee shop, how he hurt her and just took off... I'd call those strikes one and two. One more wrong move and it wasn't going to matter what Thomas did or how much Tess asked me to keep my cool. He and I were going to have it out. Theres only so much disrespect a guy can take.

"Tess, get your boyfriend a stick." Vincent snarled.

I was good with that statement. More than good. At least he knew my role. She was mine. Not his. I felt the tension release in my arms. She shook her head at him. "Go Vincent." She ordered. She tugged at me from behind as he walked away.

"Thanks." She whispered.

"For what?"

"For letting it go."

"He's impossible."

"I know."

"What's his deal?"

She lowered her eyes. She was helpless. And definitely at a loss for words how to justify his actions. I knew all too well what his problem was. It was jealousy. Which is weird if they live together as bother and sister. But in all reality they weren't actually related and she was more than beautiful. Still, he had no right to act like that. I felt sorry for her trying deal with him and his pathetic behavior.

"You know when it came right down to it, I wouldn't do anything to hurt you. Besides, he's your brother. I just think he needs to show you a little more respect."

"Well, thanks all the same. For keeping it together. He's not always like that you know. He can be sweet."

"Somehow I can't picture that." I chuckled softly nudging her. So tell me who's who..." I turned toward the group at her table.

"The quick thinker over there racking, that's Angelo. Sophie and Rachel are sitting at the table. I would introduce you but maybe tonight's not the best time. Besides, tonight, I want to keep you all to myself," she whispered as she nuzzled in closer to me.

"You guys up for a little wager?" Vincent challenged TJ in his typical arrogant tone. Of course, he had to glare back at me and Tess.

"Why not?" TJ replied.

"Sure, man. What's the wager?"

"How about a grand?" Vincent slammed down a stack of money. Confidence was clearly one of his stronger suits. Confidence only carries someone so far, then it becomes arrogance. The guys each check their wallets to see how much they could come up with.

"You're on, bro!" Ben confidently announced. They all groaned at Ben for accepting such a ridiculously outrageous bet.

"Ben, you better not be using rent money." I shouted.

"You better be on your game, Ben. A thousand dollars? Are you nuts?" Chris shouted as he pulled out a twenty and two ones.

"How much you got anyway?" TJ barked at Ben.

"I don't know, a couple hundred bucks. Aiden's good for the rest." He squeamishly smiled and answered. They instantly turn their focus my way. I waved them on to play. At that point I was willing to pay anything for the chance to be with her in peace with no trouble from Vincent.

I couldn't help but notice Thomas having a quiet conversation with Vincent. They were definitely not strategizing. Vincent wasn't about to take any advice from anyone. Not even Thomas. The discussion became a little more intense. Thomas was getting impatient with him. Understandably. I couldn't hear what he was saying but it was obvious that he didn't like the wager or Vincent's attitude. He shook his finger in his face pretty much scolding him. He deserved it, acting like an juvenile.

"Relax," Vincent assured him as he grabbed the cue from the table.

"Angelo, you break," Vincent ordered, tossing the ball over his shoulder to Angelo.

"I racked. They break. Who's up?" He asked setting the ball on the table with a smile.

Thomas and Angelo both knew that they needed to diffuse the situation.

Ben stepped up and took the first shot. A good break but nothing went in.

"Ben, you're going to have to do a hell of a lot better than that." TJ shrieked.

Angelo sunk a couple. Right after, TJ made two. Vincent made three trick shots while show boating the entire time. Thomas glared at the table as Vincent took his fourth shot. It was like he used some special power to direct the ball to the left missing the pocket. Vincent was furious. He knew that it should have gone in the pocket. So did I. No one else seemed to notice. But something was definitely not right with this game. Chris made one good shot but left himself nothing to follow. Angelo missed deliberately. In my opinion anyway. I knew right then what was up. Angelo was throwing the game. Maybe to avoid any more hostility between us. I could see Vincent was even more infuriated. At least this time it wasn't directed at me. Angelo seemed to be a pretty good guy. He gave Vincent a baffled look throwing his hands up as if his shot was legitimately missed.

"You must be something special, Aiden. Tess is quite smitten with you," Thomas said as he wandered over. Tess smiled and held my hand a little tighter.

"I try. But, she's pretty special herself."

"That she is."

TJ sunk a few more, high fiving Ben and Joel. Vincent chalked his stick prepared to finish it once and for all.

"Its over right here, boys." he boasted. He had a clear shot of the seven perfectly aligned with the five. He made both in one shot. He was about to win. Just the eight ball remained. I kept my eye on Thomas. Maybe I could catch him in the act. What would I see? If he had some ability to move objects would there be any way to know? How ridiculous. Man, I thought. The stuff I was coming up with… I knew I needed to quit drinking.

Vincent had an easy shot but when he took it, the eight ball hooked to the left. He hit the cue straight on. How could it shoot left? I looked around the table. No one suspected anything. I was stumped. I looked at my bottle. I brought it to my nose sniffing it for anything other than the usual beer smell. I shrugged my shoulders. It was definitely my last for the evening.

Vincent wasn't just mad, he was enraged. Breathing heavily, completely consumed with anger he leaped around the table and stood right in front of Thomas. The opposite corner erupted in cheers as Chris easily banked the eight to win.

"That's a grand, fellas," Ben announced as he celebrated with his pals.

The lights in the pub flickered a few times. The music coming from the jukebox became scratchy for a second or two. Even the TV lost its signal. The locals who were tuned into the boxing match groaned as the screen turned a snowy white. Thomas put his hand on Vincent's shoulder and within a few seconds, Vincent was calm. A hex maybe. I read something on the topic. The lights and music came back on and the television regained its signal. Everything was back to normal. The two of them quietly walked back to their table. I could have sworn that Tess' brothers had the ability to do things. Strange things. Messing with gravity, electricity, you name it. It was a little strange to say the least.

Angelo smiled at Tess from across the bar. I know she was thankful Angelo fixed the mess Vincent was desperately trying to make.

"Tess, we're heading out. Are you coming?" Thomas asked.

"Let me say goodnight."

"Nice meeting you Aiden."

"You too, Thomas."

I took her hand as we walked toward the back door. They were all watching us. It felt a bit awkward. We both knew that they were hanging on our every move so we slipped around the corner.

"I'm sorry. They're a little protective."

"It's okay, Tess. You're important to them."

"Thank you for the dance."

"It was definitely my pleasure."

I stayed close to her. My lips gently touched her. I needed a moment. I couldn't move. Slowly, I moved my hands up her back caressing her skin from beneath her shirt. She was so smooth, so soft.

"What does she think she's doing?" Vincent whispered.

"She's going to hurt now no matter what happens." Thomas replied.

"This cannot end well for either of them. She must know that," he added, as they got up from their table.

"She's taken this too far," Vincent snarled.

"So have you, Vincent. You shouldn't be so angry. It isn't good," Sofia whispered as she handed him his bottle.

"What do you think will happen if your anger continues to grow like this?" Thomas scolded under his breath.

"It's under control. Don't worry about it. I'll go and so will Tess. I'll make sure of it," Vincent insisted as he attempted to smile.

"We all worry about it Vincent." Sophia mumbled.

"There's nothing I can do for any of you," Thomas jokingly announced, as he blew out a deep breath grabbing Vincent's shoulders. "You're all hopeless."

Dr. Bennett was so intrigued. The look on her face made me laugh.

"What's so funny" She asked.

"You," I replied. She smiled as she nodded. She stood from her chair and walked toward the window looking at the statue perched directly in the center of the garden.

"What do you think of her?" She asked.

"She's the reason I come here."

She nodded her head as if she knew what I was going to say. "Makes a whole lot of sense. I definitely get it."

She turned back toward me and sat down.

"It sounds like Vincent may not be too keen on you seeing Tess,"

"Not at all. There was something about them. Something different. But, Tess... she was like their center. They gravitated toward her. Not just her family, everyone who met her."

II

Well Off Course

Later that evening Tess and the others returned to the castle. None of them wanted to talk about Aiden. They all were well aware of the mistake Tess was making, yet they were afraid to start the conversation in the presence of Vincent. Thomas waited until the others were inside with the rest of the family before he spoke up.

"Getting so close to him is a very bad idea, Tess," Thomas whispered, helping her with her jacket.

"Don't worry, Thomas. I'll be fine." She assured him.

"You're just in time. We were about to share with Dominic how far back the stories go here in the castle," Father Andrews announced, with a bit of excitement in his voice.

"Sarah, come over here and sit closer." Father patted the seat next to him. "Now, I know there's something you wanted to ask Dominic, isn't there?" he said in a tender fatherly voice.

"Where did you travel from? Were you with others?"

"Well, I've been looking for you. And yes, there are others that we have to find. They are sick and need our help. Just like I did," he told her. Her eyes grew as big as saucers.

"Where are they?" she asked with worry in her voice.

"They're out there somewhere waiting for me to come for them. To bring them here."

"This world is a very big place with only a few places to be healed. You're lucky. You have Thomas and Angelo to guide you. There were three others with me. Jowell, Isabel, and little Tien. She's just ten. She's young just like you." He touched the tip of her nose. She smiled but had a troubled look on her face. She rested her head against his shoulder.

"I wanted to bring her with me but she wasn't strong enough to travel," Dominic explained. Sarah put her tiny hand over his.

"Don't worry. My brothers will find them," she whispered.

"We will, Dominic," Vincent insisted.

"We'll map it out. They need to be found," Thomas announced. "Vincent, Angelo, let's go over the charts with Dominic. He can show us where he last saw them."

The charts were kept in a secret room in the cellar of the castle. They used them to keep track of the locations of the waters of restoration and also had details of other groups of Dominions all over the world.

"Isabella was looking for her family in Rome. She insisted there were others. But I refused to listen. I only knew of your existence here. That's why I knew I had to find you."

"There are a few other clans, Dominic," Angelo said as he stepped closer to the chart, pointing to the four gold pins.

"There is the Dante Clan in Scotland, the Tribe of elders in Austria, the underground clan in foothills of Yugoslavia and the Demetrio's in Rome."

"The clan in Rome. That's her family." Dominic lowered his head. "She knew they were there, but I didn't listen. I just left her."

"You did what you thought you had to do, Dominic. Don't give up hope. We will find them," Father Andrews whispered.

"I know how to get them here," Tess announced.

"Father, I can send Aiden. I've sent him to save others," she explained. "He's been helping me."

"What do you mean, Tess? What have you done?" Thomas scolded.

"I knew she crossed the line with him," Vincent snapped.

"Aiden was mine. I've watched over him for years. And, when it was time... I spared him."

"What do you mean, you spared him, Tess? You are not supposed to interfere," Thomas exclaimed. "He's valuable to us. He's strong. He handles every task I've given him."

"Tess, do you realize what you've done?" Vincent shouted. "I told you she's gone too far Thomas."

"What? What have I done? I couldn't let him fall. How could I?" she shouted. "He begged for his life. I chose to save him. I chose... because I love him. I've loved him for a long time. I wanted him to stay here, with me."

"Tess..." Father whispered. "You're too upset. You need to go and rid yourself of this."

"No Father. I can't lose him. I won't," she insisted. "I know what I have to do. I have to send him. He can find them and bring them here to us," she calmly finished.

"You spared him for your own selfish reasons. You've gone against every rule you've ever known," Vincent scolded. He was right. She knew it. They all knew it. It wasn't just a matter of restoring now. It was the fact that she interfered. And the ripple effect could go on for years. Decades. Even centuries.

"It may have been wrong. I'll deal with whatever has to happen to me. But not him. Nothing can happen to him. And right now, he can help us. I'll see that he finds them and brings them safely home."

"This could change things, Tess. For you, for him. For all of us," Thomas whispered.

"We must mean nothing to you," Vincent muttered as he stormed toward the window.

"Don't say that. And don't act so innocent, Vincent. You break rules. You find him just to taunt him. You're so full of hate!"

"A mortal can't go. It is completely out of the question. I will go. And I will find them!" Vincent insisted.

"Wait. Vincent, what does she mean you find him?" Thomas questioned.

"She doesn't know what she's talking about," Vincent shouted glaring at Tess.

"Vincent can go. He's strong enough," Frederic insisted.

"No. He isn't strong enough. This anger makes him weak. He would never make it," Thomas explained.

"Aiden can find them. He's strong, Thomas. Just let him," Tess pleaded.

"He will destroy everything," Vincent warned.

"I won't hear of it, Tess," Father Andrews insisted. "This is not Aiden's task to bear. It is ours."

"Father, how did we become your tasks, your burdens?" Tess asked, in a gentle voice, as she took Fathers Andrews' hand.

"I don't like this Tess. He will get too close to us. He can't know," he warned her.

"And he won't. This is what needs to happen," she insisted as she turned toward Thomas.

"Don't worry Dominic. He'll find them. He will. Let's go sit with the rest of the family. Father can we just be done with this conversation, please?" She clutched Dominic's arm and lead him up the cellar stairs. "Thomas?" she called.

"Yes, Tess. We're coming," he replied as they followed her. He and Father Andrews continued to discuss the idea of sending Aiden.

"Out of the question," Vincent groveled as he followed them up the stairs. "Please? No more about this tonight," she insisted.

The Great room of the castle was magnificent. Hundreds of tiny white candles flickered soft light all around the room. The large wrought iron chandelier hung in the center above them. Thomas sat at the piano next to Sarah and began to play a gentle tune for her.

"Thank you," Dominic whispered to Tess as they sat near the others. "Your home now. Safe. Don't worry. They'll be here soon," she replied.

Vincent spread his arms across the long wood mantle of the oversized fireplace. He stood directly in front of the fire. Much too close. His face is reddened by the heat as his eyes flicker with rage. He spun around toward Tess glaring at her with his arms folded. What a ridiculous conclusion they had come up with, he thought. How could a pathetic mortal go and retrieve three weak Dominions and bring them back here without finding out what they really were? Every part of the idea infuriated him.

12

Absent Minded

Tess woke to the sound of tapping on her door. She tossed the sheets off of her as she stretched.

"Tess?" Thomas whispered, pushing gently on her door. "You've missed class.. again. I've noticed your needing more and more sleep lately," he whispered.

"I'm fine Thomas. I'll be down in a minute."

"If you need this much sleep, Tess…"

"I'm fine, Thomas. Really, I am."

Bright and early the following Monday morning, I was comfortably perched in my chair at two minutes to eight. I was a little curious why her chair was empty. She didn't say anything about not feeling well or that she wouldn't be in class today. My mind drifted away from the steady chatter of the room. And the booming voice of Professor Williams trying to capture our attention. Today was the chapter review for the exam. If she were in her chair, I might have been be able to pay attention. But she wasn't. Thinking about her caused me to drift off revisiting the time we spent together.

"Isn't that right, Mr. McCarthy?" Professor shouted. I shot up in my chair in a panic. I had no idea how long I hadn't been paying attention. I peered around the room trying to access which material we were covering. Some students were writing, a couple had their hands raised… by the looks of it… too long.

"Right. Yes. Sir. That's right." I quickly agreed even though I had no idea what I was agreeing to. A desperate attempt to keep him from tearing me to bits in front of the class. And judging by the look on his face he wasn't about to let it go that easily.

"It would appear you've lost interest, yet again, in the class discussion. This is an exam review. I believe you are aware of that, am I right?" he asked sarcastically. I nodded like a scolded child hoping he would grant me a stay of execution, show me some form of sympathy. But I got nothing back but a cold glare. I definitely checked out. Again. And this time he wasn't going to let it slide. "Could this lack of interest possibly be that you're the victim of a love stricken condition rendering you incapable of following along? And, is it a possibility, Mr. McCarthy, that you now possess no real motive to succeed in this class?" I was afraid to respond. I quickly decided that no answer would be the best answer. "Is that the case?" I sat there silent. "It must be." He fired one after another, demeaning, rhetorical questions in a highly disappointed, bitter tone.

I sunk deeper and deeper in my chair. He stood there waiting. I seriously did not want to respond. That would only encourage him. But if he was waiting on something from me, I needed to act quickly. Otherwise this would never end. So, I took the easy way out and shook my head no.

"No? That's not the case?" he asked, raising his brows even higher, doubting my sincerity.

The entire class roared with laughter. Professor finally let up and walked past me. He began tapping on my desk with a rolled up paper and then dropped it. The grin on his face was one I was familiar with. And then came the wink. I opened the tightly rolled paper and there it was in bold red.. an "A" with a small inscription that read, "Perfectly researched, perfectly written. Well done, Mr. McCarthy."

I shot up in my chair beaming with confidence. His approach was interesting. Beating me up like that wasn't something he liked doing, but I had it coming. The tactics he chose were a bit over the top especially when his enormous ego took over. Demoralizing anyone who disrespected his classroom and his time was his standard method of punishment and something he was very good at.

"For those of you who did poorly on your essay, cheer up. You will have a chance to redeem yourselves with your thesis. Pay attention to corrective criticism. I've made some suggestions. Use them to make the changes. See you tomorrow." Every word that came out of his mouth came in the form of a suggestion. But it wasn't a suggestion. It was a command. If you wanted to get anything out of his class including a passing grade, you needed to figure that one out... day one.

Students poured from their seats rushing past him as he stood at the front of my desk. He gave me the look. The "what could possibly be happening in your pitiful life that was more important than paying attention in my class..." look.

"Two words. Follow along. You may not look like such an idiot the next time you're handed a perfect score."

"Yeah, sorry. It's this girl. You know?" I confessed.

"So... my assumption was correct. You are a pathetic love sick individual," he said, chuckling.

"Unquestionably."

"Miss. Hamilton, I presume?"

"Yes."

"Get out of here. Go. Do something constructive," he ordered.

"Alright. See you later."

"Oh, Aiden. I'm headed home for Claire's wedding on the tenth. You're still coming I hope?" he asked, eagerly awaiting a positive response.

Claire was Professor William's youngest of two daughters. His oldest daughter, Lillie was a former girlfriend of mine. We dated for quite a while back in high school. I think it would be fair to say that I had a permanent place in their family. An open invitation for marriage as Lillie so dramatically put it when we last saw each other. She still thinks we're in love. To this day, she tries to convince everyone in her family that we're still an item. I told him I would be there. He paid for my ticket. But now there was Tess and I dreaded leaving her even if it was only for the weekend. But I had to go. I needed to. Professor just stood there waiting for me to respond. And the look he gave me… I could see it in his eyes, he would accept nothing less than a "yes, of course I'm coming."

"I am. I wouldn't miss it," I shouted, running out the doors. I couldn't wait to find out why Tess wasn't in class. All I wanted to do was call her to see if she was okay.

"Hello?" Tess whispered.

"Hey there. How are you?"

"I'm ok. I can't believe I missed class this morning. I overslept," she said, giggling. "… that never happens. You have no idea how that really never happens," she added. "How was your day without me?"

"I guess it was ok. Williams caught me daydreaming."

"Oh no. That couldn't have been good."

We talked for hours. We talked about everything. My family, her family, our friends, our jobs, school, everything. There was nothing I wanted more than to see her. To tell to her how I felt. How she made me feel. How crazy she made me when we weren't together. How crazy she made me when we were. Some day when the time was right I would.

"Well, I should let you go. You need to get some sleep," she said.

"Alright. I'll talk to you tomorrow. You'll be in class, right?"

"I'll be there."

"You're definitely falling for her. She's falling for you too." Dr. Bennett whispered.

"Yeah. Hard. We fell hard. So when do you think I'll be able to get out of here?" I asked. Water seeped inside from the open window down the sill dripping onto my thin gray pants. I pushed myself far enough away to stay dry. The rain had stopped. Dark clouds began to break and warm sunlight crept through the canopy of trees above me.

"Its beautiful out here. Why would you be in such a hurry to leave the grandeur of this garden?" she whispered.

"I think it time."

Flowers bloomed all around the edges of the black fence that enclosed the grounds. The rich green grass complemented each shade. It was finally spring. Buds filled the trees and shrubs. New life came back to the garden bringing with it new hope to get back to my life.

"Talking about her, remembering her just makes it more urgent to get out of here. I need find her. I need to know where she is... that she's safe."

"You want to leave?" Dr. Bennett asked.

"Yes."

"I think you're getting closer but you're still in therapy. We're making progress, aren't we?" she asked as he knelt down beside my chair.

"Yes, but I'm done with this. This chair, this place..."

"You're getting the help you need to move on with your life outside of here. How about these dreams… how about you tell me more about them?"

I didn't answer. I held out my hand out to catch raindrops falling from the terrace roof. The dreams were difficult to revisit. I went over and over it all in my mind for months.

"You did a very good job talking about the first dream you had. It may not have been easy but I do believe it's helpful."

I nodded. She was right. It was easy to talk about Tess. About my family, my job, school… friends. That was worth reminiscing. But the times when I was pushed to the limit weren't so easy. Like in my dreams. They weren't dreams at all. We use words like "hopes and dreams" in the same sentence. Putting them together as if they belong together. Hope doesn't belong in my dreams. There was never any sign of hope. Only struggle. A constant battle to stay alive. Dreaming wasn't the word to be used to describe what I went through. Nightmare was. I glanced up at Dr. Bennett. She was still waiting for me. Always with a smile. It was her way of not pushing too hard. She was patient, I had to give her that. She didn't want to upset me. She knew I would shut down like I did so many times before. I hadn't gotten this far with any of the doctors.

No one was able to get me to open up like she did. She knew things. She understood me. Almost like she could read my mind. She was prepared for everything. And she wasn't afraid to ask questions…

"Vincent was there again, wasn't he?"

Even if the questions were difficult to ask. She'd ask them anyway. She knew the hard part wasn't in her asking. It was getting me to answer.

"Yes," I muttered.

The hard part was left to me.

13

Nothing Too Deep

I woke up in the middle of an ocean. The water was freezing. The wind and rain from a violent storm sent waves pounding against me. I struggled to stay above water. I saw nothing, nothing but the deep swells and swirling currents all around me. In the distance bolts of lightning from the heavy black clouds above me struck the monstrous waves.

Something bright was up ahead. It lit up the black sky. There was fire on the water. Just a short distance from me there was a capsized boat and it was burning. Billowing smoke rose from the flames. My arms and legs throbbed with pain from the frigid water. I couldn't move. The extreme cold seized the last bit of energy within me. I felt myself slowly losing consciousness.

In the distance I saw someone coming toward me.

"Hello?" I called out.

Maybe a survivor from the boat accident. He moved closer to me. I quickly realized it was no survivor. It was Vincent. Out of the shadows of the black night, from the depths of the ocean, he was there. He taunted me with his ability to move easily through the turbulent, icy water.

"Can you help me?" I pleaded.

He said nothing. A sadistic grin covered his face. His eyes were full of rage. There he was, in the same treacherous storm, yet he didn't struggle. He appeared to be perfectly warm, unaffected by the freezing current. I pulled my hand from the water to reach for him. My skin was a shade of bluish gray. I was definitely in trouble.

"Why are you here if you're not planning to help me?" I shouted. I grunted, gasping for air.

He didn't say a word. The only thing I could think of was that I was surrounded by evil. That's what he was. Evil. He had no intention of helping me. He was there to watch me drown. To do nothing but take pleasure in my suffering. He moved quickly around me. First in front of me and then, in an instant, he was behind me. Impossible, abrupt movements that made no sense.

"Vincent!" I screamed in one final attempt for help. That's when he shot straight up out of the water and hovered over me. He held out his hand as if offering to help. I reached out to take it when suddenly he vanished.

I heard him laughing. I couldn't see him but I knew he was still there. I could hear his sinister laugh taunting me. I searched for him in the darkness, but he was gone. At that point I had been paddling for what seemed like hours and was too exhausted to stay above water. I'm not one to give up without a fight but I had no fight left. I was completely drained. But somehow I knew it was a dream and I knew all I needed to do was wake myself up and it would be over. But I couldn't figure out how. I couldn't figure out what to do to get out of the situation. The waves continually pounded against me. I took a deep breath and went under. Lower and lower I sank waiting for whatever was supposed to happen next. I opened my eyes under the murky water and saw something ahead of me just below the surface. It was a man. He was unconscious and sinking fast. I didn't know if I had enough energy to reach him. And, if I did get to him, did I have enough left to save him. I dove down to him. I wrapped my arms around him and kicked as hard as I could toward the surface. It felt like there were a thousand tiny needles jabbing me all at once but I pushed through the pain to reach the surface.

I gasped my first breath of air as we came up. He was motionless. Maybe it was too late. I had no idea how long he'd been under but the only thing I knew to do was to keep swimming and stay above water.

That's when I heard something. A soft sound. Music. I heard music. It was faint, it was coming from far off in the distance but I heard it. And, at that point, it became my only hope. I paddled in the direction it was coming from. I could barely hear if over the storm and the waves crashing against me. The more I paddled, the louder it got. It was a violin… and it was guiding me. Like a light in the storm. My mind quickly raced to Tess. In that moment, I transported myself from the icy cold depths of this deadly abyss to a place far away from here. A place where there was nothing but calm. Suddenly I could feel her warmth. I felt a rush of adrenaline and used every ounce of strength I had to paddle.

I saw land up ahead. I was relieved. And exhausted. I towed him behind me toward the shore. The pain was excruciating. My entire body was shutting down. My legs were numb and I wasn't sure if they would even hold me up once I reached the shore but I knew I had to keep moving if we were going to survive. To give up now would mean hypothermia. And I wouldn't be of any use to either one of us. Finally, I felt the sand bottom beneath my feet. I made it. My knees buckled as I tried to stand pulling his lifeless body out of the water. I collapsed onto the beach trying to catch my breath. He wasn't moving. I leaned over him put my ear to his mouth to listen. Nothing. He wasn't breathing. I put my hands together and pressed a few times on the center of his chest. After a few compressions, I dropped down close to him to hear if he was breathing. There were giggling sounds followed by very shallow breaths. He was breathing. He made it. We both did. That's when I woke up.

"Another soul saved. Even if it was just in a dream," Dr. Bennett said in a low voice. She was trying to appear sympathetic to the frantic state I was left in sweating from most parts of my body.

"Which means nothing. It wasn't real."

"Our subconscious mind shows us what we're truly made of, Aiden. We're tested by it. It shows us our fears, our true abilities, what we're potentially capable of. And, quite often we discover our deepest desires," Dr. Bennett explained, handing me a foam cup of water and two small pills.

"Thanks, but I'm ok. No more drugs."

"You're pretty upset. They'll help settle you down."

"They don't help. They only mask."

"Okay, Aiden. No more meds. We can do this your way." She scribbled in her notebook.

"I don't want anything. I'll get out here clean. Not dependent on drugs to get me thorough a memory. Good or bad, I need to be able to handle it on my own."

"I'm glad to hear that. I'll make a note in your chart for your nurses not to offer you anything. No more meds. Not unless you ask for it. How's that?"

"Good," I mumbled. "You mentioned something about desires. Our subconscious mind shows us our desires?"

"Among other things, but yes."

"If that were the case I would see Tess. I don't see her. She's never there with me. I think the only thing being tested is my sanity. And by the looks of it... I failed. Which probably explains why I ended up here."

14

A Point of Reference

Tess spent more and more time alone in her room. She knew if she hung around Thomas and the others they would notice her changing. They would try and force her to go and restore. But if she went, she knew she would lose everything. Her feelings, her memories, she would lose the love she felt for Aiden.

She stayed nestled in her bed. Her room filled with the hazy morning sunlight. There was no way she would erase the warmth the thought of him brought. Slowly she rolled herself off the bed and walked over to open the window. The breeze blew her long dark hair away from her face. As she reached for her robe she caught a glimpse of her reflection in the mirror. She was definitely changing. The color of her skin had become lighter, thinner, somewhat iridescent. She needed to go. She knew it.

She heard a soft knocking on the door. She quickly grabbed her robe and tossed it around her. "What is it?"

"Tess, I need to talk to you," Sophia whispered through the door.

"Come in. What's wrong?"

"It's Aiden," she whispered.

"What about Aiden?" She could hardly keep still. Her mind raced with terrible thoughts. "Sophia tell me!" Tess scolded pulling on her hands for an answer.

"Aiden pulled a man from the water last night, right? You must have sent him?"

"Yes. I sent him. I had no choice. The only reason the accident happened was because of me. Because I spared Aiden. I need to fix this. Things are happening that shouldn't be happening because of what I've done."

"I understand. I do… but Tess, Vincent was there, too."

"What do you mean he was there."

"He was there with Aiden. I followed him. I knew when he stormed off last night he was angry. You've been so tired lately. I knew you wouldn't notice."

"What? Vincent was there? But how? Why? I- I slept through it all."

"That's why I went. I didn't want him to do anything crazy."

"Thank you, Sophia. Thank you for watching over him."

"You shouldn't be using Aiden like this."

"I know. But if I don't, I'll lose him."

"Tess, you need to heal. You're going to forget it all anyway, it's inevitable. You can't survive. Thomas will fix this. He'll know what to do. Let's just go… tonight. I'll take you."

"Why is Vincent doing this?"

"Just to torment him. His anger is growing. He needs to go, too. I'm sorry… but you're both doing more harm than good. To yourselves and to innocent people. Especially Aiden. You need to talk to Thomas. I'm afraid something bad will happen if he keeps following him like this. If you don't stop sending him, if Vincent continues to interfere it could be bad for all of us."

"Just once more. To find the others. That's it. I'll figure out what to do about Aiden after that."

"You have to tell Thomas. He can talk to Vincent. He listens to him."

"I will," Tess whispered.

"You used to listen to him, too, Tess. You need to go. Please," she begged taking her in her arms. "Sweet sister, I don't know what I would do if anything happened to you."

"Nothing will, I promise. I'll figure this out. Don't worry," she said softly.

Dr. Bennett peeled the wrapper off of a cough drop and popped it in her mouth. She held out her hand offering one to me.

"No, thanks," I said, smiling. We were spending much more time together going over the details of my past. It was like putting together a puzzle with ten thousand pieces. I could tell she wasn't feeling well, like she was fighting her own tiny battle.

"I've caught a bug." She said sniffling. Nonstop sniffling, I might add, using a tattered tissue she pulled from inside her coat pocket. One that couldn't possibly handle any more blowing or wiping.

"I see that. Why don't you take a couple days off? Looks like you could use the rest."

"I look worse than I feel. I'm fine. I'm supposed to be your Doctor, remember? Not the other way around." She chuckled. "Did you get any sleep that night, after the dream?"

I laid there for hours until I had to get up for class. Seeing Tess in her seat definitely helped. I sent her a quick text that I had to work after class and would call her later that afternoon. After turning in my thesis, I rushed over to the park to work. Lack of sleep was really starting to wear me down. Every muscle in my body ached. I didn't need it affecting my job like it was everything else. I tossed my knee pads to the ground as I fumbled to open my tool bag.

"Hey there," Tess whispered, as she walked up behind me. I didn't expect to see her but she was definitely a sight for sore eyes.

"Hey you."

"I didn't mean to startle you."

"You didn't. I'm really glad to see you."

The stress and fatigue I felt faded away whenever I was around her. She had a way about her. Something that gave me strength, energy, everything I needed at exactly the right time.

"Well good," she said with an affectionate smile. "I wanted to make sure that I would see you tonight at the gallery." Were you still planning on coming?"

"Absolutely. Williams and I are going to grab some dinner and then head over."

"Terrific. I'm so glad," she said gleaming with excitement. "Well, I'll let you get back to work."

"I'd rather work on you," I said, snatching her in my arms.

"I have to go. But I'll see you later," she said as she pulled from my embrace and darted away.

That night Professor Williams and I planned to have dinner at his favorite spot downtown not too far from the gallery. I would've cancelled if it were anything other than something Tess invited me to. Even if I was overly tired, I was definitely excited to go.

"I'm glad you called, Aiden. I would have been on the couch all night. I completely forgot all about the premiere," Professor admitted as he drove through town. I wasn't very good company mainly because of lack of sleep but I was also eager to get there. My hands were clammy and no matter how many times I wiped them on my pants they still felt damp. He couldn't help but notice my nervous energy.

"She's going to be there tonight, I suspect... this love interest of yours?"

"She is."

As we pulled into the gallery, Professor spotted a unusually small parking spot right near the door just big enough for his convertible. It was a sixty-nine corvette. A classy little car that still looks and runs like it just rolled off the show room floor. He referred to it as his trophy wife. Front row parking was one of the many perks of owning a toy car and never having to wonder if it will fit. It always fit.

Making our way inside, Professor Williams headed straight for the bar which was very predictable. He had an order to things. The way he went about his nights out.

"First, we scope the room. Make sure to be seen before heading to the bar for a drink. Order a double thus eliminating the need to rush right back. Finally, talk to five people — preferably female — per hour." And that, my boy, is how you advance in every category of life. And I do mean every..."

He was a master of each of his crafts. Meeting new people was one he definitely mastered. He should have answered his true calling and got into politics.

The atmosphere was nice. Professor Williams already seemed to be in good hands. He found himself deep in a one sided conversation with two lovely women. And it would seem by the way they gazed at him that they found him fascinating.

I wandered over to where a pianist was playing in the reception area. As I walked closer, I noticed that it was Thomas and he played exceptionally well. He noticed me watching him. He nodded a quick hello. I waved to him. I scanned over the crowd looking for Tess. Thomas gestured toward the stairs that led to the lower level. He must have been okay with us seeing each other to point me in the right direction.

"Nice." The Professor grinned and said as he came up behind me. There was a jazz band playing an upbeat mix and with guests streaming to the dance floor, it would seem they were a hit. Professor nodded his head to the beat.

"Now, Jazz interestingly enough can turn a dull environment into a livelier one instantly," he announced aloud clicking his fingers. He looked like the fifth member of the rat pack with his undeniable vintage swagger. And the way he swayed to the tempo as he walked... he was completely in his element. The two women stuck closely to each arm as they strutted away.

The lower level glowed with candlelight. It had a slight retro feel, very chic and contemporary. Most of the work was on display in the reception area upstairs but some of the larger paintings were set up in the lower level. Tess' sister was quite talented.

I spotted Sofia and Angelo sitting on a long red sofa. I remembered meeting them at the pub. There was no sign of Tess. Angelo was completely surrounded by several lovely young women. They must be her other sisters. I cased the group for Vincent. I definitely didn't want to run into him here. Tess tried to convince me that Vincent's problem was with her, not me. But after the dream in the water, I found that hard to believe.

Professor Williams was perched at the bar. He smiled at me and held up his glass. By this time, he had drawn a small crowd of women eager to hear tales of his glory days. It's no wonder my father became friends with him. He gave Professor Williams the nickname "Willie" when they were in college together. I thoroughly enjoyed giving the Professor a hard time about the stories my father told me. But I did find it difficult calling the respected Professor Williams "Uncle Willie" around here. So, I came up with a shorter version — "Will." It was easy and respectable. Professor liked it too. We were like family. Especially when we were out socializing together.

I noticed Dominic near him at the bar. I remembered meeting him at the ballet. He looked much better that he did that night. He was chatting with a couple of guys I didn't recognize. As I walked toward the bar I saw her. She didn't notice me. Not yet. She looked so beautiful. I felt an intensely warm rush of emotion run over me. She was absolutely breathtaking in a full length gold strapless dress. Her hair was tied to one side with curls cascading over her shoulder.

"Champagne, sir?" I couldn't seem to break from my stare. I was mesmerized by her. I'd never seen her look more beautiful.

And I loved that fact that she was expecting me that evening. "I'm sorry. Yes, thank you," I replied as I sat my empty wine glass on the server's tray. I took a glass of champagne. This moment definitely called for a toast if only with myself. I stood there for a moment shaking my head absolutely taken back by her sheer exquisiteness. I wanted to hang back and just watch her. That was short lived once she noticed me staring. And when her eyes met mine, her face lit up.

"Aiden!" A gleaming smile covered her face. She rushed over to me and threw her arms around my shoulders.

"You're here."

"Of course I'm here."

"Come on, I want you to meet everyone." She took my arm and directed me over to her group.

"Tess…" I whispered as I held her still for a moment. "I…. I… " I know I sounded like a babbling idiot. I couldn't find the words to tell her what I was feeling. She leaned herself in toward me.

"I know… me, too," she whispered into my ear. I felt my body melt. I had absolutely no inner strength to remain standing. She shook my arm. "Come on. They all want to meet you."

"Great," I whimpered as she tugged me closer. She was so happy. I was so nervous. What about Vincent, I thought. She didn't seem at all worried so maybe I shouldn't either.

"Everyone's here except Nathanial. He's at home with Avery. You can meet them later. But everyone else is here, come on. Come meet them!"

As we approached the group she held my hand tighter so I couldn't let go. I had no desire to let it go. "Dominic, you remember Aiden?"

"I do. It's nice to see you."

"You're looking much better Dominic." I said shaking his hand.

"I'm feeling much better, thank you."

"And, this is Frederic," Tess announced.

"Frederic. It's nice to meet you."

"Hey, you too, Aiden," he replied.

Tess turned to her sisters waiting for a break in their conversation to make the introductions. Just as I turned to take a seat next to Tess, a man came up behind me and put his hand on my shoulder. "Excuse me but have we met? You look so familiar," he asked with a puzzled look on his face. It was covered with white strips covering deep cuts across the bridge of his nose and one on the corner of his lip. He was in bad shape. Definitely a rough looking guy by all accounts.

"I don't think so." I answered. "I'm Aiden. It's nice to meet you." I answered slightly startled by his appearance.

"Oh, I'm sorry, I must look pretty alarming. I was in a car accident. I saw you come in. I probably shouldn't be here but you looked so familiar, I thought maybe... Well, where are my manners, my

120

name is Bruce, Bruce Mason." He held out his hand. I took it gently and shook it. "Are you sure we don't know each other?"

"I don't think so. I'm sorry."

"Please don't apologize. I didn't mean to disturb you. Would you excuse me?" He said as he walked away.

"Who was that?" Tess asked as she stood next to me.

"I'm not sure. He looks a little familiar, but I don't think I know him. Poor guy. He looked pretty messed up. He said he was in a car accident. He thought he knew me from somewhere. I guess I looked familiar."

"Aiden, come. Have a seat," Frederic shouted as he slid down next to Sofia making more room. Tess quickly sat on the red velvet sofa across from them sliding to the end.

"Here, sit," she demanded as she patted on the cushion next to her.

"Hello Aiden, I'm Sofia. We didn't get a chance to meet the other night. It's really nice to meet you."

"You too." Aiden smiled as he sat next to Tess.

"And I'm Rachel. I think we met at the Premiere of James St. Clare last year. Am I right?" she asked.

"We did. Your right. You're the curator."

"I am. And I believe that I met your Father that evening as well. Your family owns the Benevolence Gallery in Boston?"

"That's right. It's nice to see you again."

"You too, Aiden," Rachel replied.

"And here's our star of the evening, Elaina." Tess stood snatching her by her arm proudly escorting her toward me.

"It's a pleasure to meet you, Elaina. Your work is incredible. You're very talented."

"Thank you, it's so nice to finally meet you."

"I'm Daniela. I saw you at the ballet."

"Yes, I remember seeing you. You play beautifully," I said as I shook her hand.

The youngest of Tess' sisters, Sarah came sprinting in our direction running directly into me. She gripped onto my legs tightly as she tried to hide from a young boy. She peeked around me to see if he was gone.

"He won't leave me alone." Sarah cried as she looked up to see who she was clinging to. She gazed at me realizing that she ran directly into a complete stranger. A look of sheer terror came over her face.

"Excuse me," she said in a soft, frightened tiny little voice. I knelt down in front of her. A ringlet of her auburn hair had fallen into her eyes making it difficult for her to see.

"That's okay. I will protect you from little boys who won't leave you alone," I whispered, pulling a flower from the vase on the table behind me. I handed it to her. She smiled as she took it from my hand.

"Aiden, meet Sarah." Tess said softy as she reached down to caress Sarah's cheek.

"Sarah, this is Aiden."

"Hello," she blurted, swinging her dress side to side.

"Hello Sarah. It's very nice to meet you. And may I say what a beautiful dress you're wearing."

"Thank you. Did you know that Tess and I made it? All of this lace, and these beads… we sewed it."

"Very impressive work," I replied, looking closely to the tiny detail.

"Sarah, look. That little boy is sitting all alone. Go sit with him. He looks so sad," Tess whispered to her.

"He wants to play with you," Sofia added.

Sarah's little face scrunched up with anger. She looked over in the corner where he sat with his arms folded in his lap. She scowled. He sat there pouting, waiting for her to feel bad enough to return. Sarah looked up at us. She then let out a big sigh and shrugged her shoulders. She spun around and stomped toward him.

"You're all so talented. Father Andrews must be very proud," I said, taking Tess' hand.

"I am," Father Andrews proudly boasted as he approached us.

Sarah heard his voice and forgot all about the little boy in the corner. She ran to him with her arms held wide open.

"Well, well, well… what are you up to little one?" he asked, lifting her high into the air. "And how are we all doing this evening? Have you met everyone, Aiden?"

"Yes. I believe so," I replied.

"All but Nathaniel and Avery. He's probably overwhelmed," Tess whispered.

"You have a beautiful family. Father. I had no idea how talented they all were."

"They are indeed," He replied, bouncing Sarah in his arms.

A large crowd was forming at the bar. The main attraction was Professor Williams. I could make out a bit of the conversation. He started speaking in French. That was definitely a sign that it was time to go.

"It was nice meeting all of you," I announced as I pulled Tess aside to say goodnight privately. "Thank you."

"For what?" she whispered.

"For introducing me to your family. For making me feel so welcome."

"You are welcome."

I brought her close to me. I gazed into her deep blue eyes. I had one wish. I didn't want this moment to end without showing her how I felt. She just stood there holding onto me. I knew she wanted me. It was the way she looked at me. Almost as much as I want her. All I wanted was to kiss her. My heart began to race. I felt like it was going to explode out of my chest. Her lips were so soft, so tender. She moved her tongue across them inviting me to get closer. I ran my hand across her cheek. She closed her eyes as I touched her. I wanted to savor the way she felt in my arms. I've waited for so long for this. Slowly my lips touched hers. All that went through my mind was how good she felt. How warm she was. I pulled her tighter kissing her. The passion grew between us making it hard for me to stop.

But, for Tess, it wasn't the right place, the right time. I felt it when she pulled away from me. A tender smile crept over her lips. As the night went on I had the opportunity to spend some time getting to know her family. They were the most interesting group of people I had ever met. I felt slightly underachieved after hearing about their successes and travels. But I knew I had it made with a girl like Tess at my side. There's only so much traveling, so much success and fortune one needs in life. I knew that from the successes my family had experienced leaving me aspiring to simply keep the pace. But I knew deep down there was much more to it than that. More to it than obsessing over things with price tags, or adding credentials to your name. Those things won't bring a true sense of happiness. I knew that. All the self-help books, the personal development seminars, they all pointed to one thing. The materialistic world is meaningless in the end. Sure a hefty bank account and a shiny red sports car or two wouldn't suck, but the true secret to life is making that inseparable connection with someone. Not just anyone. Someone meant for you. They may not be what you've expected all your life, maybe you had an idea of what they'd be like so you go about it looking for what you expect them to be. But its not in the looking that will help you find them. Its in the feeling. I think thats why so many relationships don't work. It's why my relationship with Lillie never amounted to a lasting commitment. I expected something from her that just wasn't there. That feeling. And until you meet this one person, this special someone, you wonder if there is such a thing as a soulmate. Someone made, built, programmed, designed for just you. And it makes sense once you've found them why none of the others worked out. For me, without question, that someone was Tess.

"You're so right on many accounts, Aiden." De. Bennett announced. "And I feel that this therapy is exactly what you need. I understand how you ended up at this point. If she's gone, and we know she is... and she was in fact the one for you, how would anyone expect you to move on?"

Finally, I thought. A complete break through.

"Exactly." I replied. I couldn't help but feel a huge sense of relief. But to be stuck here in a wheelchair in a mental ward because my girlfriend dumped me is what everyone else thought. There was so much more to it than that. And Dr. Bennett understood that completely.

"Relationships fail. Whether two people are meant for each other or not. They fail. We all lack the emotional intelligence to see what's happening at the time, to correct it allowing us to work it out. Its so much easier to just give up."

"I didn't want to give up. I had no choice."

I know. I understand. I don't want to say something completely out of line but do you think Tess felt the same, that you were meant for her?"

"Yes. Absolutely."

"She went to some serious extremes to stay with you. And with everything you've told me so far, I have to agree with you. So, Tell me how the evening ended."

Professor actually was the one to bring the evening to a close. "Aiden, my boy… could you take my keys to prove once and for all to these lovely ladies that I have absolutely no intention of driving myself home this evening?"

I couldn't help but smile at him. Tess even felt the need to giggle. It was hard to hold it together watching the way his body wobbled as he staggered toward us. He did quite well considering he not only had to manage himself, but also his two unstable dates as they clung to his arms. I quickly snatched the dangling keys from his hand.

"And, if you would be so kind as to point us to the direction of the door. I would like to get them a cab," he chivalrously announced. They giggled gripping tighter to his arms.

"I apologize, Tess," I whispered.

"It's okay, Aiden. Go and take care of him. I'll see you later."

I pointed directly in front of Professor Williams to show him the door. He and his dates were exactly two feet from it when he asked where it was.

"Here, let me get the door for you." It was that same guy. That Mason guy who thought he knew me.

"Thanks. Sorry I don't remember you." I replied pulling the all too chatty Professor and his giggly dates through the open door.

"That's okay. I thought it would come to me. I can't figure it out. I've been having these strange flash backs lately. My memory seems to be going. Oh well, it was nice meeting you. Have a good evening," he said, waving as he jogged down the street.

"Yea, you too."

"A friend of yours?" Will asked.

"I don't know who he is. But he seems to remember me from somewhere."

"That can be scary," he snickered. "Ladies... shall we?" He opened the cab door and the two intoxicated women slid inside. He quickly hopped in pretending to have fallen on top of them. All three uncontrollably laughing like lunatics. One of the women began to yank on him so he didn't attempt to escape.

"Will?"

"Ah, yes." The plan came back to him. He remembered that he was riding with me. He removed the woman's hand kissing it gently and slid back out of the seat. As he clung to the open door, he gave instructions to the driver handing him a large quantity of folded bills.

"Take care of this precious cargo, my man. Here's plenty for the fare. Keep the change. Keep them safe."

"You got it." the driver blurted. He sorted through the stash happy with the extra tip.

"Au revoir, ladies. Make sure you keep in touch, now." He waved goodbye as he slammed the cab door shut. He spun around and pointed at me.

"Well hello, Aiden!" he shouted, stumbling over to me latching on my arm.

"You are certifiably insane," I said, laughing at his inability to function.

"Did she kiss you?" he asked with a foolish grin on his face.

"That's absolutely none of your business."

"Come on now." He winked elbowing me over and over. "She did, didn't she?" he slurred.

"What's the matter with you?" I scolded. I reached into his coat pocket yanking his handkerchief from inside to wipe a splatter of his saliva from my face.

"Seriously. We're not having this conversation." I shook my head in complete horror.

"He's quite a funny guy, Professor Williams. Isn't he?" Dr. Bennett asked as she wiped her nose.

"Yeah, he is."

"We would really get along, I'm afraid," She said smiling.

"You definitely would."

"So, you have confided to him about Tess and her family?"

"Yes. Professor Williams is one of the few people in town that didn't have negative things to say about them. The town is pretty conservative."

"I can imagine."

15

Tunnel Vision

"I had another dream that night, after the premiere. It wasn't so bad. Not at first anyway," I said, as I looked at Dr. Bennett.

"She was there; I take it?" she whispered with a grin.

"Yes… in the beginning," I answered. "She looked so beautiful. She wore a satin nightgown standing in a candlelit room. Sheer curtains blew around her in the gentle breeze through the open windows. They surrounded her. I took her in my arms and held her close. I gently moved her dark hair away from her face. I caressed her tender cheek and ran my fingertips across her lips. I started kissing her gently around her face feeling her warm breath on my mouth as I touched her lips with mine. My body rushed with weakness. I took her to the bed feeling every part of her against me. She felt so real, so warm. This was too perfect to be a dream, but one that I welcomed. I was so glad to be with her.

"I heard her whisper. I could hear her, but her lips didn't move. She just smiled and looked deep into my eyes. 'Find them, she said softly'.

"I asked her who.. expecting her to speak but she said nothing. 'I'll show you' I heard her voice but still no words crossed her lips. 'Don't worry. I'll be with you, Aiden.' I had no idea what she wanted me to do. At that moment I didn't care. She slid her fingers in through my hair and over my shoulders pulling me to her. Her hands slid under my arms and up my back thrusting me tightly to her. Her touch sent an uncontrollable sensation over me. I couldn't move. Whatever she wanted, I didn't care. I would do anything for her. Anything.

Seconds later, I realized I was no longer in the comfort of her bed. No soft sheets, no burning candles. I turned to see where I was and to see if she was still with me. I spun around in the darkness. There was no sign of her. Behind me I saw a tunnel. A dim light lit the entrance. I began to walk toward the opening moving my feet through the shallow water. I knew that I was searching for someone. Tess told me to find them. Them meaning someone. All of the dreams started out the same. I first had to figure out where I was. This one was different. She was with me, somewhere. She told me she would be.

A foggy mist rose from the distance as I moved toward the light. As I entered the tunnel I heard the soft violin. The same sound I heard when I was in the water, after seeing Vincent in my dream a few nights before. It reminded me of Tess, of her sister Daniela and the soft sound of the ballet. I didn't know where it was coming from. It didn't matter. It helped that's for sure.

As I moved into the tunnel, I heard voices up ahead echoing in the distance. 'Hello?' I shouted.

"Who's there?" A voice called back. A woman's voice. It was faint, but I could hear her. "My name is Aiden," I told her.

"Aiden, do you know where the others are?"

"The others, what others?" I questioned pushing against the murky water as I walked closer toward her voice.

"We're lost."

I could hear her crying. There was another voice, a child's voice. I could hear them up ahead.

"Don't worry, I'll get you out of here." I shouted. "Where are you?" I could see nothing but darkness in front of me. It was hard to keep my balance. The ground beneath me was constantly changing. At first it was a shallow stream of water, then it got deeper, rising up over my feet. Next, it felt like slippery shallow mud which slowed me down. It kept changing. I moved as quickly as I could but had to focus on each step not knowing what was ahead potentially blocking my path. I needed to be prepared for anything. My fingertips grazed the cold brick as I moved along the side. The water was consistently shallow near the wall. It guided me as I made my way deeper and deeper into the tunnel.

Up ahead there was a dim light. I could see the opening. Thick fog rose toward the moonlit sky as I walked closer. I couldn't hear them. The crying stopped. I moved quicker pushing harder against the murky water eager to reach them. To reach the light. It began to get colder and colder the closer I got to the outside. The temperature was dropping so fast. I could see my breath in front of me.

That's when I heard him. Only one person could make the cold sadistic laugh I heard echoing in the darkness, and that was Vincent. I knew it was only a matter of time before he would be there. Somewhere lingering, waiting to show himself. I could hear him. I couldn't see him but I knew he was there. The soothing sound of Daniela's violin disappeared. It was silenced by the repulsive echo of evil. I clenched my fists and kept walking. The only thing I needed to do was get to them before he got to me.

"Keep coming. You're getting closer," she cried. "I can see you."

"I'm almost there, hang on."

As I neared the opening, the shallow icy water turned to mud. Thick mud. My feet sunk deeper with each step slowing my pace. I sunk farther and farther as I tried to move closer to the opening of the tunnel.

Vincent's faint laughter bounced off the brick walls.

"Are you there?" I shouted, clutching to the side as I get closer pushing my way through the mud. She didn't answer. At that point it had reached my knees. I could barely move thorough the sludge as I approached the end of the tunnel. The light grew brighter the closer I got to them. His laughter echoed louder and louder as the mud rose up from underneath me. I had to keep moving.

Finally, I could see the night sky. The full moon above me cast a brilliant light all around the opening. Instantly, the muck I was drudging through disappeared. His laughter stopped. He was gone. Along with the cold, the fear, all of it… just like that, it was gone.

"Where are you?" I shouted.

"We're here," she cried, looking up at me. Her face was covered with mud. They all were. There were three of them, lying on the bank too weak to move.

"Can you help us?" She was holding a young man who seemed to be unconscious. Next to her sat a little girl. I rushed down to the boy placing my fingers on his neck. He had a very faint pulse. He was alive. But barely.

"Are you alright?" I asked the young girl.

"Yes." She said wiping the dirt from her tiny face. She couldn't have been more than nine or ten. Her long black hair was tangled and matted. She looked exhausted and weak. I did what Tess instructed. I found them. Now I needed to get them somewhere safe and dry and soon.

I lifted the boy and ordered the others to follow close behind me. There wasn't any other option but to go back the way I came. Through the tunnel. There was no way of going around it. There was no "around"… only back through.

The mud was gone and that eased my mind a bit. There was no way I could carry him plus help the little girl and the young woman make it through three or four hundred yards of waist high mud. No way. I could barely get through it myself. It was an easy walk at that point. Just the cold water surrounding our feet. I was definitely cautious as we started though the tunnel. I didn't know what would change but there was no way we could sit around waiting for Vincent to do absolutely nothing while this boy slowly died.

"Hold onto me. Both of you!" I ordered. We moved deeper into the darkness. I could hear the young girl sniffing as she followed closely behind me latched securely to my waist. It was almost unbearable not knowing what to do, where to take them. I just had to keep going until we reached the other side. I closed my eyes for a second struggling to carry the lifeless boy. He had to be in his teens. He wasn't much smaller than I was. I tightened my grip and shifted him higher in my arms and kept moving. I saw a light flicker up ahead. Finally, someone was there. Someone to help. We moved closer to the light that was waving in the distance. A shadow of a man came running toward us.

"Please, let me help you." He said. He wore a heavy overcoat. I couldn't make out his face. It was too dark. But as you can imagine, I was relieved. I don't think I could have carried him another step. My hands trembled as I handed him his lifeless body.

He took him into his arms and carried him the rest of the way. I bent down and lifted the young girl. She wrapped her tired little arms tightly around my neck as we exited the tunnel.

"Can you hear it?" The young girl whispered. I could hear the soft violin playing. "I hear it. It's beautiful. You're going to be alright now."

"Thank you," she whispered into my ear.

"You're welcome, little one."

"Thank you for finding them. We couldn't have done it without you," the man said in a deep voice.

"I'm glad I could help."

"Don't worry, I'll take them from here. They're going to be alright… thanks to you."

I knew they would be safe. My job was done and I could wake up. As I watched him take them away I saw the silhouette of a beautiful young woman ahead in the distance. She stood under the moonlit sky. Her long hair flowed in the delicate night air as she stood waiting. I knew it was Tess. There were others waiting with her. Dark shadows in the far distance. A dense mist rose up from behind them.

"This one was different. It was different from the others." Dr. Bennett spun around in her chair and stood up.

"Yeah. It was."

"Tess was there. It wasn't violent." She folded her arms.

"No. It wasn't."

"Vincent stayed away."

"Yes."

Dr. Bennett smiled. "Maybe because she was there with you."

"Maybe."

I woke in my bed. Not hers. Unfortunately. I looked out my window rubbing my eyes. It was still dark. I reached for the clock on my nightstand. Glowing red numbers displayed 2:21 am. I ran my hands through my hair and squeezed my eyes shut.

I tossed and turned for a while trying to get back to sleep, but realized that it wasn't going to happen. I rolled out of bed and turned on my lamp. As I stumbled past the mirror over my dresser, I gazed at my reflection. I looked beat. I had heavy dark circles around my eyes. The lack of sleep, the dreams were really starting to get to me. I popped two aspirin in my mouth and reached into the shower to turn on the water. Maybe I could call Will. I needed some company and he was a night owl. He required little sleep. And he was a great listener. Professor Williams would be the first to admit that he had absolutely no life. He was probably still up channel surfing after dropping me off earlier that evening. A shower wasn't what I needed. A friend with the willingness to listen... that's what I needed. I quietly crept down the stairs and snatched my cell phone from the coffee table.

Like every other night, Ben was sprawled across the sofa. Limbs dangling from corner to corner with drool trickling onto his pillow. Ben would wake up. He may even be okay with listening. But not without whining about how late it was. I needed to call Professor Williams. He was my best bet for solid advise.

"Hey Will," I whispered into the phone.

"What's up kid?

"I could use some advice. Can you meet me at the diner?"

"Sure. You ok?"

"Yea, I just want to talk. Were you asleep?"

"Nope, just reading. I can be there in five minutes. I'll buy you a cup of coffee."

"Thanks. See you in a few." I flipped my phone closed,. jumped into the Jeep, and headed for the diner.

A cluster of bell chimes made an obnoxious ringing as I entered the diner. The regulars were pretty unfriendly especially to the non-regulars that came in after midnight. Immediately I spotted Professor Williams waving from a booth in the back.

"Hey, thanks for meeting me," I said, sliding into the seat across from him.

"I'm glad you called. Whenever you need me, day or night. You know that."

"Yeah, I do."

I began telling him about my dreams. I told him how I thought I was being tested. Finding people, saving people. And how I felt completely run down, drained of my energy when I woke up.

"I just need to sleep. That's all. I need a break. Somehow I need to get them to stop just so I can get some sleep."

"You do look like crap." He chuckled and stirred his coffee. "I ordered one for you. Black right?"

"Yeah, thanks."

'Here you are." The waitress slid a cup of in front of me. "Would you like anything to eat?" "No thanks, just the coffee."

"You should see a doctor. Get a prescription... something to help you sleep."

"Maybe. The one tonight, Tess was there. At least I thought it was her. I think she sent me."

"What do you mean she sent you?"

"She was there, in the beginning. She asked me to find them."

"Who?"

"The three that I found in a tunnel," I explained.

"A tunnel?"

"Yeah. Dark, wet and cold. They're all like that. Either I'm battling extreme elements or I'm involved in an accident of some sort where I'm saving people. And, then, there's Vincent."

"Vincent. Doesn't he live with Father Andrews?"

"Yes, with Tess and the others," I replied.

"He's not there to help. His sole purpose is to make things worse. More difficult."

"What do you mean?"

"Like tonight. I heard crying. I knew I needed to find whoever it was. I could tell they needed help. I didn't see Vincent, but I could hear him laughing. A haunting, sinister laugh. In the dream I had a few nights ago, I saved a man from drowning, he was there, too. I was in the ocean struggling to stay alive. He was there. He refused to do anything to help. He had one objective and that was to make sure I failed."

"How strange," Professor whispered, rubbing his whiskered covered face.

"Stressful is more like it. The first one I had, I saved a young girl. We were on a bus and it crashed into a river. I was completely exhausted when I woke up. It was like I was actually there, physically, saving her. Struggling to stay alive."

I rubbed my hands over my eyes.

"Well, coffee isn't the best thing for you right now." He reached over and pulled my cup toward him. "My pull out may be better. Come stay with me. I'll make sure you get some rest. And… see a doctor."

I nodded. He definitely helped. I felt better just talking to him.

Later that night after I returned home, I snatched the study guide from my bag and attempted to read through it. I was just too tired to concentrate. I moved the curtain away from the window and noticed a strange man standing at the edge of my driveway. He was smoking a cigarette. His shaggy hair spilled over his collar from under a hat. After a minute or two, he strolled away.

I wondered who he was but didn't think to much about it. I lived close to plenty of establishments that stayed open well into the morning hours to have the occasional random passerby at all hours of the night. It wasn't too out of the ordinary.

Dr. Bennett sat back in her chair and crossed her legs. She rested her chin on her palm and gazed at me.

"What are you thinking?" I asked.

"You told Professor Williams about your dreams."

"Yes. I needed advice, I needed something."

"He didn't give you much did he?" She said, chuckling.

"No. But I didn't expect much. Just sitting with him made it all a little more manageable. Knowing he was in my corner, helped."

16

Similarities

Nathaniel was the man who came to help in the dream that night. He returned to the castle with the three along with Tess, Sophia and Thomas.

"Angelo, Fredrick… Father, we're back," Nathanial called out. Angelo and Frederic rushed to help. As they opened the doors Father Andrews and Dominic hurried down the stairs toward them.

"Isabel, Tien! You're here! I'm so glad that you're safe. Where's Jowell?"

"Dom…" Jowell answered in a very faint whisper as Frederic and Thomas moved him toward the window. "They need to go. Now!" Thomas shouted.

"I'm sorry. I should've listened to you," Isabel whispered softly. "This is my fault." Dominic raced to her side and held her.

"None of that matters. You did nothing wrong, Isa. You're safe now. That's the only thing that matters." He touched her face wiping mud from her cheek. He noticed wetness coming from her eyes. "You have tears, you must go now," Dominic insisted.

"He's right. You're going to be alright now. You're safe," Father Andrews whispered.

"Angelo, you take Jowell with Thomas," Nathanial ordered. He rushed to the window with Tien in his arms.

"I'll follow with Isabel," Dominic whispered as he took her by the hand.

"I'll help you." Frederic announced taking Isabel by the arm.

Daniela, Alaina and Rachel followed them. Sofia moved slowly toward the window and glanced back at Tess. "Tess?" Sofia whispered as she stepped onto the ledge.

"It's okay, I'll stay here with Father."

Thomas and Angelo lifted Jowell to the window. "Are you coming Vincent?" Thomas asked. Vincent glared over to Tess.

"I told you, when she goes, I'll go," he groaned.

"Tess... please," Thomas begged. He was concerned for the both of them.

"Not now. Take the others. I'll go soon. I will," Tess promised. She rested her head on Father's shoulder.

"Go with them Tess. Please." Father pleaded.

"Not now. I'm fine. We need to worry about getting them. Now please, go."

Thomas and the others ascended into the night sky. Beyond the castle, high above the mountain, past the river, farther than anyone could go by foot. They traveled to a hidden place, far away from the eyes of mortals. A place where they gather to restore. To rid themselves from all emotion. Everything that distracts them. Everything that causes them to lose sight of their purpose. Hurt, sadness, sickness anything that builds inside them living their mortal lives. Desire, anger, greed, lust. It was all washed away under the moonlight sky, in the mist of the falls.

Tess gently brushed her fingers over the soft white curtains hanging over the windows. She was relieved they were found in time.

"You need to go. You both do," Father whispered.

"We will, won't we Tess?" Vincent grumbled.

"This just isn't like you Tess, to wait this long. I realize you've become very close to Aiden. But you know what has to happen."

"I do. Please, don't..." she whispered.

"I'll be in my study if you need me," Father said in a low voice as he walked out of the room. "The sooner you break this with him, the better it will be for the both of you." Father added closing the double doors behind him.

"Just because he found them doesn't mean that he is worthy of you, Tess," Vincent shouted. His anger grew. "He's still just a mortal."

"Stop. Don't say any more," she shouted, as she stared out the window.

"Look at you, you're so weak. And you refuse to heal... for what, for him?"

He was so angry. She saw a burning rage in his eyes and this time Thomas wasn't there to help.

"And you're any better? You don't heal because you want to hate him. Why is that Vincent?"

"You and I are the same, Tess." He grabbed her by the arm. He whispered into ear forcing her to listen. "We're exactly the same."

"We aren't! I'm nothing like you!" she said in an angry whisper pulling away from him.

"Yes, you are. You're just like me. We're defenseless." He clutched her chin squeezing it tightly. "We can't help ourselves. Just a little taste of mortal emotion keeps us begging for more. Isn't that right?"

"Stop it, Vincent. Stay away from me." She demanded turning away from him. You don't know what you're talking about. You don't know anything."

"You feel the need for this love... this lust for this weak mortal! And I'm given no choice but to hate just to stop you from destroying yourself! Pathetic isn't it?"

"I said stop! Please, Vincent! I'm not like you!" she adamantly insisted, trembling to defend herself. "We're nothing alike... nothing." Suddenly, she felt the warmth of a tiny teardrop as it fell onto her cheek and trickled down her face. "Hate has no room here," She turned back toward the window. "Not near me. Not ever," She mumbled, wiping the tear away.

Father Andrews stepped out from his study. Tess glanced at him. Her eyes filled with tears. "I'm sorry, Father."

He had never seen a look of sadness on her face before.

"I'm not sure if I can help. But, I do know this... I can't stand around and let you shout at each other. In all my years in this house, I have never heard any of you raise your voice. I suggest you both go. It's late, I'm heading to town," he said as he pulled his coat over his shoulders. "I'll be home in plenty of time to greet them when they return."

Tess stood staring out the window. "Vincent, no more tonight," She warned. Vincent turned away refusing to respond. "Tess?" Father asked.

"We're fine." She whispered.

"Why am I not convinced?"

"Really, it's okay," Tess insisted as she led Father to the foyer. "We won't discuss it any more tonight. Just go."

Father Andrews placed his hand under her chin raising her face to the light of the burning candles. Tears shimmered around her lashes and cheeks.

"Tears?" Father let out a sigh as he shook his head. He glared at Vincent. "No, it's not him. It's me. Please... just go."

"Promise me Tess, you and your brother will go."

"We will. Don't worry."

Vincent slammed his fists as hard as he could against the wall. He tossed a chair across the room moving swiftly toward the open window. He soared into the night far away from the castle, from Father, from Tess.

"Don't worry. He'll be fine," Tess assured Father Andrews. This was unchartered territory for all of them.

Father Andrews volunteered at the Catholic Church in Princeton. Confessionals were open three times a day. He took the latest hour. Many of the homeless, hopeless, needy and in often cases, desperate would come at night. And he worked so well with them. He helped out as much as he could. Over the past week or two, every night he came in to help with confessions, he noticed the same man sitting alone in the last pew. He knew him. He remembered visiting him in the hospital a few months ago. He was a police officer. A highly respected officer in the department. Father Andrews remembered everything about him. How he had been involved in an accident that nearly took his life. An accident that claimed the lives of his family. He lost his wife and young son. He'd been in a coma for weeks. Father visited him many times during his recovery. He remembered his obsession with a strange man who he believed caused the accident. When he woke from his coma, it was all he remembered, the only thing he talked about. Not about the loss of his family, not how it happened... nothing but the man who was to blame. His only concern was who he was and how he would make him pay.

Father was glad to see that he was better physically. But his emotional state clearly didn't heal as well. He sat alone in the pew weeping.

"May I sit down?" Father Andrews asked in a soft voice.

"Yes," he whimpered, wiping his face with his sleeve.

"Do you remember me?" Father asked.

"Yes, Father. I do. And I wanted to thank you for coming to see me while I was in the hospital."

"I see your injuries are healing. That's good." Father noticed several deep cuts across his forehead partially covered with white tape. He sat hunched forward holding his black hat in his hands.

"Would you like to share your troubles? It may help lift your heavy heart."

"Yes. Maybe it would. I lost my family, Father. They're gone." His voice cracked as he broke down weeping in sadness. "I lost them in that accident. My wife and my son." His voice trembled as he struggled to speak.

"I am so sorry for your loss."

"There's a man. He did this. He's to blame, Father."

"No one is to blame for this."

"Yes, there is. He caused this to happen. I can't stop thinking about him." He wept uncontrollably covering his face with his hands as he spoke.

"I used my badge to get to him. I did things that I shouldn't have. I lost my family. I lost everything, all because of him, because of what he's done."

"You will heal. It will take time." Father whispered reassuring him.

"But I can't think of anything but his face," he cried, clenching his fists.

"Whose face do you see? Was it the driver of the other car?"

"No. A man... a strange man... in my car. I saw him. Just before the accident. I never saw him before. He was there. If he actually exists, I have to find him. I need to know why he was there... why he didn't stop it from happening? Why he didn't save my family?" He wiped the steady stream of tears from his face with his sleeve.

"Maybe he wasn't real. Maybe you imagined him?" Father questioned.

"I don't know. I drew him. I drew his face on a piece of paper." He pulled out a crinkled up drawing from his coat pocket. He spread it out smoothing it over his knee. Father Andrews knew the face all too well. It was Vincent. He had drawn a sketch of Vincent's face.

"I will find him. However long it takes," he vowed. He closed his eyes tightly and held the emotion that welled within him. Quickly he stood and put on his hat. "Thank you, Father." He tipped his hat toward him and left.

Later that evening, Father Andrews returned home anxiously awaiting their return. He wanted to see that Jowell, Tien and Isabel were better. And, he also needed to talk to Thomas about the drawing of Vincent.

Tess waited with him by the open windows. He didn't want to bring it up to Tess. She had enough to worry about besides the fact that her health was deteriorating. Any more stress would only make matters worse.

The stars lit up the night sky guiding them back to the castle. One by one, they came inside. "Welcome back!" Father Andrews announced.

"Let's celebrate. Shall we?" Angelo exclaimed as he patted Thomas on the back. "I'll get the sodas."

"Thomas I need to speak to you for a moment… in my study," Father said.

"Sure thing," Thomas replied. He gave Angelo a quick shove as he walked past him to loosen his tight grip from Frederic's throat.

A bit of rough housing always broke out especially right after they returned. Having a fresh outlook and renewed strength created a high energy that radiated throughout the castle. And with three new family members safe and sound, it brought a whole new level of excitement. Fredrick was smaller, younger and an instigator. Always starting something with his older, stronger brothers.

"That's not funny, Angelo. Let him go," Thomas demanded, trying not to smile. It was all in good fun but it had happened once or twice where things got out of hand and required a quick trip back to heal.

"What is it?" he asked Father Andrews, closing the door behind him.

"I'm afraid we have a situation that may need to be addressed rather quickly."

"What's going on?"

"Well, it seems Vincent has put himself in a situation."

"He has nothing assigned to him. He's too unstable lately. He doesn't have any situations to get involved in. What do you mean?"

"Not his own, I'm afraid. It seems he's interfered with someone else's. He was seen. He was remembered. And now this man is searching for him."

"How did you hear about this?" Thomas whispered.

"He came to confessionals tonight. He showed me a picture he drew of the man he saw during the accident he was in with his family. He survived. They didn't. He blames him. It's Vincent. And he's looking for him."

"It's my fault," Tess whispered from the doorway.

"Why would you think that?" Father asked.

"I sent Aiden and Vincent followed. Sophia told me. I was trying to stop the ripple effect I caused from saving Aiden."

"I wish you wouldn't have involved him, Tess," Father whispered. "I know. But it was the only way...I can't lose him." She cried.

"Did he see him... he remembers Vincent?" She asked wiping her tears. "I'm afraid so."

She felt herself weaken inside. She couldn't hold herself up. She felt she was to blame for this and didn't have the strength to handle it.

"We'll fix this," Thomas assured her. He took her in his arms and held her. "Don't worry, Tess. It's going to be alright. Vincent just needs to go away for a while... until things settle down."

"Right," Father Andrews agreed. "Tess, my dear. You must end this with Aiden. For his own good. He's too involved."

She nodded in disagreement, "I can't. I won't send him again. But I won't lose him."

Both Father and Thomas decided not to push her to make any decisions. She was too emotional for her own good. Thomas just held her.

"No more worrying tonight, Tess. We're going to take care of this. Just do go far from the castle. Not until you're stronger."

"I'll call the hospital tomorrow." Father whispered, "and see if I can get any information about this man. I spoke with him during his recovery and for the life of me I can't remember his name. He may be seeing a psychiatrist. I'll find out what I can."

"Where is Vincent?" Thomas asked.

"He was here with me earlier," Tess answered. "We had a disagreement. He left. He was so angry."

Thomas was the one that protected them from anything that could threaten them and their existence. He was able to sense danger. If they felt it, so did Thomas. From anywhere, he felt what they felt. He took care of them in a way Father Andrews couldn't.

He wanted to find Vincent. If someone was looking for him, Thomas needed to get to him first and take him away. Everything else would take care of itself. He closed his eyes tightly trying to feel anything from Vincent. There was nothing. For the first time he felt nothing.

"I can't tell where he is. I don't think that has ever happened before," he admitted.

"He was so angry, Thomas. His rage had taken over," Tess whimpered.

"Maybe it's too late."

"That's not possible. He wouldn't do that to himself. He would go to the falls before he ran out of time," Thomas insisted.

"Unless he was discovered. What then?" Father asked.

"I would sense it. I don't. He's angry and without healing he's farther away from what we are. I can sense us, what happens to us, what we feel. And because he refuses to go, he's becoming something else. He's fading, like Isabel, Jowell and Tien. I couldn't sense them. Once they reached a point where they were too weak, I can't help them. Which is probably why I can't feel anything from Vincent."

"He will age then... and quickly. I hope you're right, Thomas. I hope he would go heal himself. For his own sake."

Suddenly, visions flashed through Thomas mind. Visions of Vincent. "I see him."

"Where is he, can you at least sense that?" Tess asked.

"It's dark. I can't tell where he is. We don't need to share this with the others. Not yet. It would only create panic with the new ones. They need to feel a sense of security here. Agreed?" Thomas asked.

Father Andrews and Tess nodded in agreement as they rejoined the others.

As they came out of the study, Sarah came tromping down the stairs shouting. "Welcome back! Welcome, Tien," Sarah said as she took her by the hand.

"Thank you." Tien replied.

"Are you feeling better now?"

"So much better."

"Wasn't that great? I like the ride. It's my favorite part," Sarah said beaming.

"It was really great. I liked it too."

"Do you want to see my room?"

"Sure, I'd love to!" Tien replied enthusiastically as she walked with Sarah toward the staircase.

"I can't go to get better by myself, but that's ok. Tess said that its better when you can share the ride with someone you love. Maybe we can go together next time?"

"That sounds nice, Sarah. I would like that."

"Do you want to share a room or would you like your own?" Sarah asked.

Tien bent down and whispered into her ear. "Would you like to share your room with me?"

"Oh, yes! I really would!" Sarah nodded in excitement.

"Okay, it's settled then. We will share your room," Tien said with an enormous smile. Sarah's eyes grew as wide as ever. Her excitement just couldn't be contained. She began waving her arms and flapping her little hands in excitement. Just the thought of having a new friend, a new sister to share her room with was more than she could ever have wished for. Tien giggled at Sarah's private little celebration. Tien was happy, too. She was the youngest for so many years. Not anymore. Sarah was much younger. Sarah needed her. Tien was finally the big sister she always wanted to be. Sarah danced all around her circling her, holding, squeezing Tien's hands as she swung them side to side, twirling around again and again.

Tess worried about Vincent and desperately wanted to be with Aiden. She needed him tonight more than ever. The evening's celebration was all thanks to him. He found them. He delivered them to Nathaniel and now they were home. Her emotions grew deep inside her. He was all she could think about. She wandered up the staircase wishing the others a goodnight. She was the only one who needed rest. Other than Vincent.

"Goodnight Tess," Thomas shouted up to her.

"Are you sure you couldn't stay up a bit longer?" Elaina begged.

"Not tonight. Maybe tomorrow."

"Goodnight then. Rest well," Elaina replied.

"She's too tired. Sofia, you should talk to her."

"She'll go. When she's ready." Sofia assured them.

Dominic rushed to the stairwell. "Thank you Tess. I wish I could thank Aiden too. I owe him everything."

"You're welcome, Dominic. I'm glad he was able to find them in time. Who knows… maybe someday there'll be a way to thank him."

"Maybe so. I'll welcome the opportunity. Good night then."

"Good night," she said as she turned and went up the stairs.

"Dr. Bennett, can I ask you something?" I turned in my chair and looked back at her.

"Of course, Aiden?"

"Do you think Vincent wanted me to die in my dreams?" I gripped the wheel, turned the chair around, and waited for her response.

"Did Vincent purposely put himself in your dreams to try and end your life... is that what you're asking?"

"I guess."

"That is beyond anything I could logically explain." She moved her chair closer to me. She knew I was struggling to make sense of everything. I could tell she struggled with her own thoughts.

"Did you fear him in reality?" she asked.

"I'm not scared of him if that's what you're asking," I replied confidently.

"Did he threaten you?"

"I suppose."

"Maybe you needed to confront him and put an end to his attempts to intimidate you into staying away from Tess. Maybe then your dreams would've stopped."

"I thought so, too. Everything I did... or didn't do was for Tess."

17

Withered Pages

Tess went to her room and closed the door behind her. There was something she wanted to give to Aiden. She kept her most important possessions tucked away in her closet. Underneath old trunks and neatly stacked hat boxes, she kept letters she wrote over the years. She wanted to remember the love stories she witnessed after restoring caused her to forget. Reading her own words, her thoughts, how she felt watching them, seeing how deeply they loved caused her question her purpose. They were a constant reminder that meaningful love existed but she would never be allowed to experience it. Until now.

Tess was born in 1766 in a small town east of London, England. In the summer of 1790 she became very ill. Separated from her family she was sent to a hospital to be treated for malaria. She was just twenty-four years old. After being treated for several weeks, she could no longer fight off the infection and, as she took her last breath, she was chosen. Appointed. Spared by her guardian. A guardian she doesn't remember because they never met. Most of them never lived as mortals. The few who did, were chosen to fulfill tasks. Tess was one of those few. She spent her first years watching over her family. She watched as her parents aged and passed away and many years later, her younger brother, too. Never was she questioned about her lack of aging. It was just part of the process. Something they had complete control of. In her early days, Tess went to restore often to rid herself of the grief from the loss of loved ones. She traveled over the years moving from place to place, but she always returned to where her family was buried in a small cemetery just outside London.

Thomas found her in Milan in the summer of 1872. He followed her, watching her until one day she had enough of his menacing pursuit.

"Are you following me? You were watching me while I was in the market," she said to him, "and now today, I catch you following me again."

Thomas removed his hat and lowered his head. "I beg your pardon, Miss. Please accept my apologies," he said in a low voice.

"There are laws against this type of behavior, you know. You look as though you're somewhat intelligent. I'm sure that you are aware of such laws."

"I am. However, I think that I may be able to be of some assistance to you."

"I don't require assistance, thank you. Now please, leave me be. Go about your business."

"But, I think that we may have something in common." He squeezed the edges of his hat nervously.

"Yes. We both have two legs. But I choose to use mine to travel alone. It's much easier," she said sarcastically.

"But if I may add, much lonelier as well... am I right?"

He didn't take his eyes off of her. He knew what she was. And, soon she realized he was just like her.

"A little. I suppose. But I have many acquaintances. They keep me from being lonely. I enjoy their company," she insisted.

"Interesting. Would you say that you become involved with them?" he asked. He seemed curious but she sensed there was more he was hinting toward.

"Somewhat... to the extent that I can."

153

He smiled at her. She was so different. Not like the others he had encountered. That's what drew him to her.

His voice lowered, "There is a rule, you know." His voice lowered.

"I know about the rule," she sneered, kicking dirt and rocks from under her boot. "I could never understand the concern. Would it be possible to become so involved… to actually fall in love?" she asked.

She missed certain things about her mortal life. Certain feelings that weren't allowed. Such as the excitement, nervousness when she met someone intelligent, adventurous and strikingly handsome. The butterflies that came with it. She was curious about love. Maybe it was because her mortal life was cut short. She was just beginning to enjoy the advances of certain young men who have long since passed.

"It's not only impossible, it is forbidden," he quickly answered.

"It's a silly rule, that's what it is," she whispered, kicking the lose pebbles as she walked. A larger one struck Thomas in the shin. He gripped his leg hobbling in agony.

"Oh, I'm terribly sorry. Are you hurt?" she winced, trying to console him.

"I'm quite alright." He dusted off his pants. His face was bright red after holding his breath attempting to manage the pain.

"Are you sure?"

"Yes. I'm sure. I'm very resilient." He strutted around, limping less and less. "See? Good as new."

"Well, if you're sure you're okay, I must be going." She lifted her long, dusty skirt and darted around him.

"Won't you sit with me for just a little while?"

She gazed at him. It couldn't hurt. He was the first one she had met who was like her. There were questions she could ask him.

And… she found him slightly irresistible which made absolutely no sense simply because of how annoying he was.

"Very well. I'll give you the time it takes for one cup of tea. And then I must be going."

All she kept thinking was what a wretched suit he was wearing. He had absolutely no sense of style whatsoever. If nothing else, she could advise him on what not to wear. He was clumsy, awkward and more of nuisance than anything else. But she felt sorry for him. He had such a helpless look on his face. Maybe he could become her project. He needed her, that was obvious. And for multiple reasons. And she did have the time. Lots of time.

"So, what is your name, anyway?" she demanded, nudging him.

"Thomas. And you're Tess. Am I right?"

"How did you…." She shook her head at him and scowled. He had no manners. No explanation how he knew who she was. "You are very rude."

"So I've been told."

"Of course you have. Well, if I am to travel with you, then you will need to change some things. Starting with your rudeness and ending with that suit." She started walking even faster, challenging him to keep up.

She was different. There was something about her. She was fiery, exciting, opinionated, and extremely passionate about everything which was quite uncommon for a guardian. He liked that about her.

"What's wrong with this suit?" He stopped abruptly and looked at his attire. He buttoned the top button of his jacket, adjusted the sleeves, and pulled gently on each cuff. In his opinion, he looked quite handsome. He gazed back at her with a pitiful look on his face. She couldn't help but laugh. She was brutally honest. So very uncommon but, strangely enough, he liked that, too.

She told him of her travels, he told her of his. He explained how he spend his years searching for others like them. That was his job. His priority. She enjoyed his company. He was funny in his own way and could easily make her laugh. They sat for hours and quickly formed a bond. A bond that would remain strong for hundreds of years.

Tess pulled a tiny footstool from the corner and sat inside her closet. She began digging through trinkets and keepsakes looking for the letters. There were old pictures and postcards, pocket watches and coins. Little keepsakes that she saved from decades that had passed. Tucked neatly below were the letters wrapped with ribbon. She wanted to share the letters with Aiden. She wanted to tell him everything. How long she waited for him. What he meant to her and what she did to keep him.

She gently pulled one from the bundle and began to read it.

Seventh of June, 1894

I witnessed something wonderful again today. James Arthur is in love with Miss Adele. He held her, confessing that she indeed was the one he wanted. She fought his advances knowing she agreed to marry another. Even so, she let him kiss her. In that moment, she belonged to him. The passion they shared... I long for it. I admit, I do. ~Tess.

And she opened another...

Fifteenth of September, 1841

It cannot be described, this love I long for. I know who you are. I've imagined you. You will show me in due time. Until then, I shall wait for you. For as long as it takes, I shall wait. ~Tess

She felt tears well in her eyes as she touched each letter. Thankful she didn't have to wonder what it was like. She finally knew.

She came upon a light blue envelope. She knew the letter. It was one she didn't write. It was from a young man, an artist that she met centuries ago. He had the ability to see her differently. He was gifted. He saw her for what she was, in her true form. He drew her, he painted and sculpted using her likeness… how he saw her. In her image. He felt them around him, he connected with them bringing them to life in his art.

She began to unfold a crisp paper she pulled from inside. It was covered with faded swirls of pastels. A hand painted postcard of a tiny villa on a lake where Tess, Thomas, and Vincent lived in Rome. He often would paint her portrait there near the water. He was a teacher to her and a friend. On the back of the paining he wrote a note that read…

"Dearest Tess, thine angel with me~

I have witnessed thou longing for true love. I have but few words to share. 'Tis not what is seen with thine eye for it cannot fulfill what thou truly desires. It is that which one possess from within… for it is what shall deliver divine fulfillment. Listen to the soul and listen well, for it speaks only in silence." ~M. Angelo

Tess folded up the letter. She placed it inside the box along with the others. Turning the key and locking them safely inside. She felt a cool breeze whirl around her from the open window. She couldn't help but think of Aiden. She stepped onto the ledge and floated out into the night sky.

Nothing had ever felt like this. Nothing. It consumed her, the love she felt for him. She glided through the night air to his open window as if he was expecting her. She moved herself closer to him, watching him as he slept.

"No dreams tonight, Aiden. Just rest." She whispered gently slipping in beside him. The full moon lit up his room, casting a soft light onto his dark hair, his broad shoulders, his strong arms. She touched him brushing fingertips across his back slowly stroking him. She wanted him. The desire burned deep inside of her. She delicately placed her lips on his shoulder tenderly kissing his soft warm skin. She moved her fingers over him gliding them down his spine to the lower curves of his waist.

He abruptly rolled over and was facing her. He was beautiful. His full lips, his tanned skin, his warm breath. The desire she felt made her tremble. She moved closer trying not to wake him. She wondered if he would be startled by her presence but the way it felt being that close to him outweighed the fear of him waking. She was his. He was hers and for now nothing else mattered.

Suddenly, he reached for her. With her waist in his grasp he wrapped himself around her pulling her into him. He knew she was there. Maybe he thought he was dreaming. Maybe that's why he didn't wake up. He held onto her like he would never let her go. She stayed with him that night for hours. It was the rest she needed. But she knew she couldn't stay. She gently pulled herself from his arms and headed for the window. The brisk air surrounded her. She gazed back at him as she glided away.

"Are you okay, Aiden?" Dr. Bennett asked softly. She could see I was upset. My eyes welled with tears. I quickly wiped them and refocused my attention back to Dr. Bennett.

"I've dreamt of her. Holding her close to me." I tried clearing my throat. A big lump formed making it hard to talk. "Just talking about her now with you… she brings me back to life."

Accepting Probability

"So, Aiden. Tell me about the trip with Professor Williams." Dr. Bennett stood there holding a cup of coffee.

"Alright."

Professor Williams pulled into my driveway blaring on his horn. The professor's daughter, Claire was getting married on Saturday. I was happy to be going back home to visit but didn't want to leave Tess. I picked up my bag and headed for the front door.

"Hey, Ben? I'm leaving! Try to stay out of trouble while I'm gone," I shouted in my typical parental tone.

"Ok, see ya later!" Ben yelled from upstairs.

I darted across the front yard, tossed my bag into Professor's tiny car, and jumped in.

"You ready?" Professor asked as he pulled his dark shades over his eyes.

"All set, let's go."

Professor and I made it to the airport in record time. He was excited to see his girls. It'd been a few months since he had a chance to visit. That particular weekend however, he had to give his daughter away and that had him a bit on edge. We rushed through security and settled into our seats aboard the plane.

"First class? You've got to be kidding," I blurted jokingly fastening my seatbelt.

"Is there any other way to travel? Besides, my daughter's getting married tomorrow!" he announced. A few passengers seated near them began clapping and cheering.

"Can I get either of you a beverage?" the flight attendant asked.

She was what the Professor would refer to as "stunning." Very attractive for her age, very tall and very blonde. Definitely his type. And, by the creepy grin on his face, this was the perfect start to what was to be a perfect weekend.

"Well, aren't you a welcome sight." He smiled and gave her a wink. "I'll take a double martini."

"Dirty I take it?" She asked flirtatiously.

"You know it."

"And for you, sir?"

I didn't respond. I wanted to send Tess a quick text before we took off.

"Sir?" She repeated.

"His name is Aiden, and he'll have the same." Professor answered driving his elbow into my side.

"Oh, yes. Thank you." The same will be fine."

"What did we get?"

"Martini's my boy. A couple of Martini's to kick it off!"

The Professor's future son in law, Matthew Murphy, was on the championship rowing team last year at Harvard. He and I were old friends. We attended prep school together, played rugby and baseball together — always on the same team. And, now, he was marrying Claire. Professor William's youngest daughter.

"Truth serum." Professor blurted staring into his glass.

"What do you mean?" I asked trying not to laugh.

"Haven't you ever heard the term?"

"I suppose I have."

"When one consumes alcohol they become more aggressive. Inhibitions fall to the wayside. And, in my case, a superhero emerges." He chuckled. "When I'm out with a woman and we have a drink or several, it seems I become more attractive to her. I can do no wrong. I'm much more exciting," he boasted as he sipped.

He was somewhat a philosopher. Especially when he had moments like this, moments of clarity.

"I can see that," I replied, grinning at him. "You can add less manageable to your list."

"To moments of bliss," he held up his glass proposing a toast. "To the moments when the brain is released from duty. A short lived escape from a desperately insane reality. Here's to those short lived escapes." The Professor held his glass toward mine. I had to agree with him. Reality could be a hard game to play at times. I turned toward the window. In the distance, through an opening in the clouds, was a brilliant beam of sunlight that streamed into the plane.

"So, have those dreams stopped?" Professor asked with a genuine look of concern in his eyes.

"They haven't stopped. But they've gotten better. I've had a few dreamless nights. A few about Tess, too," I grinned, winking at him. "You know... she's got something over me. I can't get her out of my mind." I finished my drink and held it up toward the stewardess as she passed by.

Professor held up two fingers ordering a couple more. "I like the way you think," he said with a smirk. "I have something I

161

want to show you." He reached down and pulled out a book from inside his briefcase.

"Here, read this. It's very interesting. I've had it for years. After we met at the diner, I remembered I had it and wanted to give it to you." He handed me the book. It appeared to be old. I hadn't ever seen one quite like it before. On the heavily worn gray cover was an outline of an angel sculpture. It was hard to see at first, the way it blended into the background. The faded colors were so similar.

"Where did you get this?" I asked, brushing my hand over the cover.

"I don't remember. It's a book about Dominions."

"Dominions? So, you do believe in this kind of thing?"

"What it is to believe or not? We need to ask ourselves what it takes to believe in something we can't understand simply because we can't see it. That's where true knowledge stems. In dreams we're more susceptible to believe anything. Any suggestion, any idea, any concept. What do we really know about the subconscious mind? We don't question the possibility of what can actually exist or not while dreaming. We simply comply with the dream. So what is there to believe in? The fact that you're having dreams is real, right?"

"Right," I answered.

"The fact that you're saving others seems real, right?"

"Right."

"So, you're questioning what you're dreaming. If you're dreaming. The reality of it. If you're in fact dreaming the events or are they actually happening."

"Yea, I guess I am." I answered as I thumbed through the pages.

"Then you should read the book, Aiden. It may introduce

another scenario. Other than the possibility you're losing your sanity questioning what's real and what isn't."

"Do you think I'm crazy? I gazed at the Professor with a disturbed look on my face.

"No. You're not crazy. I'm crazy. And you're nothing like me, right?" he whispered, elbowing me in the arm.

"Nothing like you," I said chuckling.

I opened the book and began turning the withered pages. The pictures were incredible. Page after page of ancient sculptures from around the world. Descriptions of each piece, more history than in any book I'd ever seen. I turned to a picture of a sculpture from Wescott Park. It was a photo of the angel that I was working on. My angel.

"She's in Princeton. At Wescott. How ironic."

"I know. That's why I knew you would find it interesting."

"I wish you would have shown me sooner."

"Everything in its time. Not too soon, not too late." He was always so dramatic.

"Who is the author?" I flipped through it. Nothing on the inside. No credits, no author's biography. "There's no author?" I was completely puzzled.

"Author unknown," he said. "It happens."

"Where did you get it?"

"I've had so long, I honestly can't remember. Someone gave it to me when I was a boy. My ideologies as a professor were based on the premise of this book. On the possibilities. It fascinated me," he confessed.

"Interesting. I never knew you were so open minded. Cool Will, cool." I pressed the light button over my seat lighting up the gold pages. Within seconds, I was completely enthralled.

The professor slipped his reading glasses out from inside his shirt pocket. He rested them on the tip of his nose as he glanced at each page.

The attendant came back with our drinks. He grinned at her as she handed him the glass.

"I think angels do exist," he said, winking at her once again. His eyes fixated on her as he spoke. She began to blush. "… and they can fly, too." He added raising his glass to her as she handed him his napkin.

I thumbed through the pages. Each filled with incredible images of Dominion angels. Dominions were referred to as guardians. And the book was filled with recorded encounters and stories of their existence. I was speechless.

"I think they may be using you in your dreams. That's what I think. If you tell anyone that I said that, I will deny it all. They could force me into retirement or worse, put me in a nut house just by the mere rumor that I had this discussion with you." He lifted his brow, grinning as he sipped his drink.

"I know. Don't worry. Your insanity is safe with me," I laughed, as I gazed back at the book.

"Let's not discuss this anymore this evening. Let's just sit back, enjoy and toast to everything imaginable."

He toasted to so many things that we nearly ran the modest bar completely out of vodka. But he was still able to acquire the phone number of our overly accommodating flight attendant.

"… and that is how it's done." He proudly held out a beverage napkin revealing her number she jotted down. "Listen and learn, my boy. Listen and learn." He stuffed her number into his pocket and pulled his briefcase from the overhead compartment.

He was something else. Definitely a dying breed.

"He sounds like a real character, your professor," Dr. Bennett said, as she opened the shutters to the windows in the terrace. The clouds covered overhead casting darkened shadows over the peaceful garden.

"He is. He's a good guy. You'd like him," I replied, peeling the label off the bottle of cream soda. Made me think of Ben. I looked back at Dr. Bennett. She held her own bottle. I smiled at her. I found it funny how well she listened to even the tiniest details.

"He gave you a book about Dominions?" she asked.

"He did."

"Does he believe that they exist?"

"I think he does."

"How about you, what do you think?"

Even after the months we've spent talking, after everything I've shared with her, I was still hesitant to answer.

"I don't know. Maybe I do. It sure would answer a lot of questions."

19

Boston's Lillie

After arriving in Boston, the Professor and I spotted his ex-wife Mary and his two daughters as we came through the terminal.

"Daddy! Over here!" Claire shouted, waving.

"Hey, there!" Professor dropped his bags. His arms spread out to greet them.

There she was. As perfectly preserved as I expected. Lillie was a knock out and she was looking as gorgeous as ever. She smiled as me as our eyes met. We and I dated on and off ever since high school. Through the years we remained very close friends. She really was a fantastic girl. Smart, witty, fun, and at the same time, demanding and overbearing. Which is why it didn't work out the half dozen times we tried.

Professor Williams often mentions that Lillie still refers to me as "the one." He also said that she refused to get too deeply involved with anyone in hopes of one day rekindling our romance.

"There they are… my girls!" Professor shouted wrapping his arms around Claire. He reached out attempting to pull Lillie in but she ran right past him and straight for me.

"Huh. What do you know... passed up for a younger man. Can't say I blame her," Professor said jokingly. "Mary, how are you? You're looking as divine as ever." He leaned into her, kissing her on her cheek.

He still loved his ex-wife. They seemed to make up whenever he returned to Boston. She loved him, she never stopped. Moving away to Princeton was all his idea. She didn't want him to go. She begged him to stay. Twelve years in a rocky marriage was enough for Will. Mary had a slightly suffocating personality. He wanted a fresh start. But, when he came back to visit, it was easy for him to fall right back into the husbandly role with his ex-wife. She adored him and he loved that.

"Hello, Jack." She returned the kiss. "Well, what do you know, martini's," She snipped after smelling the vodka on his breath. "So, you had a nice flight I take it?" she asked sarcastically as a grin crept over her face.

"Perfect. Thank you for asking." He smiled and nudged her just a little. She gave him a wink. She knew him too well. That's the one thing that the Professor missed most about Mary. The way she allowed him to be himself. It didn't matter to her if he chose to act like an idiot, which happened to be most of the time.

Lillie had me cornered. She just stood there, staring at me.

"Hi, Lil," I blurted. She didn't respond. She was a tough one to read.

"Don't be so rude Lillie. Say hello…" Mary waited for Lillie's first words. So… was I at that point?

"Lil?" Professor whispered. She didn't say anything. She just stood there, staring. She gazed at her father and then at back at me. I don't think we had an argument the last time I was home, however it was somewhat hard to recall since it was so long ago. After I thought about it for a second or two, I remembered the last time I saw her. She came to visit me in Princeton. We had a terrific time together.

She met Ben, Maggie and most of my friends. We went hiking, I took her to the lake, we had a great time together. It was casual, nothing too deep, which I liked and she knew it. Maybe she wanted more. She didn't bring it up. I assumed things would simply stay unchanged. No rules, just better than good friends who occasionally spent a few intimate weekends together. I couldn't imagine what was causing her to just stand there staring at me like she was. Maybe I should have called her back after she left. We weren't serious. We considered our relationship "casual." We agreed that we were okay with seeing other people. It was her idea. It sure sounded good to me at the time. I didn't want the stress of a long distance relationship. Life was stressful enough.

"Where's the car?" Professor hesitantly asked. No one of them responded. Claire and her mother were too busy waiting on Lillie. They knew something was brewing in that sweet little head of hers.

"A-hem," Professor whispered. It was pretty obvious that he was growing more and more impatient.

"I think your Dad is trying to say hello," I told her. You never knew what you were going to get when it came to Lillie. She could be a bit moody.

"Oh." She shook her head in confusion. "I'm sorry." Lillie turned and gave him a smile. "Hey, Dad," she said, squeezing him tightly.

"Did we park or did we keep it running?" Professor asked as he threw the strap of his briefcase over his shoulder.

"We pulled up, Daddy," Claire answered. "Just outside. Matt's waiting."

Matt was Claire's fiancé. He was a great guy, extremely lucky, too. Claire and Lillie were everything to Will. He couldn't be more proud of them. Claire was an Executive Director at a large accounting firm and Lillie had just made partner at a prestigious law firm. Both worked in downtown Boston. Both daughters were, in his opinion, "too good for any man."

But Matt was as good as they came according to Professor

Williams. "He's a terrific accountant with a promising future," he boasted. Claire started dating him when she was first hired in several years ago.

"How's Matt doing, anyway? This wedding hasn't driven him away yet?" Professor teased.

"He would never leave. He loves me," she whispered. "Besides, he's too afraid of you to leave." She and Mary giggled.

Finally, Lille broke from her stare as she reached out her hand and pulled the handle of my suitcase. "That's okay, Lillie. I can get that." I took her by the arm and snatched the handle.

"Don't be silly, you take your backpack. I can get this," she insisted.

"Thank you," I whispered. She smiled at me. One thing was for certain, she had an incredible smile.

As we reached the door, Professor Williams spotted Matt. He was waving frantically trying to get our attention. He stood in front of a town car with its hazard lights on.

"You look amazing, Lil. Really, you do."

She looked at me. She didn't say anything but at that point, I knew what she was thinking. I could see her cheeks redden as she passed in front of me as I held open the door. I should've called.

"So, how've you been?" I asked.

"Good. Busy with the wedding, but good. How about you? How's college life? Are you still glad you went back?" I could see it in her eyes. She was still upset that I went back. We decided to break off our relationship and two months later, out of nowhere, I left for Princeton.

"Yea. No regrets. It's busy, you know."

"No regrets, huh?" she mumbled.

"Lil…" I sighed. Clearly I didn't want to go there. Not again.

"Never mind, forget I said anything," she snapped. "How's your roommate, Ben? It is Ben, isn't it?" "Yeah, Ben's good."

"Hey Matt, what's up?" I happily shouted as we reached the car. Anything to get out of the instant drama Lillie was begging to start.

"Hey there yourself, stranger," Matt replied, snatching my suitcase from Lillie. He reached out and shook my hand. "How ya been?"

"I'm good. Busy. And you… you look good, man. Congratulations."

"Thanks. We're glad to have you back. It wouldn't have been the same without you." He was a super guy. He and Claire were a great match.

The short drive to the hotel was quite a pleasant reunion to my surprise. Professor seemed very happy to be with his family. As we arrived, I noticed my father waiting just inside the lobby door.

"I'll see you later, Aiden," Lillie whispered, clutching my hand.

I knew that look. I couldn't encourage her. I simply smiled grabbing my bags as I got out of the car. I had to say something. And I needed to say it soon. She had to know.

I said goodnight and ran into the hotel. I rushed over to my father and hugged him.

"Hello, son."

"Hey, Dad. I've missed you," I whispered and held him tightly.

"Missed you, too. Good trip?" he asked.

"Yea, pretty good."

"I got us a table over by the bar. Unless you're too tired."

"I'll have one and then head up to the room." I collapsed in a comfortable chair and exhaled. "I could use one."

My father chuckled. He completely understood me.

Professor Williams kissed Mary and his daughter's goodnight after unloading the suitcases to the curb where a bell hop loaded them onto a cart and followed him inside to the lobby.

"Hey, Will!" My father shouted.

"How are ya pal? You're looking good!" Professor replied after tipping the bell man.

"Of course I am. You've got those goggles on again don't you? Everybody's looking good by now!" He and I laughed as the Professor came strutting over. "How've you been?"

"I'm good… really good." Professor Williams replied confidently. He quickly fixated his attention to three women walking into the hotel. His stare clearly offended them. Their scowls were a pretty good sign that they weren't impressed nor interested. He smiled anyway seemly unaffected. He couldn't help himself.

"Wow. Not a thing has changed, I see," my father teased. "I've missed you, Will."

"Same here partner."

I needed to crash. They had a lot to catch up on and I wanted to get up to the room, get comfortable, and call Tess.

"I'm going to head up. I'm beat."

"Of course. We're on the fifth floor… five-seventeen. Here's your key. Go on up, get some rest. I'll keep this old guy company," my Father said jokingly.

"Who you calling old?" Professor snapped. With a scandalous grin, he pulled two cigars from inside his coat pocket.

My father checked in earlier that afternoon. He rarely left the gallery but thought it would be easier to stay downtown for the weekend. And a suite at the Drake was just we needed.

"Hey. I'm glad you called. How was your trip?" Tess said.

"It was okay but I'm missing you already."

"Good… then were even."

She began to tell me about an argument she had with Vincent. She explained how he stormed out and hadn't returned. She and her family were beginning to think that something may have happened to him.

"He'll be alright. It is Vincent we're talking about, Tess." I tried to reassure her but I could tell she was upset. "Don't worry. He'll be back." I definitely was missing her.

They had the next day all planned out. First, there was a round of golf, followed by a luncheon, and later in the evening, an extravagant dinner. I could tell Professor Williams was glad that I came. So was Lillie. Every chance she could she tried to get me alone to work her way back in. She was good at it. She waiting for just the right time to get closer. But I kept my distance. I wasn't interested. The problem was I hadn't found the opportunity to tell her about Tess. I suppose I was afraid of her reaction. I didn't want to spoil any of the wedding activities with a tantrum. She's done it before and she was definitely capable of doing it again. If I kept distance between us, maybe she would get the hint.

During dinner, her advances became a bit more aggressive. She finished her glass of champagne just as the server brought another tray. She snatched one and turned toward me. She didn't need it. Her behavior began to bother me. The way she rubbed her foot on my leg under the table… the way she kept glaring at me. She was acting ridiculous. So, I took it from her, sipped a little, and set it on the other side of the table.

"So…?" She started to speak but decided instead to picked up my fork and poke at the last bite of cake on my plate.

"So, what?"

"You have someone now… is that it?"

"I do. And you've had enough."

"Come on, Aiden, it's me you're talking too. I know when I've had enough," she snapped reaching around me for the glass.

"The wedding is tomorrow. You need to slow down."

She sat back in her chair and folded her arms. I immediately regretted opening my mouth. I knew that face, very well in fact. She had a temper. And if she was pushed even just a little at the right point in time, she would snap. Dinner was over. Guests were mingling amongst themselves. No one would notice… so that would make it the right point in time. Her brow furrowed as she stared at me searching for just the right words. I could see her contemplating the use of profanity in her defense.

"Slow down? Funny. That's really funny, Aiden," she snipped. "You're the one who needs to slow down!" She lowered her voice to a gruff whisper. "What's up with you anyway?"

"Come on, Lil. Don't get mad." I was desperate not to create a scene.

"I'm not mad!" she shouted. She threw her napkin onto the table. "I'm not mad," she repeated in a quieter whisper. She finally noticed a few people around us staring. "I'm not the one who needs to slow down, Aiden. I'm simply trying to get your attention."

"Well, you have it. Along with several others, as well," I said in a low voice, looking around the table. She didn't seem to care. I on the other had was humiliated. I needed to take a walk and she needed to follow. Continuing the conversation, regardless of how much I dreaded it, didn't require an audience.

I stood up and calmly, excused myself, and placed my napkin in front of her. She took the bait. Within four or five steps she came up behind me barefoot with an opened bottle of champagne and two glasses.

"So, come on… tell me that you're no longer the lonely Aiden I know and adore." She tugged on my coat sleeve as we came to a bench near the pool. She sat and pointed her finger at the open space next to her.

"I'm not lonely, Lillie," I answered as I sat down.

She had quite a bit to drink during dinner. Glass after glass of wine, champagne, whatever they were pouring, she was drinking. She had a dominant personality. Never backed down from a fight. Litigation was the only thing she ever wanted to do. She made a living arguing. That's how good she was. She was already fearless and with alcohol she was invincible. Just like her father. Or so they thought.

"So… what's she like? I'll bet she's pretty." I didn't want to discuss Tess with her.

"Come on, Lillie. I'll take you back to your room." I grabbed the bottle from her one hand and the two glasses from the other. I sat them on the bench and pulled her to her feet. She quickly fell into my arms and looked at me with her big green eyes.

"Now that is what I've been waiting to hear," she slurred, throwing her arms over my shoulders.

There was something I found irresistible about her. But not this time.

"Come on, Lil. Be serious." I gripped my hands around her tiny waist attempting to stabilize her as she wobbled. "We didn't work, remember? We tried over and over but it just was too damn hard."

I looked into her eyes trying to catch a glimmer of understanding. There was nothing but a haze. A drunken haze.

"You didn't try hard enough. Besides, things are different now. We're older. I'm better, more mature. I'm ready to settle down," she insisted.

I thought about the scene she just made. "More mature… and to back that up you throw a fit at the dinner table in front of everyone?" I snickered. She picked up her glass and the bottle and began to pour but was too angry, too intoxicated, and in a too big hurry to storm off. Only a small amount actually made it into her glass. The majority spilled all over. Satisfied with what little she had, she slammed the empty bottle on the bench next to me and wobbled off. I waited a second debating whether to go after her or to leave it alone. I smiled as I watched her stagger across the lawn of the country club, barefoot, in what I imagine was a very expensive red dress. I couldn't leave her. She was someone who meant a lot to me once… and still did. She wasn't in any condition to go off on her own. I darted up behind her snatching her drink from her hand.

"Give me that… who do you think you are?" she shrieked, grabbing for the glass. "You are not my boss, Aiden McCarthy. I'm not that naive little girl anymore. You can't just order me around." She headed for the lobby. "I'm a grown up now. And I have needs." She took the glass from me sipping it after spilling a bit on the floor. "I'm a highly respected, highly compensated attorney. I work for the most respectable firm in Boston. I even made partner in three years. Do you have any idea how impossible that is?" she shouted, pointing at me with her glass and waving it aimlessly around spilling champagne all over the polished marble floor, "… which means that I am highly respected and ridiculously compensated." She shouted shaking her finger in my face coming within inches of poking me with it. Her confidence reached an all time high, along with her eyebrows. I batted my eyes at her attempting to appear apologetic. For what… I hadn't a clue. I was completely baffled by her rant. All I kept thinking was how she was still so adorably impossible to manage. "… and I don't need you following me around telling me what to do." It appeared as though she was finished. I held back the urge to laugh. Her dramatic facial expressions alone were too much to handle.

"Okay, Lil," I calmly whispered, giving her a nudge along with a gently smile. In that moment, I figured out why I spent so many years with her. It was obvious, she was just like her father.

"Jackass," she muttered with a smirk.

She was ridiculous. She knew it, I knew it, and the front desk clerk, who was dialing housekeeping to clean up the mess, knew it.

"Sorry about the spill," she announced. "Could you tell me… is the bar still open?" she asked, swaying from side to side. Everyone stood around watching her, whispering wondering if the show was over. By this time a few from our dinner party had wandered over to see what the commotion was all about. Lille could barely stand. She had enough excitement and champagne for one night. The show was definitely over.

"You don't need anything now but sleep," I whispered to her. I scooped her up in my arms and carried her toward the elevator.

I knew they were watching. I also knew what they were thinking. Will, Mary and Claire… even my father and grandparents… they all wanted me to marry her. They were hoping for a miracle that weekend and with her in my arms headed up to her room, it looked as if they might get their wish.

"I'm on two. I'm in two thirty-six."

"Okay." I could feel her nuzzling her nose closer to my neck as I held her. She was still thinking I would cave in like I always did and stay with her.

"Have you even heard of Sterns, Ross, and Hadley?" she asked. The elevator doors opened. "Do you have any idea how prestigious we are?" she slurred. I glanced down at her. She picked her head up off from my shoulder gazing at me. Her soft blonde hair had fallen over her eyes cascading down her pale skin. She knew how to accentuate her best features. And one of hers was her smile. Her full lips were perfectly outlined and colored with her favorite shade. A very deep red.

"I have heard of it, Lillie. I went with you to your Christmas party two years ago, remember?"

"Oh... yes, that's right. I do remember." She giggled. Her head dropped back against my shoulder. Lillie was one of a kind. Some things never change and in her case, that was a good thing. She had a great sense of style... like old Hollywood. Glamorous but classy. She definitely knew how to make it work to her advantage.

I cradled her effortlessly in my arms as we waited for the elevator doors to open. Lillie had a petite frame, curvaceous but petite. She was a tiny little thing with an attitude ten times her size which guys found extremely sexy and annoyingly irresistible.

"Are you coming in?" she asked as the doors to the elevator closed. She reached inside the top of her dress pulling out the room key. I smiled and shook my head. She was direct I had to give her that. She never felt the need to beat around the bush.

"Yes," I whispered. Her face lit up with excitement. "... to put you to bed, where you belong." I quickly added. She threw herself back heartbroken as I carried her down the hallway. I kicked the door open and carried her to the bed pulling the comforter over her.

"You be a good girl and get some sleep. Claire's getting married, tomorrow. She's depending on you," I whispered, pushing her hair off her forehead. She laid there gazing at me with her sappy, puppy dog eyes. "Crazy... she's getting married... I swear she was just fourteen a few months ago."

I laughed. "Do you remember what we got her for her birthday that year? We took her to that concert, remember?"

"Yeah, I remember," she nodded. "It rained so hard we were covered in mud. You carried me the entire way back so I wouldn't ruin my shoes," she said, smiling. She reached up and brushed her hand across my chin feeling the stubble with her fingertips.

"I miss your face, Aiden," she whispered. "Why does everything have to change?"

"Time makes everything change Lil. Situations change. But deep down, people don't."

She nodded and scooted herself deeper into the bed. A tear slowly trickled down her cheek. I reached over to the nightstand for a tissue.

"Here," I whispered, gently bringing it to her face. She had too much to drink. That was for sure.

"Stay with me," she begged.

"Lillie."

"Don't say no, not tonight."

"Lillie, I'm not going to stay with you."

"Why?"

"Why what?"

"Why does it have to change?" she shouted. "Let's just pretend it's the same." She pulled me down close to her.

"You're tired."

"You're not going to sleep with me are you?"

"No."

"Could you at least lay here with me until I fall asleep?" she asked. She opened the sheets next to her. "Just lay with me," she begged. She looked so sweet. Under different circumstances there would be no way to deny her. But things were different. I pulled the blanket back up over her folding it under her chin.

"Sleep now, Lillie," I whispered as I leaned in to kiss her on her forehead. She closed her eyes. She didn't seem to be angry, she was too intoxicated. Sleep was what she needed. I was right and she knew it.

The wedding was beautiful. Professor Williams was choked up most of the afternoon mostly because Mary wouldn't let him drink before the wedding. But seeing Claire in her wedding gown really got to him.

The reception went well. Lillie looked as gorgeous as ever. She kept a safe distance between us which allowed for a drama free evening. She knew she needed to behave for her sister's sake. Probably a tiny bit humiliated by the rejection the night before. She never heard the word "no" and she sure wasn't going to hear it two nights in a row. By the end of the evening it appeared as though she forgot all about her hurt feelings and had moved on to the next prospect. I spent the last hour of the night watching her dance provocatively with a more than willing groomsman.

"It sounds like you had a nice visit," Dr. Bennett said as she strolled over to my chair.

"It was nice."

"It's a beautiful day outside, how about if we head out?" she asked, glancing out the window behind me.

"Sure," I mumbled. I was perfectly comfortable but she seemed eager to get outside to enjoy the bright spring morning.

"Would you like me to push you?"

"No, thanks. I got it." I reached down and released the brake on the wheel.

The sun came in through the massive windows that covered the front of the hospital. Trees, covered with white and pink blossoms, swayed in the warm breeze. She was right, it was a beautiful day to be outside.

"So… Lillie tried to rekindle the old flame?" Dr. Bennett asked, smiling. She took a seat on the bench.

"She's stubborn. But, thankfully she figured out that she wasn't going to get her way. We went to breakfast the next morning. It gave us the chance we needed to chat before I left. She didn't think my relationship with Tess would last. She didn't say it specifically in those exact words, but I knew that's what she thought. Wishful thinking on her part, I imagine. She didn't get it. There was nothing else but Tess."

20

Visually Impaired

I called Tess after we landed. I was glad to be back and couldn't wait to see her. The return flight was a little less celebratory. Taking the last flight out was Will's idea. He passed out the second he sat in his seat. His snoring made it impossible to join him... not only for me but for the majority of the passengers in first class. He needed it more than I did. He had to give a lecture in less than five hours. It was definitely going to take more than a couple hours of sleep to recuperate from his weekend of overindulging.

After he dropped me off, I raced into the house. All I wanted to do was sleep. I was beyond exhausted. As I came in I heard loud music coming from the kitchen. I peeked in and noticed Ben and Maggie playfully feeding each other whatever it was they were cooking on the stove. I gave them a quick wave and darted up the stairs surprised. Through the floor, I heard thumping coming from the speakers downstairs. It was turned up so loud it actually shook the house. I heard Ben's shrieking laughter as he chased her around the living room. It was almost 3 am. How two people could be so oblivious, so obnoxious puzzled me. But I was too tired to do anything about it. As soon as my head hit the pillow I was out.

As the music faded I found myself wandering along a wooded path. Light from the full moon lit the night, reflecting off the dense fog as it lifted all around me.

Up ahead I could see Tess. I felt no hesitation like in the other dreams. There was no reason to. It was just us. Her blue eyes guided me as I walked closer toward her. She was sitting on a blanket smiling at me. As I got closer, she held out her hand. I knelt down beside her and she gently pulled me down onto the blanket next to her.

"What took you so long?" She touched my hair with the tips of her fingers.

"What do you mean?"

"I've been waiting for you."

"Well, I'm here now." I stroked her cheek. She shut her eyes as I touched her.

Suddenly, she grabbed my wrist and pushed me away. She got up and ran off. I tried to grab her but she moved so fast. She looked back at me as she faded in the distance. She wanted me to follow her.

Something in her eyes, the way she looked back at me.

"Where are you going?" I shouted, chasing after her. I could hear her calling me. There was just enough light to see her graceful silhouette running in front of me. I could see the curves of her body through her sheer white dress. The spirals of her long dark hair stretched through the air. I followed her as she weaved in and out of the trees.

Suddenly, everything began to move in slow motion. Clouds formed overhead darkening the woods. Up head in front of Tess, I saw someone in the distance. I caught up to her and held her back. It was Vincent. He was bleeding, bound and gagged tied to a tree.

"Vincent!" she shouted. Breaking from my grasp, she rushed toward him pulling on the rope around his chest trying to loosen it.

"Tess wait!" I screeched. "It isn't safe!"

"He's my brother. He's in trouble."

He didn't move. He had a blindfold wrapped tightly around his eyes. He had been beaten. Severely beaten and left unconscious. I moved closer to him to see if he was breathing. His face was mangled. He was alive. Whoever did this wanted him to suffer. I looked around for any sign, any trace of who could have done this but there was none around. Nothing but a dead silence. And something that told me it wasn't safe.

I quickly turned to her and pointed in the other direction. "You have leave this place!" I ordered.

"Not without him and definitely not without you!"

I pulled her back away from Vincent but she fought me trying to get to him.

"Just go, please! You have to trust me!" I shouted, pleading with her. She shook her head clutching my arm tightly. When I turned back to help Vincent, he was gone. There was no trace of him. It didn't make any sense. In all the other dreams I was able to save them. But not this time. This time it was all so different. I couldn't help Vincent. Maybe I was too late.

I woke in a panic. My hair dampened with sweat. I looked around my room searching for her. I was so confused. It was so real. More real than the others. My hands trembled. My entire body shook. I got up and walked over to the window that I had left open. I couldn't figure out what to do. I just stood there helplessly gripping the window frame, glaring to the dark street below. I closed my eyes rubbing them with my hands. There must have been something I missed. For him to just disappear like that made no sense. He was unconscious. He was blindfolded, bleeding… helpless. It was surprising how much it mattered. I mean, it was Vincent. The most evil of all evil. Maybe he got what was coming to him. He was her brother and she was afraid for him. Something was out there. I felt it. Something worse than Vincent and I needed to figure out how to get back to him. Maybe I woke too soon. That was it. I had to get back to sleep. I reached over and snatched a small bottle of pills from my night-stand tossing two into my mouth hoping they would help me sleep. Maybe taking Will's advice and seeing that Doctor was a good idea. I guess we would see if it helped.

Dr. Bennett sat there on the bench hanging on my every word. Her hands stuffed into her pockets of her lavender sweater. She pulled out a wadded up Kleenex and wiped her nose. She stretched her legs out in front of her crossing her ankles.

"Strange. This time you weren't able to help," she said as her eyes widened.

"I couldn't. There was no time. He needed help. But then he vanished and I woke up. No Tess, no Vincent. Nothing."

"Did you ever get back to sleep… back to the dream?"

"No."

My phone began to vibrate. It shook the tiny nightstand and then fell to the floor. I had no idea who could be calling so early in the morning. I couldn't get the image of Vincent out of my head. He was so badly beaten. It may have been bad enough that he didn't survive it. Maybe that's why he disappeared. He could have just died there tied to that tree.

My phone continued to vibrate from underneath his bed. I tugged myself to the edge reaching for it. It was Tess.

"Hello?"

"Hey. I'm sorry to wake you."

"It's ok. I wasn't sleeping. Are you okay?"

"I need to see you."

"I'll be right there," I said as I threw back my sheets.

"I'm already on my way." She whispered.

This was a good thing. I needed to see her. I wanted to know if Vincent was still missing. I wanted her to tell me everything. I know she wanted me in that dream. I honestly think she brought me there. Maybe she brought me to the others. Things sounded crazy in my mind but the dreams were becoming more and more real. I needed answers. The book that Professor Williams gave me on the plane made perfect sense. If the dreams were helping Tess, then it was all worth it. I would do anything for her. But I needed answers. I needed to figure out a way to talk to her without sounding crazy or pushing her away. I was hoping that she cared enough about me to listen. Hoping she would trust me enough to answer my questions and tell me the truth.

I rolled over facing my bedroom door when I saw her. Just like that, she was there. Standing in my doorway knocking quietly on the frame. Maggie and Ben slept in the room across the hall and she knew if we wanted privacy we had to be quiet. I hopped out of bed and rushed to her. I held her tightly as I pushed the door closed. She felt weak in my arms. She dropped her head against my chest. I knew something was definitely up.

"Tess?" I asked. I felt dampness on my skin. She was crying. I held her tighter when she didn't answer. She looked up at me. She was pale. Faint dark circles surrounded her eyes. There was definitely something wrong. I had no idea what it was. A sadness had come over her. Maybe it was Vincent. Maybe he had done something or worse... maybe he hadn't returned.

"What is it?" I asked her.

"I don't know," she whispered softly.

I held her close to me. I could feel her heart racing.

"You're upset. I don't want you to be upset. What can I do?" I begged for her to let me help her. To let me in, to trust me enough to tell me what was wrong.

"You're everything that I need right now, Aiden." She tried to smile. "Just promise me one thing."

"Anything, Tess. Name it."

"Promise me that you will remember this. What we have." She lowered her eyes to the floor. She wanted to tell me, I felt it. The way she looked at me. She wanted to tell me everything.

"Aiden, I love you," she said in a soft voice. I barely heard her. And those were three words I wanted to hear.

"What was that?" I asked in a playful tone. My insides churned with excitement. I felt such an amazing connection to her. Finally, I thought. I could finally tell her. I wanted to tell her from the moment I first saw her. At that moment she belonged to me. I wouldn't ever let her go.

"I love you, too," I whispered.

"Promise me."

"Ok. I promise. Is this why you're upset? Because you love me? This can't be good," I whispered with a snicker, trying to get her to smile.

"No." She let out a deep breath. Something was upsetting her.

"It's Vincent, isn't it? Is he alright?"

"I don't know. It's just not like him to be gone like this."

"So, he hasn't come home?"

"No." Tears trickled down her cheek. I brushed them away with my fingers and pulled her toward me.

"It's ok. Don't worry. He's definitely one who can take care of himself, Tess. But we'll find him," I assured her. "We will find him, Tess," I insisted.

"Ok," she whispered. She pressed herself against me. I just stood there, holding her. I touched her soft shoulders moving them down her arms caressing her as I took her hands into mine.

"Stay with me tonight," I whispered. I stepped backward toward my bed pulling her with me. I sat on the edge of my bed holding her as she stood in front of me. I ran my hands over her feeling her warmth under her satin gown. She closed her eyes as I touched her. I pulled her against me.

She never told me what was happening. Not all of it. But she stayed with me. Something I prayed for since I first saw her. I just wanted to hold her in my arms... to let her rest. She couldn't describe what was wrong. What was really happening. She knew she was becoming weak. She was feeling emotions that were all new to her. She was afraid for Vincent, and afraid for the love she felt for me. But in that moment, I was all that she could think about.

I knew she felt the same. The way she felt was indescribable. It felt the same for both of us. I felt her heart pounding. Just like mine. She shook as I touched her.

She gently pressed her hands against my shoulders and pushed me back onto the bed. Her long locks fell all around me. I knew I could get lost in her, in the moment. I didn't want to push her to do something she wasn't ready for but I have to admit, I wanted her more than ever. I closed my eyes and gently moved my hands over her. The softness of her skin stimulated me. The warmth of her body was intoxicating. So very tempting. I gazed up at her. She was so beautiful. I decided to let her show me what she wanted. I wouldn't push her. I would just let her take what she needed. She ran her fingers over my lips. My breathing became more labored as she touched me. She climbed onto the bed straddling me. I couldn't breathe. I couldn't move. I'd never seen anything so perfect. So flawless. She caressed my chest, running her hands over me. I sat up holding her. Kissing her. She moved her hands up and down my back, over my shoulders. The way I struggled to control my breathing was more than she could handle. She wanted me. But the way I wanted her... looking at her as she leaned into me was more than I could handle.

It was nearly impossible to maintain my composure. Every inch of me wanted to ravage her. She felt it. I could see it in her eyes. I could feel it in the way she moved on me, she was desperate to feel me. All of me. She leaned in kissing my neck and shoulders, moving the tips of her lips gently over my ear. The warmth of her breath stimulating me even more. I wanted to take her right then. I gently grabbed her laying her on the bed quickly shifting myself over her. She looked up at me with an innocence I'd never seen before. It was as if she had no idea what to do with the aching she felt inside. She gently touched my face. The way she looked at me... I knew she would give me anything I wanted. She was so innocent, so frail and at that moment all I could do was take care of her. I knew she needed to rest. I moved closely behind her shadowing her tightly with my body. I held her close to me. It would wait. Everything would have to wait. She was going to stay that night and that was enough for me. For now.

Dr. Bennett sat there in a daze. Maybe I said too much. It appeared as though I lost her. Just then she snapped back from where ever the all too intimate details had taken her.

"So, nothing happened?" she asked, sounding somewhat disappointed.

"No, that was it. She fell asleep in my arms. I gently stroked her face as I watched over her. For hours I held her as she slept. I couldn't believe that she was right there, next to me. I had no desire to sleep. I wanted to take care of her. That's all I wanted to do. Not just that night but every night."

21

Cutting it Short

I promised Maggie that I would be at the sorority party. It was a big annual thing that took months and months of planning. Who knows why? It turned out the same every year. A big bash that drew in nearly every student on campus. And... it was that evening. I didn't want to go. Not really. But I told her I would go. She typically kept Ben in line which made the possibility of having an okay time a little more probable. And I was thinking Tess would be there too. Both Maggie and I invited her. I was wondering about Vincent. Maybe she and her family wouldn't be doing of anything unless he returned. And I hadn't heard that he had. I called her to check on things. To check and make sure she would be at the party. If she wasn't I really didn't want to be there. I figured I could bail and come up with an excuse later.

"Hey, Tess. Any word from Vincent?" I asked.

"No. But I've been thinking... you're right. He can take care of himself," she adamantly announced. She seemed to be feeling better. At least she sounded better.

"Daniela and I were just talking about you," she giggled, "but don't worry. We were just discussing this party we've been invited to. Maggie's party. Isn't she dating your roommate?"

"Yes. She is. Who knows why?" I chuckled. "I was just calling to invite you to come."

"Then we'll see you there?"

"Absolutely," I replied. I was pretty excited about going now that I knew that she'd be there.

Tess hung up the phone and rolled over next to Daniela. They were looking at pictures sprawled all over her bed. Dozens of pictures. Everyone were of Aiden.

"You really do want to love him, don't you?" Daniela asked.

"I actually do," Tess whispered.

Her eyes lit up whenever she thought about him. But as the love she felt for him grew, she became weaker by the day.

"I'm happy you felt it. That's what you wanted. Now it's time to let it go. You have to… you're getting sick. I can tell. And if I can tell everyone else will, too."

"I know. Don't remind me." She jumped off the bed. She gazed at her reflection in the mirror. She tucked a strand of hair around her ear. The bags under her eyes were getting harder and harder to conceal. "So, do you want to go with me to this party or what?" Tess asked batting her eyelashes.

"Of course. It'll be fun." The two giggled and headed into Tess' closet to find something to wear.

"How about this?" Tess pulled out a very sexy but very tiny black dress. She draped it in front of her and reached over snatching a pair of black stiletto's to go with it.

"That may be a bit too much. Or too little, I should say," Daniela teased. "Maybe you should just grab a pair of jeans and a t-shirt… the poor boy is in for it already. Why make it worse by torturing him?" she added, chuckling at her.

The party was packed. Cars were parked blocking the street. Some even parked on the lawn of the sorority house. I had just finished adding ice to the keg barrel, turned my back for a second to toss the bag in the trash, and a ridiculously long line formed in front of me. That was disappointing. I should have filled a glass before refilling the ice.

"Hey, bro," TJ announced patting me on the back.

"Hey, Teej. How's it going?"

We stood there catching up while the line slowly moved. Ben and Chris crashed in front of us pushing and shoving making a huge disruption. Everyone behind us began shouting some of the worst words imaginable. Cutting in line at a party this size was a bad move. More dudes than girls, more bodies than beer… and more testosterone in one line than needed. Enough to level the house if it got out of hand.

"You guys are idiots," TJ said. "Ever hear of beer line etiquette?"

"Sorry. Who knew that there would be so many haters in one line? Yo, Aiden. Where's your girl? She show or what?" Ben asked obnoxiously as he elbowed me three or four times in the ribcage.

"Not yet. She'll be here. And you need to stay away. I mean it." I shoved Ben just enough to show him that I was serious.

"Whatever, dude. Just let me know when she gets here. I'd like to say hello." He snatched the tap just as I reached for it, filled both his and Chris' glass and disappeared into the madness. I heard him as he spotted Maggie.

"Hey, Mags!" Ben shouted. "What's his deal?"

TJ and I noticed her forcefully escorting a party crasher down the stairs. "You know this guy or what?" He added in a jealous tone.

"Yes, Ben. He's my best friend. That's why I have him in a head lock escorting him off the premises! Wow, are you that clueless?" she shouted, scolding him.

"What did he do?" Chris asked sympathetically.

"He's a total jerk. No one knows who he is… AND he took all my Jello shots! There were like twenty in the frig! How rude!" she shouted, yanking on his arm pulling him down the steps. "Ben please get this guy out of here," she demanded.

"Hang on Mags…" Ben shouted as he and Chris sprinted for the bag boards. They were waiting for it to open up and a group of guys just finished their game.

"Hey, thanks for your help there, Benny," she said to herself in disgust.

"Hey Maggie, let me help you," I said, as I took the guy by his jacket.

"Coming uninvited, taking the little ladies Jello shots? Not cool bro. Not cool." I scolded. I escorted him to the end of the yard. I wanted to make sure that he was actually going to leave without any trouble.

As I turned back, I saw a man. He just stood there with his hands in his pockets watching me. "Can I help you?" I announced.

"Hello, Aiden," the man said in a low voice. I walked closer. Right away I recognized him. It was the man from the Gallery. The one who insisted we knew each other. He just stood there. My guess is he'd been following me. I'm thinking he was the man in my driveway the other night, too.

"It's Bruce, right?" I asked.

"Right," he answered.

It didn't take long for me to notice a large red stain on his shirt. It looked like splattered blood. At that point I thought maybe he was hurt.

"Are you ok?" I asked.

"I'm fine," he nodded. His hands were shaking making it hard to zip his coat in an attempt to cover the stain. He nervously pushed his hair back away from his face. "I'm just trying to find Father Andrews. I went to the church but he wasn't there. There's something I needed to talk to him about."

He had trouble standing still. There was definitely something not right with this guy. "Have you seen him tonight? Father Andrews, I mean?"

"No, I haven't," I answered, "but I may be able to get a hold of him."

"That's okay. I can see you're occupied. I don't want to bother you." He backed away from the fence. I noticed his knuckles were scraped and bloody like he had been in a fight. "I'll just give him a call tomorrow." His voiced was trembling.

"Are you sure? It looks like maybe you're injured."

"No, no. I'm fine. I hit an animal with my car," he mumbled.

"Okay, well as long as you're alright. Have a good evening," I said as I turned to go back to the party.

"Thanks, Aiden. You too." He lowered his head and walked away.

Maggie waited for me on the porch and noticed the man I was talking to. By the concerned look on her face it seemed she didn't approve.

"Who was that? He's super creepy."

"Yeah, he's a nut case. He's looking for Father Andrews. Keep your eye out. He seems a little off. We don't need a guy like him lurking around after dark." I took one last look across the yard to make sure he was gone.

"Your roommate is really something, huh? I can't believe he doesn't feel the need to watch out for me like you do," she whined shaking her head.

"He does, come on. He adores you," I said, nudging her. I threw my arm around her shaking her. We took a seat on the porch swing.

"Yeah." A tiny grin crept over her face. Maggie was sweet. She put up with a lot when it came to Ben.

"How was your trip to Boston?"

"Very nice. It was good to see everybody."

"That's good. I'm jealous. I so need to get out of here. Soon. Visit the family. Take a break from this madness, you know?" She looked at me in a daze brought on by either the first round of lemon drops or from her increasing level of disappointment in Ben.

"Take some time. Go home, Mags. Take a long weekend. It helps."

"I'm going to. And soon. Before Ben makes me crazy."

"Thanks for inviting Tess. Have you seen her?"

"Nope. Not yet. Don't worry she'll be here," she said.

I looked around for her. I noticed Thomas standing near the road. "I'll be right back, Mags." I quickly shouted.

"I'm going to check on Ben," Maggie announced, heading back into the house.

There was something unapproachable about Thomas. He was an okay guy, don't get me wrong… from what little I knew about him. But there was just something about him that made you feel unwelcome. He had an intense yet very sophisticated demeanor, somewhat stuffy like an old man. He wasn't likely to strike up a friendly conversation only because he seemed to be too busy, too preoccupied in his thoughts. But, I'm an outgoing guy. I could get even the toughest nut to crack.

"Hey there, Thomas. Did Tess come with you?" I shouted from the steps.

"Yeah, she and Daniela went around back looking for you." He looked a little uncomfortable. He stood there alone by the curb as if he was going to stand there all night and wait for her. That wasn't happening. Tess was with me. He didn't need to hang around, if that's what he was thinking.

His hands were nestled in his overcoat. A little dressy for the party. He looked around at all the various activities happening. A dunk tank, a kissing booth, beer pong… the party had definitely reached maximum capacity. And then some. I'm sure this wasn't his typical Saturday night scene. I wandered toward him to try and make him feel a little more welcome.

"How are things, Thomas?"

"A little hectic but nothing we can't handle. Can I ask you something?"

"Sure, anything."

"That guy you were talking to, do you know him?"

"No, not really. I do know his name is Mason, Bruce Mason. I met him at the Gallery the night of Elaina's premiere. He insisted that he knew me from somewhere, but I didn't know him. He just keeps showing up. He asked about Father Andrews. He's trying to find him for some reason. He seems kind of odd."

"I think he's looking for Vincent," Thomas murmured, lowering his head.

"Vincent?" I asked. The last thing I needed was trouble. And the dream was, in fact, just a dream. Maybe it was a trick. Another one of his illusions. My stomach instantly knotted, my hands started to shake. Thomas noticed as I clenched my fists. His attitude wouldn't fly tonight, not here.

"I feel the need to apologize for the way he's been acting around you. Let's just say he's got a lot of issues."

"There's no need for you to apologize. It's not your fault. But it may not be in his best interest to show up here tonight," I warned him. "I know he's just looking out for Tess. I can respect that. But if he comes around here with that shitty attitude, I can't guarantee his safety. Not everyone is as understanding as I am."

"I know. And it's true. He is just looking out for her. He won't let anything or anyone hurt her. He's very protective. We all are."

"I get it. She's very important to you guys. But she's everything to me," I admitted. "So, what makes you thing this guy is looking for Vincent? Do you think he's in some sort of trouble?"

"I'm not sure. Maybe." He spoke with low voice.

"He hasn't returned I take it?" I asked. He looked at me a little surprised that I knew Vincent was missing. Maybe Tess told me too much about their private lives. He tossed his head trying to deciding what to say.

"No. He hasn't. It's not like him. He's been gone for days." Thomas lowered his head. He was definitely worried. From what I knew of Vincent, it was clear that he had serious issues. I could see how his temper could potentially land him in a bad situation, one that he couldn't fight or intimidate his way out of.

"Father Andrews thinks that maybe something has happened to him."

Right then I had a flash back of Vincent tied to the tree. Maybe it was some kind of message. I thought about it, how upset Tess was. Maybe I should tell Thomas. But, maybe it would only make him worry more.

"We should call the police," I suggested.

"Mason is the police," Thomas quickly replied.

"He's a cop? Man. Maybe that's how he knows me."

The news of this guy being a cop instantly stressed me out. I began to panic rubbing my forehead trying to think of anything that I may have done to get this psycho cop to start following me. I stood there trying to recall every run in I ever had with the police. Thomas remained completely calm watching as my anxiety level reached an all-time high.

"It's not you he's after, Aiden," Thomas whispered, "it's Vincent."

"How do you know?" I asked. I felt a tiny flash of relief come over me. I'd rather he had a problem with Vincent than with me.

That may have been a selfish thought but I didn't care. I wasn't the one who had the whacked out anger issue.

"Mason went to confessionals. He spoke with Father Andrews."

"What did he say," I asked.

"He told Father that he thought that Vincent had something to do with the death of his family."

"Why would he think that? Does Vincent even know this guy?"

"I don't think so. It's possible that he may have run into him at some point in time. Maybe he had a confrontation with him in the past and now has him confused with someone else."

"That's strange. That's what he thought the other night... at the gallery. He thought that we knew each other but I don't remember ever seeing him before."

"That is strange." I could see Thomas was very concerned. If this guy really believed that Vincent had something to do with losing his family who knows what he could be capable of. "I just wish I could find Vincent."

"Well, there may be something..." I whispered. At this point, I wanted to help. I decided to tell him about my dream. Even if he thought I was crazy, I was going to tell him.

"What?" Thomas quickly asked.

"I had this dream about Vincent." I began to explain but abruptly stopped. "Man, forget it. You'll think I'm crazy," I said shaking my head. I couldn't do it. I couldn't tell him. It was too risky. He would think I was a nut case and order Tess not to see me.

"Trust me, Aiden. You don't know crazy until you've spent some time with us," He admitted with a smile.

"Really?" I asked.

"Really… beyond crazy."

"Okay, well I saw him. I saw Vincent in a dream and he wasn't doing so well. I know that sounds strange but I've been having some crazy dreams lately," I confessed.

"That's not so crazy. Actually, you may be of some help to us. We should talk, Aiden."

"There are things going on. Things that you should know."

That was an understatement. Finally, someone was going to fill me in.

"We can get out of here, Thomas. I'll go inside and see if I can find Tess and Daniela."

"Sounds good," Thomas replied.

I shoved my way through the crowded living room. I quickly spotted Tess and Daniela as they headed right for the beer saturated sofa. The dress Tess was wearing definitely did not belong on that disgusting couch.

"Hey, wait, maybe you shouldn't sit there!" I warned snatching Tess by the hand pulling her back up.

"Why?" Tess said softy. I spun her around and showed her the large brown wet spot right where she was about to sit. Maggie came running over to greet the girls. She immediately noticed the soaked cushions.

"Okay, wait, what is that?" Maggie shouted pointing to the sofa. "Is that beer?" She screeched. She pressed her hand over the wet cushion and brought her fingers to her nose. Her face shriveled in outrage. "Come on! Who dumps their beer and just leaves it? That's just wrong! Disgustingly wrong." She scolded everyone holding a cup in the vicinity of the wet sofa. She continued to express her disapproval as she walked toward the kitchen.

"Let's go outside, it's crazy in here." I whispered. "I wouldn't want someone spilling on your amazing dress." I winked at her as I took her by the hand.

"I'm glad you like it."

"I do. But I have to admit, I get nervous when you look this good in a crowd this big packed full of dudes with one thing on their minds." I reached for her waist while we walked pulling her closer to me.

"Where are we going?" Tess asked.

"Thomas is waiting for you both outside." We made our way through the crowded room.

"Thomas is here?" Tess shouted over the blaring music glaring at Daniela.

"Wow. That's a first," Daniela snickered. "He doesn't ever crash parties like this."

In the middle of the room a dance competition was well underway. I tried to block out Ben's embarrassing robot moves hoping Tess wouldn't notice. But, by the way she and Daniela were whispering and giggling I knew they saw him. The only thing that came to my mind was, why did I know the guy?

Maggie stood by watching batting her eyes in disbelief asking herself the exact same thing.

As we reached the porch, Ben came rushing up behind us. I knew we wouldn't get away that easily.

"Hey, what's up? Where you guys going?" He asked.

"We gotta go, Ben." I attempted to let him down easy. "Something's come up!" I shouted. There was absolutely no way he would let me off that easily. His eyes squinted and his brows flared.

"Something's come up? What do you mean? What's more important than hanging with me?" he whimpered.

"Sorry, Ben. I'll make it up to you. We have to go. Hey, nice dance moves by the way," I said patting him on the shoulder. A grin slowly crept over his face. He was thrilled that someone noticed.

"Really? You think so?" I did it again. I inadvertently diffused the situation. He didn't care if I was serious or not. He was going to take it as a compliment either way.

"Oh, for sure," Tess said, smiling in agreement. That was it. That's all it took. He was so happy that we actually noticed his self-taught robot moves and that they were referred to as "nice". His eyes twinkled with delight. He was satisfied. He needed nothing else to happen that evening.

"I'll call you, Ben."

"See you later," Tess said. A shade of pale white washed over his face. Within seconds his cheeks reddened and he shut his eyes. His disturbing smile grew. Just as I was about to say something I felt a quick jab to my rib. She poked at me playfully.

"Nice seeing you, Tess," Ben replied opening his eyes. "Your friend, too. Hey, wait! Who's your friend?"

"Hey there, Thomas. What's up?" Daniela asked as she took Thomas by the arm.

"We're going to find Vincent," Thomas replied.

"We are?" Daniela looked puzzled. Maybe she was surprised that Thomas was willing to discuss the situation around me.

"Yes, and Aiden is coming with us," he firmly added. Tess stood in front of me squeezing my hand. I could tell that she was elated by Thomas' statement.

"He is?" Daniela asked even more surprised.

"Yes. He may be able to help." Thomas smiled as he patted my shoulder.

"I'll do whatever I can," I muttered. I sure didn't want to let them down. I didn't know if it was possible to help or not but I had to try. Just the way Tess looked at me, I needed to do something.

Dr. Bennett cleared her throat. She had a smile that completely covered her face.

"I used to enjoy our sorority parties," she confessed, thinking back to her college days. Her eyes darted back and forth from her note pad back to me realizing her lack of professionalism. As she flipped back through her notes a somber expression replaced the tiny grin.

"It's okay, you know," I whispered. I flipped the brake off the wheel as she slowly moved my chair toward her.

"What's okay?" She tucked her pen inside the flap of her folder trying to pull herself together. She patted her fuzzy hair away from her face to regain her composure. She glared at me waiting for my reply. I didn't answer.

"Aiden?" She asked again. This time in a gentler voice.

"You can smile. You don't have to be so professional all the time."

"I do smile. I just shouldn't bring up my past."

"Why?"

"It's my job to listen. Listening doesn't require commenting unless there's a question to be asked."

"That may be true if you don't care at all about what you're listening to."

I know she didn't want to come across as uncaring. She didn't want that at all. As a matter of fact she cared a great deal. She and I were making the best progress. I told her things that she didn't feel comfortable telling her staff. Unbelievable things that she deliberately kept out of my chart. I appreciated her honesty, her loyalty and her unquestionable desire to help me.

"I do care." She scooted her chair close enough to touch my

hand.

"Don't be afraid to show me," I whispered peeking at her through the thick stands of my shaggy brown hair. I reached for her hand. She reluctantly gave it to me. I pulled it toward my chest. She attempted to pull it back, but she couldn't. I gripped onto it tightly. I knew what she was thinking. This could go very bad very quickly.

"I have a heart. Can you feel it? It pounds in my chest just like yours. I am living, Dr. Bennett. I just need you to be…" My voice cracked as I tried to speak. "You're asking me to be honest with you, to tell you everything," I whispered as I held her hand tighter to my chest.

"I want you to," she insisted. She knew that she needed to maintain control of the situation. She reached out and grabbed my other hand taking it firmly into hers. Her brows lowered as she gazed at me. She was in charge, she needed me to remember that. I was her patient, her responsibility. As I stared into her eyes she could see that I'd become desperate. "I do care a great deal about you, Aiden."

"I'm good with that," I whispered, nodding. She didn't leave me. She didn't budge from her chair even when I freaked out and grabbed onto her. She didn't call for an orderly to put me in restraints nor did she make an attempt to stick me with a seda-tive. She was calm.

"I'm glad, Aiden," she replied in a gentle voice.

"I just need you to be normal. You know, human."

"Okay."

"Maybe even telling me a thing or two about you once in a while."

"Fair enough."

22

Desperate Predicament

"Do you mind if I come in Aiden?" Dr. Bennett asked, poking her head through the terrace door.

"Not at all." It wasn't time for our session. Not for another two hours. "It's not a big deal, but you're early, aren't you?" I said, spinning my chair around.

"Yes. I just wanted to make sure you were okay. I'm sorry about last night."

"Don't be. I'm the one who needs to apologize. I shouldn't have acted like that. I'm sorry."

"It's okay. We're gaining each other's trust. And we're covering a lot of ground," she said softly. "I brought muffins." She held out a tiny brown bag.

"Nice. Thank you."

"You're welcome. Normal, right?" she said, chuckling searching for a napkin to wipe her fingers. She was really trying.

"Right."

"I like to bake," she confessed. She blew at a single strand of hair hoping to get it out of her face. It was pretty obvious. She was definitely out of her professional comfort zone. "That's one thing about me. Now if you don't mind we can start a little early today…"

"Works for me. I don't have anywhere to be."

"What happened after you left the party. You went with the others to find Vincent?" She scooted her chair over to the window where I sat. She nibbled on a muffin waiting for me to respond. There was a truce happening between us leaving the doctor/patient relationship behind and on to a trusting friendship.

"Yes. I went with them."

"They must have trusted you."

"They did."

I was parked around the corner. I offered to drive. "Aiden, tell Tess and Daniela what you told me earlier."

"Tell us what, Aiden?" Tess asked as she hopped into the passenger side of my Jeep. I froze for a second. She had never been in my Jeep before. She always had a ride. I just sat there unresponsive, staring at her next to me. She looked at the tiny picture I had stuffed behind my visor. It was a picture of the two of us that Maggie had taken after the row competition. She smiled at me snatching it to get a better look.

"I don't want you to worry, Tess, but I think that Vincent may be in some kind of trouble." I explained as we pulled away.

"What do you mean?"

"I had this dream. We were in the woods somewhere. He was tied to a tree."

"Why didn't you tell me this before?" Tess asked.

"How was I supposed to tell you? Oh, I'm dreaming about your brother Tess... it sounds kind of creepy, doesn't it?" I argued. She smiled at me. I did have a point. "Don't worry. It was just a dream," I whispered to her as I stroked her cheek. I glanced back at Thomas and Daniela sitting in the back seat. They didn't appear to be too convinced. There was definitely something they weren't telling me.

We made it up to the castle. It was unbelievable that I was there with them. That close. The front gates began to open as we approached. I pulled up to the front doors shining my headlights toward the entrance. The entire castle was surrounded by the mountain. The stone doors must have been at least fifty feet tall. It was better than I ever imagined it would be. And Tess sitting next to me clutching my hand made it surreal.

"I'll get the others," Daniela shouted as she headed inside.

"Is there anything else you remember Aiden?" Tess asked. I didn't want to say anything more to upset her. But I knew I couldn't lie. My mind raced with what to say.

"Aiden?" Tess whispered as she gently squeezed my hand.

"Maybe. I'm not sure if any of it will make any sense."

"It's okay. Anything you might remember could be helpful," Thomas assured me.

"Well, a while ago, I dreamt I was in the ocean. A man was drowning. I was trying to save him and Vincent was there."

"In the ocean?" Tess asked.

"Yes. I was freezing. I struggled to stay afloat. I remember seeing Vincent. He stood on top of the water, hovering around me."

I tried not to go into too much detail. I didn't want to hurt her by telling her that Vincent was a psycho in my dreams just like he was in reality.

"He didn't help you, did he," Tess whispered. By the look in her eyes she knew. I didn't have to tell her a thing.

"No. He never seemed to want to help. Not in any of my dreams," I confessed.

"You saw him before?" Thomas asked.

"Yes. All of them. Ever since they started."

"I'm sorry, Aiden. I feel like it's my fault," Tess confessed.

"It's not your fault. I must have a real problem with him. Why else would I dream about him like this?" They both just glared at me. Hanging on my every word.

"Aiden, when you were saving the man in the water, do you remember seeing anything around you?" Thomas asked. I thought for a moment.

"Fire. I remember fire in the water. All around me. Burning wreckage, like from a boat accident. You know? And a light, a really bright light in the distance. It would turn on, and then off. I could see it. In an instant it was so bright it lit up the dark water. That's when I found the man. When I grabbed him and came up, it was dark again."

"I know where he is!" Tess shouted, slamming herself back into her seat.

"Where, Tess?" Thomas reached around and opened his door. He quickly opened hers and took her by the arm.

"I don't know why I didn't think..." She let out a deep breath. "He's at the light house... the light house on Fire Island!" she shouted. "He goes there when he's angry, and the night he left he was really angry! That's where he is. And that man! The man Father Andrews told us about, the one who was looking for him, maybe he found him."

"We did see him tonight outside the sorority house," Thomas added. "He was looking for Father Andrews."

"You both saw him, tonight?" Tess's voice was shrill.

"I'm sure it's just a coincidence. Maybe he was just trying to find Father Andrews." I tried to calm her.

"But… you did say he had blood on his shirt." Thomas was quickly putting things together.

"He did. But, I'm sure it has nothing to do with Vincent. He's a police officer. He wouldn't hurt anybody," I tried assuring them.

"I wouldn't be too sure, Aiden. He was pretty desperate to find him when he spoke with Father," Thomas whispered.

"Why would he be looking for Vincent?" I asked.

"Who knows? Vincent has a little trouble staying out of trouble," Thomas admitted.

"Yeah, but I have to believe that he could take care of himself when push came to shove. Don't worry, Tess. We'll find him." I took her in my arms and held her close to me. She was trembling. "Maybe it would be a good idea to call the police. If someone has him, we may need help," I suggested.

"It's more complicated than that." Thomas said.

Tess pulled away from me glaring at Thomas. What were they not telling me? Maybe they were a bunch of criminals. Maybe that was their big secret. Living way up here in such secrecy. And who was this Bruce Mason? A paranoid cop poking around town for information, maybe trying to find the where abouts of these law breakers living up here with the kind, yet naive priest who never asks questions. A crazy cop stalking me day and night swearing that he knows me from somewhere. He could even be some freak ex-con who shared a cell with one of them at one time or another. Maybe even with Vincent. And now he's just out for him for who knows what reason. More than likely a legitimate reason by the way Vincent asks for trouble everywhere he goes. This wasn't good. My mind was racing. At that point Tess wouldn't look at me. She folded her arms and turned her back toward me. Something wasn't right. I could feel it in the pit of my stomach. I needed answers.

"What do you mean more complicated?" I asked, trying to keep my cool. Thomas shook his head and headed for the front doors. The way he kept glaring back at Tess made me edgy.

"We don't have time for this. Not now. You have to understand," he murmured in a low voice as he walked away.

"I know this is confusing to you. I need to tell you, and I will. I promise. But not now, okay? Just please trust me," Tess pleaded. She had a desperate look in her eyes.

"You know I do, Tess," I reassured her. She took me by the hand as we followed Thomas.

"We will answer all of your questions, Aiden. But right now we need to get to Vincent," Thomas announced from the steps.

I could feel her hand shaking in mine. I needed to help them find him. No matter what else was going on up here.

As the enormous doors opened I couldn't say another word. I just stood there watching as my dormant mountain, my sanctuary came to life. I felt like I was in another one of my dreams. For years I climbed this mountain. For years I was obsessed with this very place. And as she led me toward the front doors I thought, here I go. I'm about to enter a place I've only dreamt about.

"I'll bet you were thrilled to be there." Dr. Bennett said. Her eyes were as wide as ever. She was definitely listening.

"You have no idea." My voice cracked as I spoke.

My story was unlike anything she had ever heard before. I wasn't crazy and she knew it. She stood up from her chair and wandered toward the window. Heavy clouds gathered over the garden where the sunlight quickly faded. She gazed out as raindrops began to fall.

Something had happened to me. She understood that. The lost look that consumed me, my thin pale face, my frail body that once was able to move a boat across a lake in record time... something had happened. I had given up. It was in this story that I was lost. Somewhere along the way she knew I had been thrown away, disregarded. Without knowing, without warning, I was simply chosen by someone or something.

For what purpose was still unclear to her. But I was definitely chosen by something larger than she could comprehend.

She turned back to the window. Wind sent the rain droplets slamming against the glass. She peeked out to the dark gray statue in the garden. The sculpture some of the nurses had recently referred to as mine... as "Aiden's Angel." Rivulets of water streamed down over her marble face. Her mighty, yet gentle, wings lowered as she hovered over the garden and those who came here. Dr. Bennett turned back to look at me. Once again she found me staring out the window at her.

"Tell me what it was like, Aiden."

Thomas left the doors opened just wide enough to catch a glimpse inside. As we reached the massive stone steps, I could feel a rush of adrenaline race through me. Tess took me by the hand. Instantly, we were surrounded with a soft glowing light. A giant wrought iron candlelit chandelier was suspended from the hand painted ceiling above us. Her skin glistened as the delicate light cascaded over her. The sweet aroma of vanilla wafted through the air. It was invigorating. The floors were made of polished marble etched with gold angelic figures. Countless paintings covered the stone walls. I was absolutely mesmerized by it all. I couldn't take my eyes off the magnificent angelic sculpture in the center of the circular foyer. She towered above all those who entered the castle. Rich moldings and deep recessed arches, hand carved columns that framed the entry of each room. The spiraling staircase with a marble banister that led to the three levels above each with a balcony circling the foyer. Everywhere I looked, everything I could see was covered with some unique angelic detail. I had never been anywhere like it before.

"Did Thomas tell you? We know where he is!" Tess shouted.

"Where?" Father asked, walking with her toward the great room.

"At the lighthouse," she answered in a faint voice. Her lack of restoring was beginning to show. They could see that she was aging. The worry over Vincent was causing the effects to come more rapidly.

"Are you sure?" he asked. He was concerned for both Vincent and Tess. She needed to rest.

"Tess, sit here next to me.," Father ordered as he sat on the sofa. She knew she was running out of time. She felt it with each passing hour. But she needed Aiden and Vincent needed her desperately. She couldn't think of herself. Not now. First they must find Vincent. She knew she had to restore. She would go as soon as he was safe.

"We searched there," Angelo exclaimed. "There was no sign of him."

"Why do you think he's there Tess?" Father asked.

"Aiden saw him," Thomas blurted out.

"He saw him in a dream. He's dying." She brought her hands to her face to catch the tears that fell from her eyes. I ran to her. I held her as she spoke. "That's why Thomas can't sense him. He doesn't have any strength left. We have to get to him before it's too late," she whispered, lowering her head against my chest. Father glared at me as I held her tightly in my arms. I wasn't about to let her go. I didn't care how awkward he made me feel. I didn't care how anyone them felt about me being there.

"Well, well, who do we have here? Aiden. What a surprise!" He stood looking at me with no real expression, just a look of disbelief.

"Hello, Father."

Father Andrews couldn't believe what he was seeing. It was pretty obvious I wasn't supposed to be there. Not at that particular moment. I had no idea what they were saying. It really made no sense to me. It didn't have to. I needed to be with her. She felt so weak in my arms as I held her. I loved her. More than life itself. I think it was pretty evident she loved me, too. I wasn't about to leave. No matter how unwelcome they made me feel. I would never abandon her, not at a time like this. She needed me and that was enough.

"Tess, please, sit. You need to rest," he insisted. I kept my arm securely around her as I helped her to the couch.

"No one has ever come here Aiden. I've made sure of it. They shouldn't have brought you here," he whispered with a low voice. I could feel my face shrivel up in confusion.

"What do you mean?" I replied as I sat closely next to Tess. It was strange I thought to myself. His statement, his demeanor. He was acting much different than usual. He's typically a happy go lucky kind of guy. He didn't really fit the normal, role of a priest. You know, quiet, reserved. But that's why I liked him. Tonight, he was different. He was so protective of this place, of Tess. What a ridiculous statement. No one had ever been there before. What did he mean? Maybe he was just trying to make me leave. That wasn't going to happen. Not unless Tess asked me, too.

"Don't listen to him, Aiden. He's just grumpy. Worry makes him terribly grumpy," Tess said with a tiny grin.

"It's okay. I'm not going anywhere." I held her tightly against me. Her smile grew.

I guess I just never gave it much thought. But he was right, after all I suppose. I've never known anyone to come here. Just the occasional stranger from out of town. Like Dominic. But Tess said he was family. Father never invited me. But, we weren't that close. I worked for him, that's it. Father Andrews was secretive. He always has been. He never goes into detail about anything personal. That's why people talked. They had to speculate and fill in the blanks because he never said anything about this place.

"That's crazy. Look around, Father. You've welcomed so many here over the years."

"There's more to it than that, Aiden."

Either they were going to tell me or they weren't. Right then and there I decided I was no longer looking for answers. I didn't care anymore. I didn't care about their secrets, about my dreams, about any of it.

They didn't need to tell me a thing. I was going to stay right there in that spot, holding Tess.

"Thomas, Angelo, please come with me. We need to speak in private for a moment. Aiden, would you please excuse us?" Father announced.

"Sure, of course. If there's anything I can do…"

"Just stay with Tess. She needs you right now."

The greatest feeling came over me. Finally, he acknowledged that she and I were together. She did need me. He cared enough about her to realize it. She rested her head against my shoulder and shut her eyes. I looked around the room. There were so many familiar faces. Those that I met at the ballet, and at the Gallery. But there was one person that I didn't remember meeting standing near the balcony. He must be another one of Tess' brothers. He was talking with Daniela. He looked so familiar. Just then it came to me. He was the man who actually helped me in my dream, in the tunnel. That was it. How strange to actually see someone from a dream other than Vincent.

Daniela saw me watching them. I dropped my eyes to Tess. I pressed my lips against her forehead.

"Father Andrews can overreact every so often. He's probably just surprised that we brought you here unannounced," Daniela whispered as she sat in the chair across from us.

"Yeah, no problem. I feel bad about that. I could tell he wasn't expecting company," I replied. I heard Thomas and Father Andrews talking as they came in from the balcony.

"Father, you may need to come along. If Bruce is there, if he has Vincent, we'll need someone to talk to him," Thomas insisted.

"Tess, take Aiden. Meet us at the light house. And Tess, tell him. He needs to know now." Tess nodded in agreement.

"Father, would you please go with her? She may need you. We'll meet you there," Thomas instructed.

"Do you think this is a good idea? Is this the only way?" Father asked.

"I believe it is. We have no other choice, too much has happened."

23

Red Dawn

The three of us headed for my Jeep parked outside. I was anxious to say the least. I could tell Father Andrews was struggling with everything that was happening.

"You probably have questions, Aiden. I'm sure. Tess you have plenty of time to answer them," Father whispered. "Can you drive, son?"

"Yeah, Father. No problem," I replied calmly. Inside I felt the anxiety building.

"We can take my Bentley." He shouted tossing me the keys.

Fire Island wasn't too far from the mountain. About twenty minutes at the most. I was eager to hear what it was Tess needed to tell me. I was a little worried, too. Maybe it had something to do with Tess and me.

"The others will be taking a short cut," Father whispered.

"Okay." I wanted to stay focused. No more asking questions. Just drive, I told myself. I could feel my hands shaking as I clutched the wheel heading down the mountain.

"I can't…. I don't know how to tell you," Tess whimpered.

"It's okay. Whatever it is, I can handle it," I said. I gently stroked her face lifting her eyes to look at me. "You know I love you."

"I'm afraid of losing you," she confessed.

"That will never happen. Do you hear me, Tess? Never!" I took her by the hand. I was no way prepared for what I was about to hear next. No way prepared.

"She's an angel," Father whispered. The tires made a squeal as I swerved off the road. I squeezed back on the wheel trying to regain control of the car. I saw Father staring at me in the rear view mirror. Nice timing, I thought to myself. I struggled to keep the car on the road battling with what he just said. I couldn't fathom what I heard… trying to drive down the mountain… definitely poor timing. Racing down a dark mountain road in a ridiculously expensive car with a priest and the woman of my dreams… and they pick now to tell me? Well, if I was meant to die in this car tonight, I was definitely in good company.

"Now? You decide that I should drive… and then proceed to tell me she's an angel? Are you crazy?" I shouted hysterically, attempting to keep the tires on the pavement. I shook my head in disbelief. I looked over to her as I tried to keep what little composure I had left. I glared back at the road, then back at her. Then the road again.

"Maybe we shouldn't have told him," Tess whispered.

"It's ok. I'm ok. I- I got it. I got this," I stuttered. I definitely wrestled with my speech, as well as my driving. The car continued to swerve down the mountain as I attempted to embrace the undeniable fact that Tess was…

"I knew it," I roared, slamming my hands against the steering wheel. "I knew it."

"How could you know, Aiden?" she asked.

"It just makes sense, Tess. The book, the statues, the mountain, the dreams. It all makes sense." A feeling of exuberance came over me, like I had been freed from a bondage that held me for too long. That took control of my life, my dreams. Everything.

"What book?" she asked.

"Professor Williams' gave me a book. A book about angels. About you. Man. This is incredible." I babbled with excitement as I floored the gas pedal down the winding mountain side.

"Maybe you should take it easy, huh, son?" Father whispered. His voice trembled from the back. I wasn't thinking clearly. My mind flooded with thoughts. So many answers to so many questions. My foot was like a lead weight but after a minute or so Father Andrews's recommendation registered.

"Oh, yea. Sorry. You're right."

"Father, how did Professor Williams get our book?" Tess asked.

"I'm not sure. It's been so many years since I've seen it. Thomas was always the one who kept it."

"Thomas, the others? They are too, aren't they?" I asked excitedly. "Yes." Tess replied.

"Man, I knew it. This is unbelievable." I shouted.

"It is unbelievable, Aiden. And before she tells you any more, I just want you to think about it. We need you to keep this to yourself. Not just for our sake but for yours. Stories like this, well, let's just say folks may start to question your sanity," Father warned. "Years ago, a member of the congregation told people that he met a real angel at the farmer's market in town. After realizing that he didn't mean an especially kind, sweet person, that he actually believed that met a feathery winged creature, his wife had him locked up at the state mental institution."

"I understand, Father. I wouldn't want anything to change or anyone to get hurt." I held Tess' hand to my lips and kissed it softly. She smiled at me. I could almost see relief in her eyes. No more hiding.

"There's much more to it, much more," Father whispered.

"But isn't it enough for now that he knows? Can't we just focus on Vincent?" She pleaded.

"Of course Tess," Father replied.

Thomas and Angelo were standing near the edge of the cliff close to the lighthouse when we drove up. It was nearly dawn. The bright light at the top circled out panning over the banks of the east river. It lit up the outer perimeter of the Atlantic as far out as I could see. Pounding waves hit with full force against the rocks sending a thick mist covering over the island like a dense fog.

"What is it Thomas?" Father shouted as we approached cautiously.

"There's a body, Father," Thomas replied, backing away from the edge. Father rushed over toward them. Tess tried to follow Father as I clutched onto her.

"No, Tess. Don't," I whispered as I held onto her.

"Thomas, is it...?" Tess shouted.

"No. It's not Vincent. It may be Bruce Mason," he answered. She let out a deep breath in relief. She quickly looked around desperately searching for any sign of Vincent. I noticed her eyes had become bloodshot. She didn't seem to be doing so well. She held onto me as though she couldn't carry her own weight. She must be tired. The worry over Vincent must be keeping her up at night.

"Angelo, you and Aiden check inside. See if you can find Vincent. If that isn't Bruce down there, he may be hanging around. Father, you and Tess stay here. Keep an eye out for him. Let us know if you see anyone." He ordered. "I'm going to check the woods. If he's tied to a tree, then he must be in that wooded area over there." He pointed to the heavily treed area near the road.

"You got it," Angelo replied.

"Thomas, maybe Angelo should stay with Tess and Father Andrews. They may need him if they run into Bruce. If Vincent's in there, I'll find him," I insisted.

"Are you sure?" Angelo replied.

"Yes. I'm sure." I insisted as I raced for the lighthouse. I looked back at Tess. She was shaking her head. She didn't agree. She scowled and headed toward me.

"I'm going with you, Aiden."

"No, Tess. You stay here with Angelo and Father Andrews," I demanded.

"I'm going with you. You're not doing this alone. Not anymore," She adamantly replied latching onto my arm as tightly as she could.

"Ok. But stay back," I ordered as I pushed her behind me.

I slowly opened the heavy steel door of the lighthouse. It made a dull squeaking noise as it closed behind us. Inside it was pitch black. I wanted to prop the door open allowing some light to come in from outside so I began kicking my feet around the floor searching for anything big enough to use. Tess found a heavy chain near her foot. I slid in into the door. For a moment it worked. The outside light lit the path toward a circular staircase. Just as we approached the stairs, the chain shifted slamming the heavy door shut. Once again we were surrounded in darkness. I couldn't move. Tess seemed to see a bit better than I did.

"I do better with my eyes shut. Feel your way like this…" she whispered moving in front of my clutching onto my hand, "… follow the wall to the stairs."

Just then something happened. Something amazing. She began to glow. A soft radiant light came from all around her that lit the way to the stairwell. I just froze standing there behind her.

I held out my hand and touched her face. A million questions raced through my mind.

"Don't say anything. Let's just find him. Ok?" she begged in a soft voice.

"Okay," I whispered back smiling at her.

I moved past her leading the way climbing the iron steps. As we approached the top I could hear the clattering of chains. Someone was up there. The last thing that I wanted was for Tess to get hurt. As we reached the top step, I held her back away from me as I crept closer to the wall near the opening. I turned to her with my finger in front of my mouth.

"Shhh…" I gestured.

She understood and nodded. Her glow was gone. Completely. Her skin looked pale, thin, transparent. She looked like she wasn't well. Not at all. Something wasn't right with her. I wanted to rush back down the stairs and take her to Thomas. He would know what to do. She was deteriorating right in front of my eyes. I didn't want to leave her nor did I want to risk her getting hurt.

She began to tremble. I held her close against me. I needed a moment to make sure she was okay.

"Shhhh… its ok," I whispered. I could feel her heart pounding in fear. I knew what frightened her. She was afraid of what we might find. I clutched her arms and gently shook her to get her back.

"Look in my eyes, Tess," I whispered. "Take a deep breath." I needed her to try and focus on what we needed to do. She looked at me in a daze. It was like she couldn't see me. "Are you with me?" She didn't answer. I felt like I was losing her. I seriously contemplated what to do next. Vincent needed help, but so did Tess. She was everything. I couldn't exist without her. She finally brought her eyes to mine. She scowled as she began to speak.

"Vincent," she mumbled.

"Okay, but stay here."

She shook her head and gripped my arm pushing me forward.

Father Andrews waited with Angelo outside making sure to keep a close eye on the wood line as well as listening for Aiden and Tess inside. He made several attempts to contact the police but didn't have a signal. He moved around waving his cell phone around in the air hoping to get more than a just a fraction of one bar.

"Hello, Father," he announced in a deep voice. Bruce stood near the edge of the rock. His hands were buried deep inside the pockets of his long coat. He had dark heavy bags under his eyes. It appeared as though he hadn't slept in days. Father noticed right away that he was even more distraught than he was the night he came to confession.

"Hello, Bruce," Father replied. Angelo came running over and stood right next to Father Andrews. Bruce pulled one hand out from inside his jacket holding a revolver. Thomas saw that they were in trouble and darted toward them. As he approached, he startled Bruce who quickly turned facing him frantically pointing the gun.

"Stay back," Bruce warned.

"It's alright, just stay back Thomas. He won't hurt anyone," Father shouted. "Bruce, no one is going to hurt you. Let's just talk, ok? Can we do that? Can we talk about it?" Father Andrews pleaded.

"It's no use, Father. It doesn't stop," he cried, shaking the gun around aimlessly.

"You don't want to hurt anyone. Bruce, put the gun down. Come on, son."

"You have no idea what I want!" he shouted as he smeared his soiled hands over his scruffy face. "You just won't listen," he cried. The gun dangled from his grasp as he wept.

"You don't want to hurt anyone. I know you don't. You're an officer. Your job is to protect…" Bruce wouldn't let Father Andrews finish.

"Protect? I was supposed to protect my family!"

Father quickly realized that he used the wrong word. Bruce became more agitated. More unpredictable. As Bruce sobbed, he staggered back and forth trying to figure out his next move. He quickly lifted his gun to his temple. He began to shake uncontrollably.

"My life is over. My family is gone. Without them…what's the use?"

"It's not over. Bruce. It's not. Let me help you," Father pleaded. "Put down the gun and let's talk."

"There's nothing left to talk about, Father. I need them back. That's it."

"They're gone, Bruce. They can't come back."

"Then, I'll go to them." He held the gun firmly against his head. Tears flowed steadily down his dingy face as he pressed the barrel against his skin.

"Not this way. Please. Put the gun down." Father's voice soothed the depressed man. He lowered his gun and slumped forward with his hands covering his face. Father held out one hand to Thomas and Angelo directing them to not move.

Thomas knew this was Vincent's doing. This whole situation was definitely caused by him interfering. When Vincent meddled in Aiden's dream, for whatever reason, he disturbed the outcome. They knew they weren't ever supposed to get involved. Vincent knew that. And now, they were definitely involved. Thomas and

221

Angelo knew they needed to stay back and let Father handle it until the police arrived.

Tess followed close behind me as we made our way around the circular room. The enormous light swirled around casting a radiant beam over us. Quickly it moved around lighting what appeared to be a figure hunched over near the wall. Moving slowly around the wall we tried to get closer. We waited for the light to cross again following it as it traveled around the room searching for Bruce. Tess reached for my hand. Finding it, she held it tightly as we waited. Once again the light lit the area. I could see someone near the mechanical box. A man. His arms lifted over his head. He was shackled by his wrists. I couldn't see his face; his head was lowered. I caught a glimpse of the tattoo covering his arm. I waited.

Tess attempted to get closer to him but I held onto her. I wanted to be sure that whoever did this wasn't around, waiting for us. One more time the light came around shinning on him. It was Vincent. He had been shackled to the wall near a large mechanical box. His shirt was covered in blood. Shocked by the sight, Tess backed against the wall slamming into a lantern behind us. I grabbed it off the ledge turning it on. The dim light lit the area. I held it toward him as we moved closer. His face was bloodied, his mouth was gagged, and his eyes were covered. Just like in my dream. Blindfolded, bound, beaten and left unconscious. Left to die.

"Vincent!" Tess shouted as she rushed over to him. "Tess, wait!"

He was slumped over suspended to the tall windows behind him. The machine made a loud rumbling sound as spun the massive light across the water. Vincent didn't respond. He didn't move.

"Aiden, help me!" she demanded, tugging on the chains. I rushed over to him lifting his lifeless body trying to release the chains from the hook above him. Tess removed the rag from his mouth. Blood had seeped from deep wounds covering his badly beaten face.

"He's bleeding so badly, Aiden! He doesn't bleed!" she cried. I reached around and untied the blindfold removing it from his eyes. I placed him gently on the floor checking for a pulse.

"Are we too late?" Tess cried as she clung to Vincent's lifeless body trying to pull his hands free from the shackles. Tears streamed down her face. He wasn't moving at all. Maybe we were too late.

"Why would anyone do this to him?" she asked, holding him closer to her. I held my finger to his neck.

"I can feel a pulse. It's faint but he's alive," I told her.

"We need to get him out of here!" I shouted above the loud humming coming from the rotating box next to us. Vincent wasn't a big guy, maybe five nine. A solid frame, muscular, but scrappy. I knew I could get him out of there on my own. I stood lifting him into my arms. Tess wouldn't let him go. She held his hand as I carried him toward the stairs. Vincent began to come around. He slowly opened his eyes. He tried to hold his head up to see what was happening.

"Tess?" he mumbled.

"Yes, Vincent. We're getting you out of here," she whispered to him.

"I'm so glad you found me." he said in a low voice. He started to cough. I put him down onto the floor. He began to choke hunching forward in pain.

"I was beginning to think this was it for me, you know?" he said with a smirk. Blood seeped from his mouth.

"No way, Vincent. You have too many important things to do," she assured him. She took her dress pulling it to his face and wiped the blood that smeared around his mouth. He turned his head to look up at me.

I didn't know what to think. Up until that point he didn't seem to like me much.

"You?" he whispered. He tried lifting his weight to sit. He gripped his side and moaned as he looked at me with a frown.

"Vincent…" Tess tried to explain.

"You found me didn't you?" Vincent whispered. He smiled at me as tears welled up in his blackened eyes. He reached out placing his hand on my shoulder.

"Yes. Tess did too. We need to get you out of here, Vincent," I told him. "Can you stand?"

"I think so." I lifted him up. Tess wrapped his arm around her shoulders taking his other side. She was so weak. They both were.

"No, it wasn't me Vincent. It was Aiden. Without him we wouldn't have been able to find you," she whispered.

We took each step with caution, knowing that the maniac that did this could show up at any time. Tess couldn't keep up. She struggled with each step. I felt his legs buckle in my grasp so I leaned in scooping him into my arms taking him the rest of the way down the stairwell.

"Tough guy, huh?" he murmured with a grin. I smiled at him. I felt a truce between us as I held his frail body. He felt it too. We didn't have much time. He lost a lot of blood. With each step he grunted in pain. He was definitely all broken up inside. I glanced at Tess. She followed close behind us.

"You okay, Tess?" I asked.

"Yes," she whimpered. I could hear her, she was crying. There was definitely reason to worry. I didn't know what would happen. I was afraid we were going to run into Bruce. It must have been him. It all fit.

His bloody shirt, his nervous behavior standing at the fence. He took Vincent. He chained him here, beat him and left him to die.

"You need to go, Vincent. You have to... Soon," she warned.

"Tess," Vincent muttered.

"Don't worry Vincent, he knows. It's ok. Father told him."

"So, the wonder boy knows our secret. Good," he said groaning. "You know, I owe you," he added. I did appreciate his gratitude. This was definitely one I owe you I could use.

Tess raced in front of us and reached to open the door. I warned her to open it slowly. As the morning light poured into the stairwell Tess peaked her head outside. She looked back at me shaking her head. She didn't see anyone. I lowered Vincent. He stood, his body swaying as Tess came rushing back taking him by the arm. We tried to be as quiet as possible as we exited the lighthouse. I caught the heavy metal door with my boot preventing it from slamming behind us. Just then we heard shouting from around the corner. There he was. Bruce Mason. He was pointing a gun at Father Andrews, Angelo and Thomas. There was no time to think.

"It's all his fault. He took them," Bruce turned the gun in our direction. The only thing that crossed my mind was Tess. I needed to keep her safe. He waved his gun directly at Vincent.

In an instant, Tess stepped into Vincent's path to protect him as Bruce pulled the trigger. Tess was struck in the chest. I held her as she collapsed in my arms. Vincent gripped onto her as she fell to the ground.

Bruce dropped to his knees realizing what he had done. As he brought his hands to his eyes in disbelief, Angelo jumped onto him, forcing him to the ground knocking the gun loose from his hand. It slid across the gravel where Father Andrews grabbed it and ran over to Tess.

"You got him Angelo?" Thomas shouted frantically as he rushed over to her.

"Yea, I got him," he replied as he held him. Bruce laid there, face down in the gravel sobbing uncontrollably. Angelo didn't budge straddling him holding his arms firmly behind his back. "Is she alright?" he shouted.

"I'm fine," she whispered, trying to sit up, "you know I'm fine."

It made no sense. How could she be fine after taking a bullet? I didn't know enough. But I knew they could get hurt. Vincent could bleed, he came so close to death. And Tess was growing weaker by the hour.

"This is serious, Tess. It's not just a little coffee burn," I argued.

"Aiden, really. It's not bad," Tess whispered. Thomas leaned in and slid her black strap of her dress away from her chest exposing a tiny area where the bullet struck. It should have been much worse. She was losing blood but it wasn't what I expected to see.

"She's lucky," Thomas whispered kneeling beside her. "Thankfully you had enough strength left to stop it. A few more days Tess and you wouldn't have been able to." He softly brushed her hair away from her face.

This was the closest he'd ever come to losing any of them. And tonight it wasn't just one… it was two.

I sat there holding her. I think I may have been in shock by the whole ordeal. I had just witnessed something I couldn't explain. But the important thing was that she was alright. I moved my hand gently over her skin. There was nothing left to see but a slightly red circle where the bullet hit. The bleeding had stopped. The wound appeared to be healing. Within just a few minutes it was almost completely gone.

"You're right, Thomas. Enough is enough," Father Andrews said softly as he took Tess by the hand gently stroking it. He pulled Vincent toward him. "I'm so relieved you're safe."

The sound of police sirens came blaring up the drive. A feeling of relief come over me as one of the officers ran to help Angelo. Within a few minutes Bruce Mason was in handcuffs. His partner rushed over to where we were gathered around Tess.

"We need backup. And send an ambulance, west side of the lighthouse on Fire Island," The officer barked into his radio. "Is she ok?" he asked.

"It's just a scrape. She'll be okay," Father said as he leaned into her.

"Maybe she should go and get checked out just as a precaution," he suggested. He quickly noticed Vincent. "This young man needs a doctor." The officer said crouching down beside Vincent.

"We'll take them both," Father assured the officer. He clutched Tess' hand tightly smiling at her. "Here's his gun. Please let the chief know I'll be downtown later this afternoon to see him?" Father Andrews added.

"Sure thing, Father. We're going to need to get your statements," he blurted out, walking over to where his partner held Bruce against the ground. "What do we have here, Officer Mason? Kidnapping, attempted murder?" The officer groveled, pulling Mason to his feet.

"Hey, we got a body over here!" Another officer announced from the edge of the rocks. "Now, you're looking at murder, Mason. Shoulda got the help when we offered it to you."

Within a few minutes the area was covered in emergency vehicles. More officers arrived on the scene taping off the area. Paramedics rushed over to us pulling blankets and equipment from their bags. Thomas, Father Andrews, and I were moved back out of the way to allow them assess their injuries.

"Hey, is this the guy that did this to you?" The officer shouted to Vincent before placing Mason in the back of his squad car.

"Yea, he did. But it's not his fault," he grunted holding his side. "Let's let a judge decide that, shall we?" the officer scolded.

"Hey, captain…." a voice shouted from below the rock wall. "It's his ex-partner, its Bridges."

Vincent tried to take a deep breath to speak. He was surrounded by medics attempting to get him onto a gurney.

"I'm alright." He shouted pulling off the blood pressure cuff.

"Please. Leave him. We'll take him to the hospital. His injuries look far worse than they are, I assure you," Thomas insisted.

"He showed up. He followed Mason. I saw him coming, I shouted to him… that's when Mason put the gag in my mouth. I'd already taken a heavy beating by then," he admitted. "My hands were tied. I couldn't move. He went for Mason's gun," he explained struggling to breathe as he spoke.

"Can't we do this later, officer?" Father Andrews pleaded.

"They struggled. The gun went off. He lost his footing and went over the edge."

"Is that it?" the officer questioned as he finished scribbling down Vincent's statement. "Yea, that's it," Vincent mumbled.

"You should to take a ride in the ambulance."

"Nah. It's not my style."

He took my hand pulling himself up. Thomas lifted him tossing his arm over his shoulders.

"Glad to see you, brother," Thomas whispered pulling him tightly. Vincent moaned as his affection was more than he could handle.

"Yeah, you too. Now take it easy."

I helped Tess to her feet. She could barely stand on her own.

"I'm so glad you weren't hurt, Tess," I whispered taking her into my arms. I felt her collapse against me. I scooped her up and held her close. She threw her arms around my neck burying her face into my chest. She needed to do whatever it was they did to get better. I held her tightly, pressing my lips against her forehead. Just then the morning sun began to rise. The sky lit up with reddish glow. I heard about the red dawn on Fire Island. I've seen pictures but they failed to do it justice. Nothing compared to the real thing.

It seemed appropriate, nostalgic. Thomas walked Vincent over to the edge of the cliff. Angelo quickly joined him helping Vincent to stand. The rising sun broke through the clouds casting a powerful, brilliant red light over the island. I felt privileged to be here with them. To know what I knew. To understand and yet know nothing.

Father put his hand on my shoulder. He had a look of relief in his eyes as he gazed at them. They were going to be alright. And so was Tess.

"What's the saying?" Thomas asked. "Red sky at night, sailors' delight?"

"Red sky at morning, sailors take warning," Vincent whispered, smiling at Thomas.

"Well then, it's a good thing you're not a sailor," Thomas grinned. "Let's get you out of here, shall we?" he added latching onto his arm.

"Father, Nathanial is coming for her," Thomas announced. "Dominic and Sofia, too."

"Very good, Thomas," Father Andrews replied.

"They're going to take you, Tess. You have to go," Thomas ordered. I had no idea where she needed to go but I trusted Thomas.

"I need to go home first," she insisted. Thomas shook his head as he glared at her.

"You need go now, Tess." Father whispered to her.

"Vincent, can we just go home? Just for a little while? Please?" she begged. Tears trickled down her cheek.

"What's an hour? Come on," Vincent said. "We'll both go then together, right Tess?"

Tess nodded. "We'll both go. I just need time to talk to Aiden. That's all, just a little time."

"That's all you have, Tess. A little time," Thomas said in a low voice. "I'll take her, Angelo you help Vincent." Thomas took Tess from my arms. She gazed at me. Her eyes quickly filled with tears. She seemed so afraid. My mind raced with questions but I trusted Thomas. He would keep her safe.

"I'll see you in a little while." I kissed her on her forehead. She squeezed my hand and he pulled her away. She wouldn't let me go.

"It's okay, angel. I'll be there," I whispered pulling her hand from mine. "Take care of her Thomas. Don't let anything happen to her."

"I'm only giving her this hour because she has something she needs to tell you." His voice was cold. He glared at me as he walked away.

"Father. You and Aiden take the car. We'll see you at home," he said.

"Tell me what? What is it?" I shouted. "She's going to be alright, isn't she?"

"Yes, Aiden," Father said pulling me away. "She's going to be okay. Let's go, son. You're going to see her soon," he assured me.

My mind raced with thoughts. Worried about Tess, hoping she would be okay. Getting her better, getting her back to me safe and sound. She was mine. Nothing would change that.

I always imagined what it would be like. What they would look like if they were actually real. Not made of stone, frozen in time. But living, breathing perfect beings eternally connected to this imperfect world. He held her in his arms. I held my breath. I continued to watch them as they headed toward the woods. Many emotions came over me as she faded into the morning mist. Worry, disbelief, anxiousness. Every emotion that comes with fear, with helplessness. I tried not to blink. I didn't want to miss any of it. I couldn't take my eyes off of her.

That's when I saw the impossible. They drifted away. They became the air, the wind in the trees, they rose high above the ground, becoming transparent like their surroundings Like a gentle breeze that came and left... just like that, they were gone.

I would have imagined mighty feathered wings extending from their bodies, soaring into the sky. But there was none of that. They simply elevated themselves and gracefully floated away.

That was it.

I could feel my eyes welling up with tears as I stood there, silent, still. I wiped them away struggling with what was happening. I felt strange. Like I was about to lose my mind struggling to understand what was real and what wasn't. I didn't know what she was but what we felt for each other... that was real.

Whatever she was, it didn't matter. I just wanted her to be safe. I wanted her with me.

24

Truth Be Told

I had just witnessed was something incredible. Unfathomable. I kept thinking it just wasn't possible. I looked around. Father was waiting for me by the car. I couldn't move. How could I be the only one to have witnessed it? Someone else must have seen it too. I gazed around at all the commotion. The officers, detectives, paramedics, the cornier, even the media. The local news team had arrived pushing their cameras into the police captains' face asking dozens of questions. It was strange. No one noticed anything. Nothing at all. This is how it was. How it's been for centuries.

"That's incredible," Dr. Bennett whispered.

"You believe me?" I asked. My eyes opened widely. I felt relieved.

"Of course I believe you," she replied with a grin.

"Professor Williams knew all along." I stared aimlessly through the glass window.

"Yes. I believe he did. He's pretty sharp. And open minded."

"Yeah. He is. He knew about them."

"He called yesterday. Professor Williams… to see how you were. He wants to come for a visit. Would that be okay with you?" she asked. "Maybe it's time for a visitor."

"He wants to come?" I asked, somewhat surprised.

"You've made incredible progress. Everyone here wants you to get well. You were unresponsive for months before I decided to take your case personally. You didn't say a word to anyone. You wouldn't take visitors."

"What was the point?" I muttered. "No one believed me. They all looked at me like I was crazy. From the second I got here."

"It was the depression that caused you to withdraw, Aiden. Eventually you lost the ability to notice anyone. You didn't recognize visitors who came to see you. Your father, your grandparents, everyone who cared about you. Father Andrews came too. He was the only one who could get an expression other than just a blank stare. You never spoke. Not even to ask about Tess. Where she was, how she was. Nothing.

Just a dull smile when Father Andrews came. But he couldn't reach you. He couldn't get through to you either.

And he was there with you when Thomas took her away. He stood next to you when they drifted into the sky.

"Father Andrews knew what you were feeling. You had to know that, Aiden."

"I suppose."

"He knew all about how it. How it had to be. The interaction they had with mortals over the ages. And situations like yours must have been few and far in between. But I'm guessing it has happened.

"Time was what you needed. We needed to be patient and give you the best care we could. That's how it had to be for the time being. Father helped your family, he helped his family deal with what happened to you. They never left you, Aiden. Never. Especially Vincent. From the moment you arrived, he's watched over you. Constantly. He told us you were bothers.

They all came. Thomas, Daniela, Angelo. Everyone except

Tess. I haven't seen her. I can't tell you why. I don't know. Maybe she couldn't.

"I believe you. I wondered myself when I saw them here. They came after hours. I could have made them leave but I thought it was best for you if I didn't. Most days they would stay out of sight. I didn't think anything of it. Either did the rest of the staff. I think they hung around to keep you from falling too deeply to a place where even they couldn't reach you."

"I knew they were here," I admitted. "I didn't want them here."

"They felt the need to watch over you. And after telling me about what happened to Vincent, I completely understand. I understand why he told the nurses he was your bother. You saved him Aiden. You found him when he was lost. And now, you need them and they know that.

"I told you Dr. Bennett, I don't want them here."

"They know that. They stay away. They have to sort it out. What happened with you. They think it's their fault," she said.

"It is. All of it," I shouted. I buried my face in my hands rubbing the wetness from my eyes. Then I looked back at her. "Will came?"

"Yes. When you first arrived. But after a while it began to sink in that you didn't recognize him. You were like a son to him making it very hard to see you like that. Lillie came too."

"She did?"

"Yes. She told one of your nurses she wanted to shake you until you snapped out of whatever it was that snatched the life from your eyes. Even Ben and Maggie came to see you. But after a while, they all stopped coming," she explained.

"I'm sorry. I need to tell them…"

"They know. Trust me. They love you very much. All they wanted was for you to get better," she whispered. She took my hand. She was so smart. She had everything figured out.

"How are you feeling right now?" she asked. "I see your hands are shaking." Dr. Bennett checked my pulse. "You've been running a slight fever for days."

"I'm okay. Feeling a little excited, I guess. I can't believe Will wants to come. It's been so long since I've seen him. Since I've seen anyone."

She held my hand tighter to stop the shaking. "I must have caused them so much pain."

"Healing is a complicated process. You didn't have the ability to know they were here. But they trusted us. They trusted the doctors here. They believed that one day with treatment, you would get better."

I watched as the tips of the trees swayed in the wind. She lifted her hand and brushed the hair away from my eyes.

"I'd say you're there," she whispered. She did care. She spent so much time listening it would have been impossible not to. I was an unexplainable case. I was sent here because I had been struck by something so powerful, so unheard of it was close to impossible to fix. Nothing they tried worked. So in a last ditch effort, she took my case herself. I respected her for that.

"When can he come?"

"Professor Williams?" she asked. I nodded. "He can be here Friday."

As she reached the door she turned back to find me smiling. I couldn't wait to see him.

The next morning I was in my chair in the terrace waiting to greet Dr. Bennett. I had prepared a little surprise for her. My hair was combed neatly to one side, hands folded in my lap. For the first time, in a very long time I got dressed. With a little help from my nurse, I pulled on a pair of jeans and a black t-shirt.

The cool morning breeze drifted through the opened door blowing all around me. I felt a heavy weight had been lifted from my shoulders. Now that she actually knew… she actually believed me, for the first time I felt like I was going to be okay. The mere fact that she didn't look at me like I was crazy, that alone changed everything.

The possibility that she believed that it actually happened was more than I ever expected. I knew now that my memories weren't just scattered visions in a series of insanely impossible dreams. One after another, night after night. The dreams were over. Tess was gone, but she was real. The confusion that had consumed me had disappeared. There was no one left to save. Nothing left to do. I could leave it all behind and get on with my life. All because this one doctor believed me. And I wanted to thank her.

I decided to make a special request. I asked the nurses for a special breakfast table to be set up just outside the terrace, in the courtyard. I wanted to surprise Dr. Bennett.

I waited patiently for her to arrive. The morning sunlight broke through the trees casing a glow over the lushly green garden. The table was set for two. Polished silver domes covered two servings of Eggs Benedict with white table linens, fine white china, and in the center, a large crystal vase filled with white roses. It was perfect. Sweet Colleen, she would do just about anything for me. She had a not-so-secret crush. I knew it. It was hard not to. She went above and beyond normal nursing duties. She would even go as far as risking her job if I needed her to. Colleen, along with a couple others battled with their code of ethics when it came to pleasing me.

Just then I noticed her as she walked toward me. She had an enormous smile covering her face. Someone obviously spoiled the surprise. Maybe she was just happy to see me in more than a faded hospital gown. It wasn't the most masculine attire. I looked better. I shaved, I worked a little on my hair. I looked good.

Colleen even asked to snap a selfie. She told me I looked like a model. That might have been pushing it. "Good Morning." I announced.

"Well, good morning, Aiden. What's this all about?"

"This is for you."

"How nice. Thank you. But, it is against the rules, you know."

"I know. I'll take my punishment. Take me off the scrabble schedule. I don't play anyway. Besides, it's worth it."

"Well, just this once. I guess it would be alright. You're on the scrabble schedule?" she snickered. "I'd like to know what happened after they took her that morning. Is now a good time?"

"I can't imagine there'd be a better time, or a better place."

25

No Escape

It was hard to function after Thomas took Tess. I could barely get myself to the car. I was pretty messed up.

"You're going to be alright, son," Father insisted as he patted me on the back.

Perfect, I thought. He sat there cluelessly attempting to remind me that I was going to be okay. I was fine! I wasn't the one we needed to worry about. He was only trying to help but he had no idea what I was going through.

"Please, Father." I quickly shifted myself toward the window. "Just... don't," I mumbled. Father pulled his hand away. My outburst came as a surprise. I don't know how he expected me to deal with it. I felt like I was suffocating. And his hand on my back only made it worse. I wasn't going to be alright. I thought. Not until she was better. Not until she was back in my arms. I didn't want this, any of this. I wanted Tess. I needed her. Father didn't seem to understand. There was no nicey-nicey pat on the back that would make it alright. But, if he too possessed the ability to leap into the sky carrying me on his back, well, then... maybe. Maybe I could deal with it better. Maybe then I would be alright. I glared at him. I think he knew what I was thinking.

I wondered about him. I wondered if he was one of them or was he simply a regular Joe, like me. A non- gifted, nothing special, standard issue, take the long way back aging, dying mortal.

He tossed his head side to side as if to tell me there was no other way back.

I fumbled around the steering column reaching for the key to start the car. They were missing. I couldn't move fast enough and it was getting harder to breathe. There was no way to keep up with them, with Tess. I felt her slipping farther and farther away from me.

This wasn't a very good plan that was for sure. Whose idea was this anyway? I thought. Ground transportation versus flight. What a joke. It was a no brainer. I dropped my hands in my lap and slouched over. This was crazy, she was probably back by now. Sick, weak, and waiting for me. And I couldn't even get the damn car started. I couldn't think. My head dropped against the cool glass of the window. I ran my hands up and down my thighs trying to feel if the key was in my pocket. It was. "I would offer to drive son, but I don't have my glasses."

"I can handle it," I muttered. He didn't say a word after that. I didn't give him much though. How he must have been feeling. I'll bet he was in shock. The big family secret was out of the bag. I felt a little angry with him for not telling me sooner. Tess should never have waited in the first place. She shouldn't be sick. I couldn't get her out of my mind. The way she looked at me before Thomas took her. Her eyes were so lifeless. The brilliant blue had turned to a faded gray as she grew weaker.

One by one the police cars drove away. I caught a glimpse of Bruce Mason in the back seat of one of the cruises. Our eyes met as he turned around to take one last look. The body of his partner was placed on a stretcher covered with a white sheet. Carefully they lifted him into the back of the ambulance and closed the doors. They used no lights, no sirens. Just a slow moving decent down the gravel drive back to the main road. We followed the ambulance for a mile or two as we made our way back to the mountain.

Father Andrews reached across and put his hand on my arm.

"She's going to be okay, Aiden. That I can promise you," he whispered. I gazed at him like a child. A very confused, desperate child. I took the wheel squeezing it tightly in my hands.

"I'm sorry I snapped at you."

"Don't apologize. You've been through so much."

He had a desperate look on his face. He was obviously worried. I needed to cut him some slack. He took care of them. It had to be overwhelming sometimes. For these unexplainable, freaky yet miraculous events to take place on a day to day basis had to be tough. There was one think I wanted to know and at that point I had to ask.

"If she goes, will she be healed?" I asked.

"Yes."

"I don't understand. Why won't she just go now? What is she waiting for?"

"She will. She first needs to talk to you."

"Why can't it wait? If she's sick, I want her to go now," I pleaded.

"She just won't. We've tried convincing her to go so many times. She refused. She won't go without telling you everything. Just trust that because she loves you, this is how it has to happen," he said softly. I nodded my head. Even if I didn't understand, I had no choice but to go along with it.

Heavy clouds rolled over head turning the dim morning sky to a gloomy gray. Not exactly the setting I needed to absorb the events that had taken place over the last few hours. Violent streams of lightning scattered across the sky ahead. I desperately wanted to see Tess, I needed to know that she was alright. I brought my hands to my face wiping the perspiration from my brow. My heart raced as we got closer to the castle. There was a break in the dark clouds casting a single beam of light down over the mountain guiding us to the castle. I watched closely toward the sky for any trace of them as we drove closer.

Everything was so familiar to me, our surroundings, and the steep, narrow road. I made this trip so many times before. But it was different. Everything was different. I caught a glimpse of the landing. The flat rock bed where I parked my Jeep so many times before. I made so many climbs unaware of the magnitude of the place I obsessed about ever since I came here. Unaware of the significance of the dwelling resting within the mountain. It was all different now. The mountain, the castle, her family, everything.

Tess and her brothers reached the castle within minutes of leaving Fire Island. Thomas came in with Tess in his arms. Angelo and Nathanial followed closely behind them carrying Vincent over the balcony, through the open French doors to the great room.

"Hey there, madman!" Frederic shouted, racing toward them.

"You didn't go, Tess?" Daniela shouted. She and Elaina rushed over to help Thomas carry Tess to the sofa.

"She wants to talk to Aiden, first. He's on his way with Father Andrews," Thomas explained.

"Close call, huh, Vincent?" Daniela wrapped her arms around him as Angelo helped him to his favorite chair near the fireplace.

"Yea. It was. Too close."

Rachel began to clean his cuts with a damp cloth. He groaned bobbing his head trying to overt her constant swiping.

"You can actually feel this?" she asked as she chased him with the cloth wiping the blood from his face.

"Yes and I don't like it," he scowled in pain.

"Of course you don't. What do you like?"

"Do you have to keep doing that?" He pushed her hand away.

He turned his head and noticed a little girl stood holding her hands to her face. She knew he must have been the missing brother she overheard everyone talking about. The one they worried about for so many days. She could tell he needed to restore. But he was hurt and bleeding. Something they didn't ever do. He frightened her a little. She saw his blood stained shirt, his bruises, and cuts covering his face. She was afraid of him.

He realized who she was. Aiden had found them. Just like Tess tried to tell him he could. He made it so hard from him to save any of them. He couldn't take his eyes off her. His face softened with a gentle smile.

Frederic came from the kitchen with a tray of cream soda. Which just happened to be Vincent's favorite. He reached for his guitar propped against the book shelf and sat down on a chair near Vincent. He began to play. Frederic loved his brother. He taught him so many things when he first came. It was hard to see him hurt but he knew he would go soon.

Vincent smiled, happy to be back with his family. He wanted to let go of the mean, hateful man he'd became. He was broken and needed to change. He welcomed change. The soft sound of the guitar released Vincent from his physical, even emotional pain just for a while. He closed his eyes resting his head on his palm gazing at Frederic as he played.

"Thomas? Can I ask you a question?" Dominic whispered.

"Of course."

"What makes him so angry?"

"His anger has been with him for so long, it's like he knows nothing else. It's a long story." Thomas shook his head gazing at Vincent.

"Tell him, Thomas." Tess mumbled. "We need something until Aiden gets here, please?" she pleaded. Anything to get her mind off of the anxiety, the reality of what she had to do.

"Has he ever been assigned a mortal?" Dominic whispered. Vincent glanced toward the sofa where they were sitting. He knew they were talking about him. He didn't appear angry or upset. That was somewhat surprising to Thomas.

"Yes. But the last one assigned to him, refused to follow his path. His name was Abner Wilkins. No matter how Vincent tried, Abner failed. Vincent could do nothing. He was released from him and was told not to interfere. Abner Wilkins became a murderer. He took many lives, innocent lives. Vincent felt responsible so he made sure that he was captured quickly. After a lengthy trial, Abner was found guilty and sentenced to spent the rest of his life in prison. It made no sense to Vincent. Not possessing the ability to stop evil from happening drove him mad. He just wanted to stop the evil. If he couldn't do that, he didn't want anything to do with being a guardian. Vincent knew there was one thing he could do. He knew that he could punish him. So that's what he did. For years he made him suffer. Not only would Abner spend the rest of his life in a prison cell, he would be haunted by the crime that put him there. For thirty-seven years, Vincent sat with Abner, in his cell. Haunting him, tormenting him until the day he died.

"But even then, Vincent wasn't satisfied. Even after Abner's death, Vincent stayed there in the tiny cell refusing to restore for months at a time. He was punishing himself, becoming a prisoner in a mortal institution, in a mortal world.

"None of the guards questioned his presence there. He was surrounded by monsters with no conscious. Cold blooded, callused mortals who took the lives of the innocent. His anger grew, often causing trouble with the other inmates. He was beaten and shackled to a wall and left for days or locked up for months at a time in solitary confinement. Life as a prisoner made sense to Vincent. To punish while being punished. It made perfect sense.

"Vincent spent one hundred and sixteen years there. That's where I found him, aged and dying. Too weak to restore. He had gone for too long. It was his ultimate punishment, he told me. I took him away from that horrible place and Tess and I brought him to restore. We needed to take him quite often for many years hoping that he would return to us, to his role as a guardian." Thomas felt a deep sadness for his brother. "He still punishes himself Abner's actions," he added in a quiet voice.

"He was a mortal, Dominic," Tess whispered. "Like you and I were. And you, of course, Thomas."

"He's very old, and very wise. He could teach you many things if you can just get past his temper. And he's very stubborn as you can see," Thomas said nudging Tess.

Vincent wasn't the only one who was stubborn, he thought. Tess snickered elbowing him back. A smile broke through the worry that weighed so heavily in her eyes.

"What are you grinning about? Your just as stubborn, Tess," Thomas whispered wrapping his arm around her pulling her tightly to him.

"No way, Thomas. He's one of a kind and you know it."

"That is true."

"How old is he, Thomas?" Dominic asked.

"He was born in Scotland in 1381." Tess smiled, resting her head on Thomas' shoulder as he spoke. She watched as Vincent teased Tien and Sarah with a sucker that he snatched from Rachel's pocket.

"He took us many times to his home town. He remembers everything about his life."

"How is that possible? I don't remember anything."

"It's not common to remember, Dominic. Don't worry. It's best if you don't. The temptation to interfere is much too great.

It's better this way, trust me," Thomas explained.

"Vincent was born to a wealthy, royal family. He was born to protect his people and his country. He's a fighter, it's in his blood," Thomas boasted.

"That's not surprising," Dominic chuckled.

Everything would be better for Vincent now. Thomas thought as he watched him with little Tien.

"What's your name?" Vincent whispered to the young girl.

"Tien," she said in the softest voice he had ever heard. Slowly she began to step backward away from him. She was afraid to get too close. He was different than the rest.

"My name is Vincent. It's okay, don't be afraid. I'm sorry that I look this way. I don't mean to frighten you." He took the rag from Rachel and pressed it against the cut over his brow.

"What happened to you?" she whispered as she moved closer to him.

"I made a mistake. And someone got very angry with me. But I'm going to be okay very soon," he assured her.

"Vincent?" A quiet voice came from beside his chair. Vincent turned to see who it was.

"Did that man hurt you?" It was Avery. He whispered so softly, Vincent could hardly hear him. Vincent reached down to where Avery was hiding on the floor. He picked him up and pulled him closer to him.

"Hey, you! What are you doing down there?" Vincent said in a soft gentle voice. Avery was especially quiet. He rarely ever spoke.

"Naw, not really. I'm pretty tough," Vincent smiled at him.

Avery was eleven, the youngest of the men in the castle. He followed Frederic around most of the time. Watching, listening, learning.

"You need to go soon. I can tell." Avery slid his finger over Vincent's bloodied scrapes that covered his arm.

"I do. You're right. Would you like to come with me?"

"Okay." Vincent smiled and held him closer.

"They're here!" Sophia announced.

Thomas met us at the door. "How is she?" I shouted.

"She's okay, Aiden. You can see her in a moment, first we need to talk. Walk with me."

I knew that I had no choice. I looked through the opening of the front door. I could see most of her brothers just inside, Nathaniel, Angelo, Dominic as if they were standing guard, protecting her. From what? I thought. I wouldn't hurt her. I couldn't help but feel a little protective myself. And a little angry toward them. After everything that happened. After all I've done for them, they think they need to keep her from me?

"I'll go inside and see that she's alright, Aiden," Father yelled as he ran into the castle. "I'll tell her you'll be in soon."

"Thanks, Father." I felt a little relief as I watched him go inside. "It's been quite a day."

"Yea, I'd say."

"She loves you, Aiden. I know she does."

"Yes, she does."

"She can't," he whispered. He didn't take another step. He stood there waiting for my response. My reaction. I didn't think that I heard him correctly.

"What?" I glared at Thomas. "What did you say?"

"She can't love like this. When she's healed, she'll forget all of it."

"All of what?"

"Her love for you."

"No way. She couldn't. I don't understand." I couldn't believe this. How could he know how Tess would feel? She loved me enough to remember me. He had no idea what we shared.

"I should have stopped this from happening. I never thought that it would go this far. I knew that she was putting you in those dreams to save others. I never thought that she... She shouldn't have done this to you, to herself."

"She did nothing wrong, Thomas. It was me. I pursued her. It was all me."

I turned back. I needed to see her. This could not be happening. How could Thomas be telling me that I couldn't love her? He didn't know anything, I thought as I started walking back toward the castle. How could she not remember? I began to walk faster hoping to stop Thomas from saying any more. He followed closely behind me.

"Aiden, if she doesn't go soon, she will die. Then you would truly be without her." I could see the worry in his eyes. He was telling me that she couldn't be with me, and if she did, she would die.

"That can't happen," I shouted.

"She wants to love you. That's why she won't go. If she restores it will all go away. She doesn't want to give you up."

"This is crazy," I whispered as tears filled my eyes.

"I'm sorry, Aiden. I believe that she would rather die than to restore and lose her love for you."

"You have to make her go, Thomas. That just can't happen," I pleaded.

"You need to tell her to tell her to go, before it's too late," Thomas begged. "And Vincent swore he wouldn't go without her. He would die for her you know. You'll be saving them both."

Right then, I realized I had to give Tess back.

"I know this must be hard for you."

"You don't know, Thomas. I can't live without her."

"You can. You have to. If you love her, you will."

He had no idea how hard this was. To give her back was something that I simply couldn't do. I'll let her go, for now. I'll take my chances… she will go. She'll restore and be healed. And when she comes back, she'll remember me. That's what I needed to think until she came back, until she returned for me. That was the only way I could do what had to be done.

We went inside where they were all gathered around Vincent and Tess. I pulled my cuff to my eyes wiping them hoping Tess wouldn't see that I was upset.

"Aiden, get over here!" Vincent shouted waving his arm high into the air.

"Wow. What a homecoming, huh? What did we miss?" Thomas asked as he hugged Sarah, Tien and Avery.

"Hey." I took Tess by her hand.

"We need to talk, don't we?" she asked with a sorrowful look in her eyes.

"Yea, maybe we do. Just let me look at you. I'm a bit over-whelmed with all of it," I confessed, stroking her face.

"I know. I'm sorry."

"Don't be sorry. I'm just so glad you're okay."

"Well, as you can see, I'm fine."

"You're anything but fine," I whispered in a low voice. I ran my fingers through her soft dark hair. She smiled at me. She knew what I meant. She needed to go soon, her skin was thin like paper, almost invisible. Her eyes were now a soft gray, no blue left at all. I took her hand and brushed it gently.

"Really, I'm ok. There's so much I need to tell you, Aiden.

Let's go to my room where it's quiet." She led me up the stairs. The others watched as I followed her. She clutched the banister trying to hold herself up. She was too weak. I didn't hesitate. I scooped her into my arms and carried her the rest of the way up the stairs into her room.

"This is going to be very hard for him. For them both," Father whispered.

26

Mine

I gently laid Tess onto her bed and sat next to her. She was shaking. I couldn't catch my breath. I took her hand and held it to my chest. My heart was pounding.

I knew what she needed to say. I didn't want to hear it. I wanted to hear her say Thomas was wrong. But I knew he wasn't. I could see it in her eyes. She was very sick. I laid next to her and held her. She felt so cold. I knew we didn't have much time. I gazed into her eyes waiting for her to speak. She struggled to hold back the tears searching for just the right words.

"It's alright Tess. Thomas told me."

"Told you what?" she whispered.

"That you have to go tonight. If you don't, you'll die."

"He's wrong."

"He's not wrong. You have to go," I insisted.

"There's something I want to show you," she said, walking to her closet. She came back to the bed holding the bundle of letters.

"I wrote them to you," she whispered as she handed them to me. I gently touched the white ribbon that held them together. I looked at her and smiled.

"I waited for a long time. I knew one day I would find you."

"I don't understand, Tess. What do you mean?"

"A love like this. What we have. For centuries I've waited, patiently. Watching. I knew you would come. And I knew you would change everything."

She caressed my hand. There was something about the way she looked at me. I'd never seen before. She was desperate. I could see it. I could feel it. She didn't want to let go. I knew she would give up everything to stay with me.

"If she stayed, she couldn't heal. And if she went, she couldn't be with you is that right?" Dr. Bennett whispered. She cleared her throat. I began to believe that Dr. Bennett was becoming emotionally involved. She took her tissue and wiped her eyes.

"Right."

"So you both knew what had to happen."

"Yes."

"She was different. She did things she shouldn't have done. Maybe there was a way she could remember... "

"Do you think I would be here if she could?"

I wanted to believe she would come back to me. That's all I kept thinking. She would defy the odds; she would break the rules again. Like she did to save me. She knew she wasn't allowed to get involved, and to fall in love with me was impossible. But she did.

I stroked her hair. The luster was gone, the smooth silky sheen disappeared. Everything about her was deteriorating. She was fading fast. I knew we were just delaying the inevitable.

"You have to go," I whispered.

"I knew your mother, Aiden."

"You did?" I sat up quickly.

"Yes. I watched over her for a long time. I was there when you were born. There were complications, I protected you both."

I couldn't believe what I was hearing. Then again, nothing that happened that night was believable. But I was living it. It was happening.

"I was with her… when the tomb collapsed."

"You were with her?" My mind raced.

"Yes," she said softly lowering her head.

So many thoughts, so many emotions went through my mind. My father's sadness for so many years, and mine. How I became obsessed with my mother's work… the angel sculptures. How much I missed her. How much time I lost with her. She was her guardian, she let it happen. I had to know why.

"You couldn't stop it from happening? Why couldn't you save her?"

"Please try an understand. It was her time. I couldn't change it. I'm so sorry."

It was obvious that I was confused by it all. The selection process, one life spared, one life lost. I didn't understand the need for them to be with us if not to protect us, to stop things like this from happening. But even as I questioned it, I knew better. I knew that in the grand scheme of it all, it came down to one simple thing and it was something my mother made sure to teach me. It's not about how much time we have. It's about having a true understanding of our purpose here. What we do and why we do it. Our impact, our lasting footprint. Our contribution to society. Whatever our purpose was, it was up to us figure out. And to use it to leave this place better off because we were here.

Because we existed. And for whatever reason... I was spared. Because of her I was still here. To question her about any of it was not my place.

"Please don't apologize, Tess."

"She saw me. She knew who I was, what I was."

"You have no idea how much that means to me to hear you say that."

"I know how much she meant to you. I was with you. Night after night when you cried yourself to sleep, I was there."

"That's so hard to comprehend. I was so young. Why didn't I see you?"

"When we watch, we're unable to be seen. It's just our way. It's the only way. In day to day life, we appear to be just like you. We can only appear in dreams or visions in our true form."

"Like on the mountain that day."

"Yes, like on the mountain."

"You were there with me. I remember you."

"Something happened. I shouldn't have but I couldn't stop myself. I allowed you to see me... to remember me. I didn't have a choice. I knew I couldn't lose you."

"All I remembered was that you saved me. You were there. And then I saw your eyes... walking that night. I couldn't explain any of it, But I knew when I saw you in the park.. the library... there was something I couldn't explain... like a centrifugal force. I knew you belonged with me."

"I broke every rule."

"And to make up for it you had to use me in dreams?"

"Yes. I know I shouldn't have. It was so wrong. And it got so complicated. I felt I had no choice. I needed to try and fix what was happening. I disrupted things... I interfered."

"I'm glad you did. I wouldn't be here with you right now if you hadn't. But that's selfish of me. You wouldn't be sick right now." I stroked her cheek as I spoke.

"It went too far. I took it too far Aiden. And, so did Vincent. Boundaries were crossed. That's what happened here, tonight. It went too far."

"With Mason you mean?"

"Yes. He was the man you pulled from the water."

"That's why I looked familiar to him! He opened his eyes... on the beach. After I pulled him out of the water. He must've seen me. But I don't understand, why go after Vincent?"

"It wasn't a boat accident like in your dream. He and his family were in a car accident. Vincent was there, in the car and Bruce saw him."

"Vincent was there with me, in my dream. He was in the water."

"I know. He shouldn't have been. Bruce Mason's family was killed that night. And he blamed Vincent."

"But it wasn't his fault."

"It wasn't, but he saw him. He shouldn't have been there. It made no sense to him. He insisted he wasn't a vision or a mirage. He obsessed over it, playing the last few seconds over and over in his mind. It drove him crazy. We're never supposed to interfere like that. Visions and dreams are one thing; reality is much different. Vincent went after you because of me."

Her hands trembled as she held out the letters to me. "Take these. I want you to have them," she whispered.

"Tess, you have to go."

"You don't understand."

"I do. He told me."

"Did he tell you that I would forget? I'd forget everything? You, the way I feel…this love… it would go away? Don't you understand? That's how it works!" she scolded as she began to cry. "Did he tell you that?"

"That would never happen," I insisted as I wiped her tears.

"You have no idea what you're saying, Aiden. Otherwise you wouldn't say it." She pulled away from me. She moved to the edge of the bed. "I can't," she whispered as she walked toward the window. She closed her eyes as the tears that trickled down her face. "I wish it would all just stop. All of it… and I could just stay here with you," she cried.

"I'll be here. I'll wait for you, Tess." I walked over to her and wrapped my arms around her. She fell back into my arms. I pressed my lips against her soft skin. Gently I moved her hair away from her neck and I kissed her. I felt her take a deep breath as she leaned against me. "It won't go away. I will love you as long as I breathe," I vowed whispering into her ear.

"Aiden, please…"

I wouldn't let her finish. I spun her around taking a hold of her arms.

"Tess, listen to me. If you die, I couldn't live. Don't you understand? I would rather have you not remember than gone forever."

She shook her head in disagreement. "Tess, please," I shouted, gently shaking her. "You have to go! For me, for Vincent, for everyone who loves you," I begged.

I couldn't believe what I was saying. I had no idea what would happen. I didn't know if I would ever see her again. But I needed her to go. She needed to get better, she needed to be here with Father and the others. I already knew all about her, about her family about this place. I would do anything to protect them. No one would ever find out about them, about what I witnessed. And nothing would touch what I felt in my heart. I'll get her back. I'd find a way. I had to.

"I'll go." Tears streamed down her face as she looked into my eyes. My heart ached inside. It was a pain I'd never felt before. "I just need tonight," she whispered. "I want this night, Aiden. With you. I'll go in the morning, Vincent and I will both go."

I wanted her to go, right then. I couldn't tell her no. She wouldn't listen anyway. "I'm so sorry for all of this," she whispered.

"Please, don't be sorry. You went against everything you were ever taught… for me." I cupped her face wiping her tears. I held her that last night in my arms watching her as she slept wishing the morning would never come.

Dr. Bennett made a whimpering sound as she pressed her Kleenex over her nose. She wiped the tears from her eyes and began to clean the lens of her glasses.

"I'm sorry, Aiden. You've suffered through so much sorrow in your life. It seems as though dealing with loss has become a way of life for you."

"Yeah."

She snatched another tissue from the box on the counter. "There was no other way," she mumbled. "You had to let her go." Her voice cracked as she spoke.

"If I wanted her to live I did."

27

Unwavering Oath

A few hours later, I woke in her bed, alone. She wasn't next to me like she was a few hours before. I was afraid they took her sometime during the night while I slept. I ran out of her room and down the stairs. I saw Thomas standing near the open doors in the great room. The morning sky was lined with hundreds of brilliant stars. Maybe I was too late. Maybe she was gone.

"Thomas?"

"She's been asking for you." She was resting on the couch in front of him. Her time was running out. "She wanted to wait till you woke to say goodbye," Thomas said in a soft voice.

"Why didn't you wake me?"

Her head rested in Vincent's lap. His skin was as pale as hers.

"We're more alike than she would ever admit," Vincent whispered. "We're willing to go to any length… even to suffer, just to feel something more."

Daniela sat on the floor close to Tess gently running her fingers over the tips of her dark hair. "She wanted to ask you something. She wouldn't tell us what it was," Sofia whispered.

Nathanial, Rachel, Angelo, Elaina… they were all there surrounding them. They would do as she wished. They gave her the time she had asked for. Isabel and Jowell stood near Frederic by the fireplace. They were new to the family but a bond had formed among them. They didn't need to understand why she waited. They were simply waiting for her to go.

"She needs to go soon, Aiden," Father said softly.

"I know." I moved in closer to her. I gently brushed her hair away from her face. "I should have made her go," I whispered. Vincent rested his hand on my shoulder. His face still covered with lacerations.

"He's unable to heal. He shouldn't be wounded at all. The years will soon catch up to them," Thomas warned.

"Aiden?"

"Yes, Tess. I'm here." I reached for her hand kissing it tenderly as she opened her eyes. She glanced around the room.

"Can I talk to him alone, just for a minute?"

"Not long, Tess. Ok?" Daniela pleaded as she and the others walked into the next room.

"Ok." Tess whispered.

"Aiden, I...I wanted to ask you something." She spoke in a very soft whisper. I could barely hear her so I moved in even closer.

"Anything. You can ask me anything."

"Your necklace... I was thinking maybe..." She was too weak to finish but I knew what she was asking. I smiled at her pulling my necklace from inside my shirt and gently tied it around her neck.

"I'll remember... and I'll come back you..." she whispered as she moved her fingers over the medallion, "...somehow." A tender smile crossed her lips as she pressed her hand to my face.

"You better," I said as I leaned into her kissing her gently one last time. I attempted to smile back catching a single tear as it fell down her cheek.

"Thomas, she's ready."

"Let's go," Thomas announced.

Daniela knelt down to Tess and looked at me. I fought back the tears with every ounce of my being. I wanted to be strong for Tess. She refused to take her eyes off me. I felt the same way. She latched onto my arms tightly as I lifted her.

"It's going to be ok, Tess," I assured her, holding her against my chest. My heart was broken but still able to pound out of control. "I love you," I whispered. I kissed her forehead and placed her into Nathanial's arms.

"I love you, Aiden. I'll remember. I will," Tess whispered as she clutched my medallion.

"I know you will."

I could do nothing but stand there as Nathaniel carried Tess to the large French doors. The morning breeze rushed over them sending the long flowing curtains into the air. Tess' dark hair blew around them as he stepped with her onto the balcony.

"Don't worry, Aiden. She'll be ok," Daniela whispered as she hugged me goodbye before stepping off the balcony soaring behind them into the sky. And that was it. Just like that, Tess was gone. I felt my insides twist into knots. I could barely hold myself up.

"Stay with Father Andrews. He'll take you back when you're ready," Thomas ordered as he and Vincent moved toward the windows. "And thank you, Aiden... for everything."

"You're welcome," I whispered, "but I'll never be ready. Never."

"Thomas, wait..." Vincent muttered. "Aiden?"

"Yeah, Vincent?"

"I'll never forget what you did for me."

"I'm glad I could help," I replied as I wiped my eyes.

"Remember, I owe you one." He shouted from the balcony.

"Vincent?"

"Yeah?"

"Bring her back to me. Then we'll be even."